BRIEF CANDLES

CANDLES

STORIES BY
ALDOUS HUXLEY

GARDEN CITY, NEW YORK

DOUBLEDAY, DORAN & COMPANY, INC.

1930

PRINTED AT THE *Country Life Press*, GARDEN CITY, N. Y., U. S. A.

C. S.

CONTENTS

BRIEF CANDLES

CHAWDRON

From behind the outspread *Times* I broke a silence. "Your friend Chawdron's dead, I see."

"Dead?" repeated Tilney, half incredulously. "Chawdron dead?"

" 'Suddenly, of heart failure,' " I went on, reading from the obituary, " 'at his residence in St. James's Square.' "

"Yes, his heart . . ." He spoke meditatively. "How old was he? Sixty?"

"Fifty-nine. I didn't realize the ruffian had been rich for so long. '. . . the extraordinary business instinct, coupled with a truly Scottish doggedness and determination, which raised him, before he was thirty-five, from obscurity and comparative poverty to the height of opulence.' Don't you wish you could write like that? My father lost a quarter of a century's savings in one of his companies."

"Served him right for saving!" said Tilney with a sudden savagery. Surprised, I looked at him over the top of my paper. On his gnarled and ruddy face was an expression of angry gloom. The news had evidently depressed him. Besides, he was always ill-tempered at breakfast. My poor father was paying. "What sort of jam is that by you?" he asked fiercely.

"Strawberry."

"Then I'll have some marmalade."

I passed him the marmalade and, ignoring his bad temper, "When the Old Man," I continued, "and along with him, of course, most of the other shareholders, had sold out at about eighty per cent. dead loss, Chawdron did a little quiet conjuring and the price whizzed up again. But by that time he was the owner of practically all the stock."

"I'm always on the side of the ruffians," said Tilney. "On principle."

"Oh, so am I. All the same, I do regret those twelve thousand pounds."

Tilney said nothing. I returned to the obituary.

"What do they say about the New Guinea Oil Company scandal?" he asked after a silence.

"Very little; and the touch is beautifully light. 'The findings of the Royal Commission were on the whole favourable, though it was generally considered at the time that Mr. Chawdron had acted somewhat inconsiderately.' "

Tilney laughed. " 'Inconsiderately' is good. I wish I made fourteen hundred thousand pounds each time I was inconsiderate."

"Was that what he made out of the New Guinea Oil business?"

"So he told me, and I don't think he exaggerated. He never lied for pleasure. Out of business hours he was remarkably honest."

"You must have known him very well."

"Intimately," said Tilney, and, pushing away his plate, he began to fill his pipe.

"I envy you. What a specimen for one's collection! But didn't you get rather bored with living inside the museum, so to speak, behind the menagerie bars? Being intimate with a specimen—it must be trying."

"Not if the specimen's immensely rich," Tilney answered. "You see, I'm partial to Napoleon brandy and Corona Coronas; parasitism has its rewards. And if you're skilful, it needn't have too many penalties. It's possible to be a high-souled louse, an independent tapeworm. But Napoleon brandy and Coronas weren't the only attractions Chawdron possessed for me. I have a disinterested, scientific curiosity about the enormously wealthy. A man with an income of more than fifty thousand a year is such a fantastic and improbable being. Chawdron was specially interesting because he'd *made* all his money— mainly dishonestly; that was the fascinating thing. He was a large-scale, Napoleonic crook. And, by God, he looked it! Did you know him by sight?"

I shook my head.

"Like an illustration to Lombroso. A criminal type. But intelligently criminal, not brutally. He wasn't brutal."

"I thought he was supposed to look like a chimpanzee," I put in.

"He did," said Tilney. "But, after all, a chimpanzee isn't brutal-looking. What you're struck by in a chimpanzee is its all-but-human appearance. So very intelligent, so nearly a man. Chawdron's face had just that look. But with a difference. The chimpanzee looks gentle and virtuous and quite without humour. Whereas Chawdron's intelligent all-but-humanity was sly and, underneath the twinkling jocularity, quite ruthless. Oh, a strange, interesting creature! I got a lot of fun out of my study of him. But in the end, of course, he did bore me. Bored me to death. He was so drearily uneducated. Didn't know the most obvious things, couldn't understand a generalization. And then quite disgustingly without taste, without aesthetic sense or understanding. Metaphysically and artistically a cretin."

"The obituarist doesn't seem to be of your opinion." I turned again to the *Times*. "Where is it now? Ah! 'A remarkable writer was lost when Chawdron took up finance. Not entirely lost, however; for the brilliant *Autobiography*, published in 1921, remains as a lasting memorial to his talents as a stylist and narrator.' What do you say to that?" I asked, looking up at Tilney.

He smiled enigmatically. "It's quite true."

"I never read the book, I confess. Is it any good?"

"It's damned good." His smile mocked, incomprehensibly.

"Are you pulling my leg?"

"No, it was really and genuinely good."

"Then he can hardly have been such an artistic cretin as you make out."

"Can't he?" Tilney echoed and, after a little pause, suddenly laughed aloud. "But he *was* a cretin," he continued on a little gush of confidingness that seemed to sweep away the barriers of his willed discretion, "and the book *was* good. For the excellent reason that he didn't write it. I wrote it."

"You?" I looked at him, wondering if he were joking. But his face, after the quick illumination of laughter, had gone serious, almost gloomy. A curious face, I reflected. Handsome in its way, intelligent, aware, yet with something rather sinister about it, almost repulsive. The superficial charm and good humour of the man seemed to overlie a fundamental hardness, an uncaringness, a hostility even. Too much good living, moreover, had left its marks on that face. It was patchily red and lumpy. The fine features had become rather gross. There was a coarseness mingled with the native refinement. Did I like Tilney or did I not? I never rightly knew. And perhaps the question was irrelevant. Perhaps Tilney was one of those men who are not meant to be liked or disliked as men—only as performers. I liked his conversation, I was amused, interested, instructed by what he said. To ask myself if I also liked what he *was*—this was, no doubt, beside the point.

Tilney got up from the table and began to walk

up and down the room, his pipe between his teeth, smoking. "Poor Chawdron's dead now, so there's no reason . . ." He left the sentence unfinished, and for a few seconds, was silent. Standing by the window, he looked out through the rain-blurred glass on to the greens and wet greys of the Kentish landscape. "England looks like the vegetables at a Bloomsbury boarding-house dinner," he said slowly. "Horrible! Why do we live in this horrible country? Ugh!" He shuddered and turned away. There was another silence. The door opened and the maid came in to clear the breakfast table. I say "the maid"; but the brief impersonal term is inaccurate. Inaccurate, because wholly inadequate to describe Hawtrey. What came in, when the door opened, was personified efficiency, was a dragon, was stony ugliness, was a pillar of society, was the Ten Commandments on legs. Tilney, who did not know her, did not share my terror of the domestic monster. Unaware of the intense disapproval which I could feel her silently radiating (it was after ten; Tilney's slug-a-bed habits had thrown out of gear the whole of her morning's routine) he continued to walk up and down, while Hawtrey busied herself round the table. Suddenly he laughed. "Chawdron's *Autobiography* was the only one of my books I ever made any money out of," he said. I listened apprehensively, lest he should say anything which might shock or offend the dragon. "He turned over all the royalties to me," Tilney went on. "I made the best part of three thousand

pounds out of his *Autobiography*. Not to mention
the five hundred he gave me for writing it." (Was it
quite delicate, I wondered, to talk of such large sums
of money in front of one so incomparably more virtuous than ourselves and so much poorer? Fortu-
nately, Tilney changed the subject.) "You ought to
read it," he said. "I'm really quite offended that you
haven't. All that lower middle-class childhood in
Peebles—it's really masterly." ("Lower middle-
class"—I shuddered. Hawtrey's father had owned a
shop; but he had had misfortunes.) "It's *Clayhanger*
and *L'Education Sentimentale* and *David Copper-
field* all rolled into one. Really superb. And the first
adventurings into the world of finance were pure
Balzac—magnificent." He laughed again, this time
without bitterness, amusedly; he was warming to his
subject. "I even put in a Rastignac soliloquy from
the top of the dome of St. Paul's, made him shake his
fist at the City. Poor old Chawdron! he was thrilled.
'If only I'd known what an interesting life I'd had,'
he used to say to me. 'Known while the life was going
on.' " (I looked at Hawtrey to see if she was resent-
ing the references to an interesting life. But her face
was closed; she worked as though she were deaf.)
" 'You wouldn't have lived it,' I told him. 'You must
leave the discovery of the excitingness to the artists.' " He was silent again. Hawtrey laid the last
spoon on the tray and moved towards the door.
Thank heaven! "Yes, the artists," Tilney went on in
a tone that had gone melancholy again. "I really

7

was one, you know." (The departing Hawtrey must have heard that damning confession. But then, I reflected, she always did know that I and my friends were a bad lot.) "Really *am* one," he insisted. "*Qualis artifex!* But *pereo, pereo.* Somehow, I've never done anything but perish all my life. Perish, perish, perish. Out of laziness and because there always seemed so much time. But I'm going to be forty-eight next June. Forty-eight! There isn't any time. And the laziness is such a habit. So's the talking. It's so easy to talk. And so amusing. At any rate for oneself."

"For other people too," I said; and the compliment was sincere. I might be uncertain whether or no I liked Tilney. But I genuinely liked his performance as a talker. Sometimes, perhaps, that performance was a little too professional. But, after all, an artist must be a professional.

"It's what comes of being mostly Irish," Tilney went on. "Talking's the national vice. Like opium-smoking with the Chinese!" (Hawtrey re-entered silently to sweep up the crumbs and fold the table-cloth.) "If you only knew the number of master-pieces I've allowed to evaporate at dinner tables, over the cigars and the whisky!" (Two things of which, I knew, the Pillar of Society virtuously disapproved.) "A whole library. I might have been—what? Well, I suppose I might have been a frightful old bore," he answered himself with a forced self-mockery. " 'The Complete Works of Edmund Tilney, in Thirty-Eight Volumes, post octavo.' I dare say the world ought to be grateful to me for sparing it *that*. All the same, I get a bit depressed when I look over the back numbers of the *Thursday Review* and read those measly little weekly articles of mine. *Parturiunt montes . . .*"

"But they're good articles," I protested. If I had been more truthful, I would have said that they were sometimes good—when he took the trouble to make them good. Sometimes, on the contrary . . .

"*Merci, cher maître!*" he answered ironically. "But hardly more perennial than brass, you must admit. Monuments of wood pulp. It's depressing being a failure. Particularly if it's your fault, if you might have been something else."

I mumbled something. But what was there to say? Except as a professional talker, Tilney *had* been a failure. He had great talents and he was a literary journalist who sometimes wrote a good article. He had reason to feel depressed.

"And the absurd, ironical thing," he continued, "is that the one really good piece of work I ever did is another man's autobiography. I could never prove my authorship even if I wanted to. Old Chawdron was very careful to destroy all the evidences of the crime. The business arrangements were all verbal. No documents of any kind. And the manuscript, *my* manuscript—he bought it off me. It's burnt."

I laughed. "He took no risks with you." Thank

heaven! The dragon was preparing to leave the room for good.

"None whatever," said Tilney. "He was going to be quite sure of wearing his laurel wreath. There was to be no other claimant. And at the time, of course, I didn't care two pins. I took the high line about reputation. Good art—and Chawdron's *Autobiography* was good art, a really first-rate novel—good art is its own reward." (Hawtrey's comment on this was almost to slam the door as she departed.) "You know the style of thing. And in this case it was more than its own reward. There was money in it. Five hundred down and all the royalties. And I was horribly short of money at the moment. If I hadn't been, I'd never have written the book. Perhaps that's been one of my disadvantages—a small independent income and not very extravagant tastes. I happened to be in love with a very expensive young woman at the time when Chawdron made his offer. You can't go dancing and drinking champagne on five hundred a year. Chawdron's cheque was timely. And there I was, committed to writing his memoirs for him. A bore, of course. But luckily the young woman jilted me soon afterwards; so I had time to waste. And Chawdron was a ruthless taskmaster. And besides, I really enjoyed it once I got started. It really was its own reward. But now—now that the book's written and the money's spent and I'm soon going to be fifty, instead of forty as it was then—now, I must say, I'd rather like to have at least one good book to my credit. I'd like to be known as the author of that admirable novel, *The Autobiography of Benjamin Chawdron*, but, alas, I shan't be." He sighed. "It's Benjamin Chawdron, not Edmund Tilney, who'll have his little niche in the literary histories. Not that I care much for literary history. But I do rather care, I must confess, for the present anticipations of the niche. The drawing-room reputation, the mentions in the newspapers, the deference of the young, the sympathetic curiosity of the women. All the by-products of successful authorship. But there, I sold them to Chawdron. For a good price. I can't complain. Still, I *do* complain. Have you got any pipe tobacco? I've run out of mine."

I gave him my pouch. "If I had the energy," he went on, as he refilled his pipe, "or if I were desperately hard up, which, thank heaven and at the same time alas! I'm not at the moment, I could make another book out of Chawdron. Another and a better one. Better," he began explaining, and then interrupted himself to suck at the flame of the match he had lighted, "because . . . so much more . . . malicious." He threw the match away. "You can't write a good book without being malicious. In the *Autobiography* I made a hero of Chawdron. I was paid to; besides, it was Chawdron himself who provided me with my documents. In this other book he'd be the villain. Or in other words, he'd be himself as others saw him, not as he saw himself. Which is, incidentally, the only valid difference between the virtuous and the wicked that *I*'ve ever been able to detect. When you yourself indulge in any of the deadly sins, you're always justified—they're never deadly. But when anyone else indulges, you're very properly indignant. Old Rousseau had the courage to say that he was the most virtuous man in the world. The rest of us only silently believe it. But to return to Chawdron. What I'd like to do now is to write his biography, not his autobiography. And the biography of a rather different aspect of the man. Not about the man of action, the captain of industry, the Napoleon of finance and so forth. But about the domestic, the private, the sentimental Chawdron."

"The *Times* had its word about that," said I; and picking up the paper once more, I read: " 'Under a disconcertingly brusque and even harsh manner Mr. Chawdron concealed the kindliest of natures. A stranger meeting him for the first time was often repelled by a certain superficial roughness. It was only to his intimates that he revealed'—guess what!—'the heart of gold beneath.' "

"Heart of gold!" Tilney took his pipe out of his mouth to laugh.

"And he also, I see, had 'a deep religious sense.' " I laid the paper down.

"Deep? It was bottomless."

"Extraordinary," I reflected aloud, "the way they *all* have hearts of gold and religious senses. Every single one, from the rough old man of science to the tough old business man and the gruff old statesman."

"Hearts of gold!" Tilney repeated. "But gold's much too hard. Hearts of putty, hearts of vaseline, hearts of hog-wash. That's more like it. Hearts of hog-wash. The tougher and bluffer and gruffer they are outside, the softer they are within. It's a law of nature. I've never come across an exception. Chawdron was the rule incarnate. Which is precisely what I want to show in this other, potential book of mine —the ruthless Napoleon of finance paying for his ruthlessness and his Napoleonism by dissolving internally into hog-wash. For that's what happened to him: he dissolved into hog-wash. Like the Strange Case of Mr. Valdemar in Edgar Allan Poe. I saw it with my own eyes. It's a terrifying spectacle. And the more terrifying when you realize that, but for the grace of God, there goes yourself—and still more so when you begin to doubt of the grace of God, when you see that there in fact you *do* go. Yes, you and I, my boy. For it isn't only the tough old business men who have the hearts of hog-wash. It's also, as you yourself remarked just now, the gruff old scientists, the rough old scholars, the bluff old admirals and bishops and all the other pillars of Christian society. It's everybody, in a word, who has made himself too hard in the head or the carapace; everybody who aspires to be non-human—whether angel or machine it doesn't matter. Super-humanity is as bad as sub-humanity, is the same thing, finally. Which shows how careful one should be if one's an intellectual. Even the mildest sort of intellectual. Like me, for example. I'm not one of your genuine ascetic scholars. God forbid! But I'm decidedly high-brow, and I'm literary; I'm even what the newspapers call a 'thinker.' I suffer from a passion for ideas. Always have, from boyhood onwards. With what results? That I've never been attracted by any woman who wasn't a bitch."

I laughed. But Tilney held up his hand in a gesture of protest. "It's a serious matter," he said. "It's disastrous, even. Nothing but bitches. Imagine!"

"I'm imagining," I said. "But where do the books and the ideas come in? *Post* isn't necessarily *propter.*"

"It's *propter* in this case all right. Thanks to the book and the ideas, I never learnt how to deal with real situations, with solid people and things. Personal relationships—I've never been able to manage them effectively. Only ideas. With ideas I'm at home. With the *idea* of personal relationships for example. People think I'm an excellent psychologist. And I suppose I am. Spectatorially. But I'm a bad experiencer. I've lived most of my life posthumously, if you see what I mean; in reflections and conversations after the fact. As though my existence were a novel or a text-book of psychology or a biography, like any of the others on the library shelves. An awful situation. That was why I've always liked the bitches so much, always been so grateful to them— because they were the only women I ever contrived to have a non-posthumous, contemporary, concrete relation with. The only ones." He smoked for a moment in silence.

"But why the only ones?" I asked.

"Why?" repeated Tilney. "But isn't it rather obvious? For the shy man, that is to say the man who doesn't know how to deal with real situations and people, bitches are the only possible lovers, because they're the only women who are prepared to come to meet him, the only ones who'll make the advances he doesn't know how to make."

I nodded. "Shy men have cause to be drawn to bitches: I see that. But why should the bitches be drawn to the shy men? What's their inducement to make those convenient advances? That's what I don't see."

"Oh, of course they don't make them unless the shy man's attractive," Tilney answered. "But in my case the bitches always were attracted. Always. And, quite frankly, they were right. I was tolerably picturesque, I had that professional Irish charm, I could talk, I was several hundred times more intelligent than any of the young men they were likely to know. And then, I fancy, my very shyness was an asset. You see, it didn't really look like shyness. It exteriorized itself as a kind of god-like impersonality and remoteness—most exciting for such women. I had the charm in their eyes of Mount Everest or the North Pole—something difficult and unconquered that aroused the record-breaking instincts in them. And at the same time my shy remoteness made me seem somehow superior; and, as you know, few pleasures can be compared with the sport of dragging down superiority and proving that it's no better than oneself. My air of disinterested remoteness has always had a *succès fou* with the bitches. They all adore me because I'm so 'different.' 'But you're different, Edmund, you're different,'" he fluted in falsetto. "The bitches! Under their sentimentalities, their one desire, of course, was to reduce me as quickly as possible to the most ignoble un-difference. . . ."

"And were they successful?" I asked.

"Oh, always. Naturally. It's not because a man's shy and bookish that he isn't a *porco di prim' ordine*. Indeed, the more shyly bookish, the more likely he is to be secretly porkish. Or if not a *porco*, at least an *asino*, an *oca*, a *vitello*. It's the rule, as I said just now; the law of nature. There's no escaping."

I laughed. "I wonder which of the animals I am?"

Tilney shook his head. "I'm not a zoologist. At least," he added, "not when I'm talking to the specimen under discussion. Ask your own conscience."

"And Chawdron?" I wanted to hear more about Chawdron. "Did Chawdron grunt, or bray, or moo?"

"A little of each. And if earwigs made a noise . . . No, not earwigs. Worse than that. Chawdron was an extreme case, and the extreme cases are right outside the animal kingdom."

"What are they, then? Vegetables?"

"No, no. Worse than vegetables. They're spiritual. Angels, that's what they are: putrefied angels. It's only in the earlier stages of the degeneration that they bleat and bray. After that they twang the harp and flap their wings. Pigs' wings, of course. They're Angels in pigs' clothing. Hearts of hogwash. Did I ever tell you about Chawdron and Charlotte Salmon?"

"The 'cellist?"

He nodded. "What a woman!"

"And her playing! So clotted, so sagging, so greasy . . ." I fumbled for the apt description.

"So terribly Jewish, in a word," said Tilney. "That retching emotionalism, that sea-sickish spirituality—purely Hebraic. If only there were a few more Aryans in the world of music! The tears come into my eyes whenever I see a blonde beast at the piano. But that's by the way. I was going to tell you about Charlotte. You know her, of course?"

"Do I not!"

"Well it was Charlotte who first revealed to me poor Chawdron's heart of hog-wash. Mine too, indirectly. It was one evening at old Cryle's. Chawdron was there, and Charlotte, and myself, and I forget who else. People from all the worlds, anyhow. Cryle, as you know, has a foot in each. He thinks it's his mission to bring them together. He's the matchmaker between God and Mammon. In this case he must have imagined that he'd really brought off the marriage. Chawdron was Mammon all right; and though you and I would be chary of labelling Charlotte as God, old Cryle, I'm sure, had no doubts. After all, she plays the 'cello; she's an Artist. What more can you want?"

"What indeed!"

"I must say, I admired Charlotte that evening," he went on. "She knew so exactly the line to take with Chawdron; which was the more surprising as with me she's never quite pulled it off. She tries the siren on me, very dashing and at the same time extremely mysterious. Her line is to answer my most ordinary remarks with something absolutely incomprehensible, but obviously very significant. If I ask her, for example: 'Are you going to the Derby this year?' she'll smile a really Etruscan smile and answer: 'No, I'm too busy watching the boat-race in my own heart.' Well, then, obviously it's my cue to be terribly intrigued. 'Fascinating Sphinx,' I ought to say, 'Tell me more about your visceral boat-race,' or words to that effect. Whereupon it would almost certainly turn out that I was rowing stroke in the winning boat. But I'm afraid I can't bring myself to do what's expected of me. I just say: 'What a pity! I was making up a party to go to Epsom'—and hastily walk away. No doubt, if she was less blackly Semitic, I'd be passionately interested in her boat-race. But as it is, her manœuvre doesn't come off. She hasn't yet been able to think of a better one. With Chawdron, however, she discovered the correct strategy from the first moment. No siren, no mystery for him. His heart was too golden and hog-washy for

that. Besides, he was fifty. It's the age when clergy-
men first begin to be preoccupied with the underclothing of little schoolgirls in trains, the age when
eminent archæologists start taking a really passionate interest in the Scout movement. Under Chawdron's criminal mask Charlotte detected the pig-like
angel, the sentimental, Pickwickian child-lover with
a taste for the *détournement de mineurs*. Charlotte's
a practical woman: a child was needed, she immediately became the child. And what a child! I've never
seen anything like it. Such prattling! Such innocent
big eyes! Such merry, merry laughter! Such a wonderfully ingenuous way of saying extremely *risqué*
things without knowing (sweet innocent) what they
meant! I looked on and listened—staggered. Horrified too. The performance was really frightful.
Suffer little children . . . But when the little child's
twenty-eight and tough for her age—ah, no; of such
is the kingdom of hell. For me, at any rate. But
Chawdron was enchanted. Really did seem to imagine he'd got hold of something below the age of
consent. I looked at him in amazement. Was it possible he should be taken in? The acting was so bad,
so incredibly unconvincing. Sarah Bernhardt at sev-
enty playing L'Aiglon looked more genuinely like
a child than our tough little Charlotte. But Chawdron didn't see it. This man who had lived by his
wits, and not merely lived, but made a gigantic fortune by them:—was it possible that the most brilliant
financier of the age should be so fabulously stupid?

'Youth's infectious,' he said to me after dinner, when the women had gone out. And then—you should have seen the smile on his face: beatific, lubrically tender —'She's like a jolly little kitten, don't you think?' But what I thought of was the New Guinea Oil Company. How was it possible? And then suddenly I perceived that it wasn't merely possible; it was absolutely necessary. Just because he'd made fourteen hundred thousand pounds out of the New Guinea Oil scandal, it was inevitable that he should mistake a jolly little tarantula like Charlotte for a jolly little kitten. Inevitable. Just as it was inevitable that I should be bowled over by every bitch that came my way. Chawdron had spent his life thinking of oil and stock markets and flotations. I'd spent mine reading the Best that has been Thought or Said. Neither of us had had the time or energy to live—completely and intensely live, as a human being ought to, on every plane of existence. So he was taken in by the pseudo-kitten, while I succumbed to the only too genuine bitch. Succumbed, what was worse, with full knowledge. For I was never really taken in. I always knew that the bitches were bitches and not milk-white hinds. And now I also know why I was captivated by them. But that, of course, didn't prevent me from continuing to be captivated by them. *Experientia* doesn't, in spite of Mrs. Micawber's Papa. Nor does knowledge." He paused to relight his pipe.

"What does, then?" I asked.

Tilney shrugged his shoulders. "Nothing does, once you've gone off the normal instinctive rails."

"I wonder if they really exist, those rails?"

"So do I, sometimes," he confessed. "But I piously believe."

"Rousseau and Shelley piously believed, too. But has anybody ever seen a Natural Man? Those Noble Savages . . . Read Malinowsky about them; read Frazer; read . . ."

"Oh, I have, I have. And of course the savage isn't noble. Primitives are horrible. I know. But then the Natural Man isn't Primitive Man. He isn't the raw material of humanity; he's the finished product. The Natural Man is a manufactured article—no, not manufactured; rather, a work of art. What's wrong with people like Chawdron is that they're such bad works of art. Unnatural because inartistic. Ary Scheffer instead of Manet. But with this difference. An Ary Scheffer is statically bad; it doesn't get worse with the passage of time. Whereas an inartistic human being degenerates, dynamically. Once he's started badly, he becomes more and more inartistic. It needs a moral earthquake to arrest the process. Mere fleabites, like experience or knowledge, are quite unavailing. *Experientia* doesn't. If it did, I should never have succumbed as I did, never have got into financial straits, and therefore never have written Chawdron's autobiography, never have had an opportunity for collecting the intimate and discreditable materials for the biography that, alas, I shall never write. No, no; experience didn't save me from falling a victim yet once more. And to such a ruinously expensive specimen. Not that she was mercenary," he put in parenthetically. "She was too well off to need to be. So well off, however, that the mere cost of feeding and amusing her in the style she was accustomed to being fed and amused in was utterly beyond my means. Of course she never realized it. People who are born with more than five thousand a year can't be expected to realize. She'd have been terribly upset if she had; for she had a heart of gold—like all the rest of us." He laughed mournfully. "Poor Sybil! I expect you remember her."

The name evoked for me a pale-eyed, pale-haired ghost. "What an astonishingly lovely creature she was!"

"Was, was," he echoed. "*Fuit*. Lovely and fatal. The agonies she made me suffer! But she was as fatal to herself as to other people. Poor Sybil! I could cry when I think of that inevitable course of hers, that predestined trajectory." With a stretched forefinger he traced in the air a curve that rose and fell away again. "She had just passed the crest when I knew her. The descending branch of the curve was horribly steep. What depths awaited her! That horrible little East-Side Jew she even went to the trouble of marrying! And after the Jew, the Mexican Indian. And meanwhile a little champagne had become rather a lot of champagne, rather a lot of brandy; and the occasional Good Times came to be incessant, a necessity, but so boring, such a dismal routine, so terribly exhausting. I didn't see her for four years after our final quarrel; and then (you've no idea how painful it was) I suddenly found myself shaking hands with a Memento Mori. So worn and ill and tired, so terribly old. Old at thirty-four. And the last time I'd seen her, she'd been radiant. Eighteen months later she was dead; but not before the Indian had given place to a Chinaman and the brandy to cocaine. It was all inevitable, of course, all perfectly foreseeable. Nemesis had functioned with exemplary regularity. Which only made it worse. Nemesis is all right for strangers and casual acquaintances. But for oneself, for the people one likes—ah, no! *We* ought to be allowed to sow without reaping. But we mayn't. I sowed books and reaped Sybil. Sybil sowed me (not to mention the others) and reaped Mexicans, cocaine, death. Inevitable, but an outrage, an insulting denial of one's uniqueness and difference. Whereas when people like Chawdron sow New Guinea Oil and reap kittenish Charlottes, one's delighted; the punctuality of fate seems admirable."

"I never knew that Charlotte had been reaped by Chawdron," I put in. "The harvesting must have been done with extraordinary discretion. Charlotte's usually so fond of publicity, even in these matters. I should never have expected her . . ."

"But the reaping was very brief and partial," Tilney explained.

That surprised me even more. "Charlotte who's

always so determined and clinging! And with Chawdron's millions to cling to. . . ."

"Oh, it wasn't her fault that it went no further. She had every intention of being reaped and permanently garnered. But she had arranged to go to America for two months on a concert tour. It would have been troublesome to break the contract; Chawdron seemed thoroughly infatuated; two months are soon passed. So she went. Full of confidence. But when she came back, Chawdron was otherwise occupied."

"Another kitten?"

"A kitten? Poor Charlotte was a grey-whiskered old tigress by comparison. She even came to me in her despair. No enigmatic subtleties this time; she'd forgotten she was the Sphinx. 'I think you ought to warn Mr. Chawdron against that woman,' she told me. 'He ought to be made to realize that she's exploiting him. It's outrageous.' She was full of righteous indignation. Not unnaturally. Even got angry with me, because I wouldn't do anything. 'But he wants to be exploited,' I told her. 'It's his only joy in life.' Which was perfectly true. But I couldn't resist being a little malicious. 'What makes you want to spoil his fun?' I asked. She got quite red in the face. 'Because I think it's disgusting.' " Tilney made his voice indignantly shrill. " 'It really shocks me to see a man like Mr. Chawdron being made a fool of in that way.' Poor Charlotte! Her feelings did her credit. But they were quite unavailing. Chawdron went on being made a fool of, in spite of her moral indignation. Charlotte had to retreat. The enemy was impregnably entrenched."

"But who was she—the enemy?"

"The unlikeliest *femme fatale* you ever saw. Little; rather ugly; sickly—yes, genuinely sickly, I think, though she did a good deal of pathetic malingering too; altogether too much the lady—refined; you know the type. A governess; not the modern breezy, athletic sort of governess—the genteel, Jane Eyre, daughter-of-clergyman kind. Her only visible merit was that she was young. About twenty-five, I suppose."

"But how on earth did they meet? Millionaires and governesses . . ."

"A pure miracle," said Tilney. "Chawdron himself detected the hand of Providence. That was the deep religious sense coming in. 'If it hadn't been for *both* my secretaries falling ill on the same day,' he said to me solemnly (and you've no idea how ridiculous he looked when he was being solemn—the saintly forger, the burglar in the pulpit), 'if it hadn't been for that—and after all, how unlikely it is that both one's secretaries should fall ill at the same moment; what a *fateful* thing to happen!—I should never have got to know my little Fairy.' And you must imagine the last words pronounced with a reverent and beautiful smile—indescribably incongruous on that crook's mug of his. 'My little Fairy,' (her real name, incidentally, was Maggie Spindell), 'my little

Fairy!' " Tilney seraphically smiled and rolled up his eyes. "You can't imagine the expression. St. Charles Borromeo in the act of breaking into the till."

"Painted by Carlo Dolci," I suggested.

"With the assistance of Rowlandson. Do you begin to get it?"

I nodded. "But the secretaries?" I was anxious to hear the story.

"They had orders to deal summarily with all begging letters, all communications from madmen, inventors, misunderstood geniuses, and, finally, women. The job was a heavy one, I can tell you. You've no idea what a rich man's post-bag is like. Fantastic. Well, as I say, Providence had given both private secretaries the 'flu. Chawdron happened to have nothing better to do that morning (Providence again); so he started opening his own correspondence. The third letter he opened was from the Fairy. It bowled him over."

"What was in it?"

Tilney shrugged his shoulders. "He never showed it me. But from what I gathered, she wrote about God and the Universe in general and her soul in particular, not to mention *his* soul. Having no taste, and being wholly without education, Chawdron was tremendously impressed by her philosophical rigmarole. It appealed to that deep religious sense! Indeed, he was so much impressed that he immediately wrote giving her an appointment. She came, saw, and con-

quered. 'Providential, my dear boy, providential.'
And of course he was right. Only I'd have dechristened the power and called it Nemesis. Miss Spindell was the instrument of Nemesis; she was Atè in the fancy dress that Chawdron's way of life had caused him to find irresistible. She was the finally ripened fruit of sowings in New Guinea Oil and the like."

"But if your account's correct," I put in, "delicious fruit—that is, for *his* taste. Being exploited by kittens was his only joy; you said it yourself. Nemesis was rewarding him for his offences, not punishing."

Tilney paused in his striding up and down the room, meditatively knitted his brows and, taking his pipe out of his mouth, rubbed the side of his nose with the hot bowl. "Yes," he said slowly, "that's an important point. I've had it vaguely in my head before now; but now you've put it clearly. From the point of view of the offender, the punishments of Nemesis may actually look like rewards. Yes, it's quite true."

"In which case your Nemesis isn't much use as a policewoman."

He held up his hand. "But Nemesis isn't a policewoman. Nemesis isn't moral. At least she's only incidentally moral, more or less by accident. Nemesis is something like gravitation, indifferent. All that she does is to guarantee that you shall reap what you sow. And if you sow self-stultification, as Chawdron did with his excessive interest in money, you reap grotesque humiliation. But as you're already reduced by your offences to a sub-human condition, you won't notice that the grotesque humiliation is a humiliation. There's your explanation why Nemesis sometimes seems to reward. What she brings is a humiliation only in the absolute sense—for the ideal and complete human being; or at any rate, in practice, for the nearly complete, the approaching-the-ideal human being. For the sub-human specimen it may seem a triumph, a consummation, a fulfilment of the heart's desire. But then, you must remember, the desiring heart is a heart of hog-wash. . . ."

"Moral," I concluded: "Live sub-humanly and Nemesis may bring you happiness."

"Precisely. But *what* happiness!"

I shrugged my shoulders. "But after all, for the relativist, one sort of happiness is as good as another. You're taking the God's-eye view."

"The Greek's-eye view," he corrected.

"As you like. But anyhow, from the Chawdron's-eye view the happiness is perfect. Therefore we ought to make ourselves like Chawdron."

Tilney nodded. "Yes," he said, "you need to be a bit of a platonist to see that the punishments *are* punishments. And of course if there *were* another life . . . Or better still metempsychosis: there are some unbelievably disgusting insects. . . . But even from the merely utilitarian point of view Chawdronism is dangerous. Socially dangerous. A society constructed by and for men can't work if all its components are emotionally sub-men. When the majority of hearts have turned to hog-wash, something catastrophic must happen. So that Nemesis turns out to be a policewoman after all. I hope you're satisfied."

"Perfectly."

"You always did have a very discreditable respect for law and order and morality," he complained.

"They must exist . . ."

"I don't know why," he interrupted me.

"In order that you and I may be immoral in comfort," I explained. "Law and order exist to make the world safe for lawless and disorderly individualists."

"Not to mention ruffians like Chawdron. From whom, by the way, we seem to have wandered. Where was I?"

"You'd just got to his providential introduction to the Fairy."

"Yes, yes. Well, as I said, she came, saw, conquered. Three days later she was installed in the house. He made her his librarian."

"*And* his mistress, I suppose."

Tilney raised his shoulders and threw out his hands in a questioning gesture. "Ah," he said, "that's the question. There you're touching the heart of the mystery."

"But you don't mean to tell me . . ."

"I don't mean to tell you anything, for the good reason that I don't know. I only guess."

"And what do you guess?"

"Sometimes one thing and sometimes another. The Fairy was genuinely enigmatic. None of poor Charlotte's fabricated sphinxishness; a real mystery. With the Fairy anything was possible."

"But not with Chawdron surely. In these matters, wasn't he . . . well, all too human?"

"No, only sub-human. Which is rather different. The Fairy roused in him all his sub-human spirituality and religiosity. Whereas with Charlotte it was the no less sub-human passion for the *détournement de mineurs* that came to the surface."

I objected. "That's too crude and schematic to be good psychology. Emotional states aren't so definite and clear-cut as that. There isn't one compartment for spirituality and another, water-tight, for the *détournement de mineurs*. There's an overlapping, a fusion, a mixture."

"You're probably right," said Tilney. "And, indeed, one of my conjectures was precisely of such a fusion. You know the sort of thing: discourses insensibly giving place to amorous action—though 'action' seems too strong a word to describe what I have in mind. Something ever so softly senile and girlish. Positively spiritual contacts. The loves of the angels—so angelic that, when it was all over, one wouldn't be quite sure whether there had been any interruption in the mystical conversation or not. Which would justify the Fairy in her righteous indignation when she heard of any one's venturing to suppose that she was anything more than Chawdron's librarian. She could almost honestly believe she wasn't. 'I think people are too horrid,' she used to say to me on these occasions. 'I think they're simply disgusting. Can't they even believe in the possibility of purity?' Angry she was, outraged, hurt. And the emotion seemed absolutely real. Which was such a rare occurrence in the Fairy's life—at any rate, so it seemed to me—that I was forced to believe it had a genuine cause."

"Aren't we all genuinely angry when we hear that our acquaintances say the same sort of things about us as we say about them?"

"Of course; and the truer the gossip, the angrier we are. But the Fairy was angry because the gossip was untrue. She insisted on that—and insisted so genuinely (this is the point I was trying to make) that I couldn't help believing she had some justification. Either nothing had happened, or else something so softly and slimily angelic that it slipped past the attention, escaped notice, counted for nothing."

"But after all," I protested, "it's not because one looks truthful that one's telling the truth."

"No. But then you didn't know the Fairy. She hardly ever looked or sounded truthful. There was hardly anything she said that didn't strike me as being in one way or another a manifest lie. So that when she did seem to be telling the truth (and it was incredible how rarely that happened), I was always impressed. I couldn't help thinking there must be a reason. That's why I attach such importance to the really heart-felt way she got angry when doubts were cast on the purity of her relations with Chawdron. I believe that they really were pure, or else, more probably, that the impurity was such a little one, so to speak, that she could honestly regard it as non-existent. You'd have had the same impression too, if you'd heard her. The genuineness of the anger, the outraged protest, was obvious. And then suddenly she remembered that she was a Christian, practically a saint; she'd start forgiving her enemies. 'One's sorry for them,' she'd say, 'because they don't know any better. Poor people! Ignorant of all the finer feelings, all the more beautiful relationships.' I can't tell you how awful the word 'beautiful' was in her mouth! Really blood-curdling. Be-yütiful. Very long-drawn-out, with the oo sound thinned and refined into German u-modified. Be-yütiful. Ugh!" He shuddered. "It made one want to kill her. But then the whole tone of these Christian sentiments made one want to kill her. When she forgave the poor misguided people who couldn't see the be-yüty of her relations with Chawdron you were horrified, you felt sick, you went cold all over. For the whole thing was such a lie, so utterly and bottomlessly false. After the genuine anger against the scandal-mongers, the falseness rang even falser than usual. Obvious, unmistakable, painful—like an untuned piano, like a cuckoo in June. Chawdron was deaf to it, of course; just didn't hear the falseness. If you have a deep religious sense, I suppose you don't notice those things. 'I think she has the most beautiful character I've ever met with in a human being,' he used to tell me. ('Beautiful' again, you notice. Chawdron caught the trick from her. But in his mouth it was merely funny, not gruesome.) 'The most beautiful character'—and then his beatific smile. Grotesque! It was just the same as with Charlotte; he swallowed her whole. Charlotte played the jolly kitten and he accepted her as the jolly kitten. The Fairy's ambition was to be regarded as a sanctified Christian kitten; and duly, as a Christian kitten, a confirmed, communicant, Catholic, canonized Kitten, he did regard her. Incredible; but, there! if you spend all your wits and energies knowing about Oil, you can't be expected to know much about anything else. You can't be expected to know the difference between tarantulas and kittens, for example; nor the difference between St. Catherine of Siena and a little liar, like Maggie Spindell."

"But did she know she was lying?" I asked. "Was she consciously a hypocrite?"

Tilney repeated his gesture of uncertainty. "*Chi lo sa?*" he said. "That's the finally unanswerable question. It takes us back to where we were just now with Chawdron—to the borderland between biography and autobiography. Which is more real: you as you see yourself, or you as others see you? you in your intentions and motives, or you in the product of your intentions? you in your actions, or you in the results of your actions? And anyhow, what *are* your intentions and motives? And who is the 'you' who has intentions? So that when you ask if the Fairy was a conscious liar and hypocrite, I just have to say that I don't know. Nobody knows. Not even the Fairy herself. For, after all, there were several Fairies. There was one that wanted to be fed and looked after and given money and perhaps married one day, if Chawdron's wife happened to die."

"I didn't know he had a wife," I interrupted in some astonishment.

"Mad," Tilney telegraphically explained. "Been in an asylum for the last twenty-five years. I'd have gone mad too, if I'd been married to Chawdron. But that didn't prevent the Fairy from aspiring to be the second Mrs. C. Money is always money. Well, there was *that* Fairy—the adventuress, the Darwinian specimen struggling for existence. But there was also a Fairy that genuinely wanted to be Christian and saintly. A spiritual Fairy. And if the spirituality happened to pay with tired business men like Chawdron—well, obviously, *tant mieux*."

"But the falseness you spoke of, the lying, the hypocrisy?"

"Mere inefficiency," Tilney answered. "Just bad acting. For, when all's said and done, what is hypocrisy but bad acting? It differs from saintliness as a performance by Lucien Guitry differed from a performance by his son. One's artistically good and the other isn't."

I laughed. "You forget I'm a moralist; at least, you said I was. These aesthetic heresies . . ."

"Not heresies; just obvious statements of the facts. For what is the practice of morality? It's just pretending to be somebody that by nature you aren't. It's acting the part of a saint, or a hero, or a respectable citizen. What's the highest ethical ideal in Christianity? It's expressed in A Kempis's formula—'The Imitation of Christ.' So that the organized Churches turn out to be nothing but vast and elaborate Academies of Dramatic Art. And every school's a school of acting. Every family's a family of Crummleses. Every human being is brought up as a mummer. All education, aside from merely intellectual education, is just a series of rehearsals for the part of Jesus or Podsnap or Alexander the Great, or whoever the local favourite may be. A virtuous man is one who's learned his part thoroughly and acts it competently and convincingly. The saint and the hero are great actors; they're Kembles and Siddonses—people with a genius for representing heroic characters not their own; or people with the luck to be born so like the heroic ideal that they can just step straight into the part without rehearsal. The wicked are those who either can't or won't learn to act. Imagine a scene-shifter, slightly drunk, dressed in his overalls and smoking a pipe; he comes reeling on to the stage in the middle of the trial scene in the *Merchant of Venice*, shouts down Portia, gives Antonio a kick in the stern, knocks over a few

Magnificos and pulls off Shylock's false beard. That's a criminal. As for a hypocrite—he's either a criminal interrupter disguised, temporarily and for his own purposes, as an actor (that's Tartuffe) ; or else (and I think this is the commoner type) he's just a bad actor. By nature, like all the rest of us, he's a criminal interrupter; but he accepts the teaching of the local Academies of Dramatic Art and admits that man's highest duty is to act star parts to applauding houses. But he is wholly without talent. When he's thinking of his noble part, he mouths and rants and gesticulates, till you feel really ashamed as you watch him—ashamed for yourself, for him, for the human species. 'Methinks the lady, or gentleman, doth protest too much,' is what you say. And these protestations seem even more excessive when, a few moments later, you observe that the protester has forgotten altogether that he's playing a part and is behaving like the interrupting criminal that it's his nature to be. But he himself is so little the mummer, so utterly without a talent for convincing representation, that he simply doesn't notice his own interruptions; or if he notices them, does so only slightly and with the conviction that nobody else will notice them. In other words, most hypocrites are more or less unconscious hypocrites. The Fairy, I'm sure, was one of them. She was simply not aware of being an adventuress with an eye on Chawdron's millions. What she was conscious of was her rôle— the rôle of St. Catherine of Siena. She believed in

her acting; she was ambitious to be a high-class
West-End artiste. But, unfortunately, she was without talent. She played her part so unnaturally, with
such grotesque exaggerations, that a normally sensitive person could only shudder at the shameful
spectacle. It was a performance that only the spiritually deaf and blind could be convinced by. And,
thanks to his preoccupations with New Guinea Oil,
Chawdron *was* spiritually deaf and blind. His deep
religious sense was the deep religious sense of a sub-
man. When she paraded the canonized kitten, I felt
seasick; but Chawdron thought she had the most be-
yütiful character he'd ever met with in a human
being. And not only did he think she had the most
beautiful character; he also, which was almost fun-
nier, thought she had the finest mind. It was her
metaphysical conversation that impressed him. She'd
read a few snippets from Spinoza and Plato and
some little book on the Christian mystics and a fair
amount of that flabby theosophical literature that's
so popular in Garden Suburbs and among retired
colonels and ladies of a certain age; so she could talk
about the cosmos very profoundly. And, by God, she
was profound! I used to lose my temper sometimes,
it was such drivel, so dreadfully illiterate. But Chawdron listened reverently, fairly goggling with rapture and faith and admiration. He believed every
word. When you're totally uneducated and have
amassed an enormous fortune by legal swindling,
you can afford to believe in the illusoriness of mat-

ter, the non-existence of evil, the oneness of all di-
versity, and the spirituality of everything. All his
life he'd kept up his childhood's Presbyterianism—
most piously. And now he grafted the Fairy's rigmarole on to the Catechism, or whatever it is that
Presbyterians learn in infancy. He didn't see that
there was any contradiction between the two metaphysics, just as he'd never seen that there was any
incongruity in his being both a good Presbyterian
and a consummate swindler. He had acted the Presbyterian part only on Sundays and when he was ill,
never in business hours. Religion had never been permitted to invade the sanctities of private life. But
with the advance of middle age his mind grew flab-
bier; the effects of a misspent life began to make
themselves felt. And at the same time his retirement
from business removed almost all the external distractions. His deep religious sense had more chance
to express itself. He could wallow in sentimentality
and silliness undisturbed. The Fairy made her providential appearance and showed him which were the
softest emotional and intellectual muck-heaps to wallow on. He was grateful—loyally, but a little ludi-
crously. I shall never forget, for example, the time
he talked about the Fairy's genius. We'd been dining
at his house, he and I and the Fairy. A terrible
dinner, with the Fairy, as a mixture between St.
Catherine of Siena and Mahatma Gandhi, explaining why she was a vegetarian and an ascetic. She
had that awful genteel middle-class food complex

which makes table manners at Lyons' Corner Houses so appallingly good—that haunting fear of being low or vulgar, which causes people to eat as though they weren't eating. They never take a large mouthful, and only masticate with their front teeth, like rabbits. And they never touch anything with their fingers. I've actually seen a women eating cherries with a knife and fork at one of those places. Most extraordinary and most repulsive. Well, the Fairy had that complex—it's a matter of class—but it was rationalized, with her, in terms of *ahimsa* and ascetic Christianity. Well, she'd been chattering the whole evening about the spirit of love and its incompatibility with a meat diet and the necessity of mortifying the body for the sake of the soul, and about Buddha and St. Francis and mystical ecstasies and, above all, herself. Drove me almost crazy with irritation, not to mention the fact that she really began putting me off my food with her rhapsodies of pious horror and disgust. I was thankful when at last she left us in peace to our brandy and cigars. But Chawdron leaned across the table towards me, spiritually beaming from every inch of that forger's face of his. 'Isn't she wonderful?' he said. 'Isn't she simply *wonderful?*' 'Wonderful,' I agreed. And then, very solemnly, wagging his finger at me, 'I've known three great intellects in my time,' he said, 'three minds of genius—Lord Northcliffe, Mr. John Morley, and this little girl. Those three.' And he leant back in his chair and nodded at me almost fiercely, as though challenging me to deny it."

"And did you accept the challenge?" I asked, laughing.

Tilney shook his head. "I just helped myself to another nip of his 1820 brandy; it was the only retort a rational man could make."

"And did the Fairy share Chawdron's opinion about her mind?"

"Oh, I think so," said Tilney, "I think so. She had a great conceit of herself. Like all these spiritual people. An inordinate conceit. She played the superior rôle very badly and inconsistently. But all the same she was convinced of her superiority. Inevitably; for, you see, she had an enormous capacity for auto-suggestion. What she told herself three times became true. For example, I used at first to think there was some hocus-pocus about her asceticism. She ate so absurdly little in public and at meals that I fancied she must do a little tucking-in privately in between whiles. But later I came to the conclusion that I'd maligned her. By dint of constantly telling herself and other people that eating was unspiritual and gross, not to mention impolite and lower-class, she'd genuinely succeeded, I believe, in making food disgust her. She'd got to a point where she really couldn't eat more than a very little. Which was one of the causes of her sickliness. She was just undernourished. But under-nourishment was only *one* of the causes. She was also diplomatically sick. She threatened to die as statesmen threaten to mobilize, in order to get what she wanted. Blackmail, in fact. Not for money; she was curiously disinterested in many ways. What she wanted was his interest, was power over him, was self-assertion. She had headaches for the same reason as a baby howls. If you give in to the baby and do what it wants, it'll howl again, it'll make a habit of howling. Chawdron was one of the weak-minded sort of parents. When the Fairy had one of her famous headaches, he was terribly disturbed. The way he fluttered round the sick-room with ice and hot-water bottles and eau-de-Cologne! The *Times* obituarist would have wept to see him; such a touching exhibition of the heart of gold! The result was that the Fairy used to have a headache every three or four days. It was absolutely intolerable."

"But were they purely imaginary, these headaches?"

Tilney shrugged his shoulders. "Yes and no. There was certainly a physiological basis. The woman did have pains in her head from time to time. It was only to be expected; she was run down, through not eating enough; she didn't take sufficient exercise, so she had chronic constipation; chronic constipation probably set up a slight chronic inflammation of the ovaries; and she certainly suffered from eye-strain—you could tell that from the beautifully vague, spiritual look in her eyes, the look that comes from uncorrected myopia. There were, as you see, plenty of physiological reasons for her headaches. Her body made her a present, so to speak, of the pain. Her mind then proceeded to work up this raw material. Into what remarkable forms! Touched by her imagination, the headaches became mystic, transcendental. It was infinity in a grain of sand and eternity in an intestinal stasis. Regularly every Tuesday and Friday she died—died with a beautiful Christian resignation, a martyr's fortitude. Chawdron used to come down from the sick-room with tears in his eyes. He'd never seen such patience, such courage, such grit. There were few men she wouldn't put to shame. She was a wonderful example. And so on. And I dare say it was all quite true. She started by malingering a little, by pretending that the headaches were worse than they were. But her imagination was too lively for her; it got beyond her control. Her pretendings gradually came true and she really did suffer martyrdom each time; she really did very nearly die. And then she got into the habit of being a martyr, and the attacks came on regularly; imagination stimulated the normal activities of inflamed ovaries and poisoned intestines; the pain made its appearance and at once became the raw material of a mystic, spiritual martyrdom taking place on a higher plane. Anyhow, it was all very complicated and obscure. And, obviously, if the Fairy herself had given you an account of her existence at this time, it would have sounded like St. Lawrence's reminiscences of life on the grill. Or rather it would have sounded like the insincere fabrication of such reminiscences. For the Fairy, as I've said before, was without talent, and sincerity and saintliness are matters of talent. Hypocrisy and insincerity are the products of native incompetence. Those who are guilty of them are people without skill in the arts of behaviour and self-expression. The Fairy's talk would have sounded utterly false to you. But for her it was all genuine. She really suffered, really died, really was good and resigned and courageous. Just as the paranoiac is really Napoleon Bonaparte and the young man with *dementia præcox* is really being spied on and persecuted by a gang of fiendishly ingenuous enemies. If *I* were to tell the story from *her* point of view, it would sound really beautiful—not be-yütiful, mind you; but truly and genuinely beautiful; for the good reason that *I* have a gift of expression, which the poor Fairy hadn't. So that, for all but emotional cretins like Chawdron, she was obviously a hypocrite and a liar. Also a bit of a pathological case. For that capacity for auto-suggestion really was rather pathological. She could make things come *too* true. Not merely diseases and martyrdoms and saintliness, but also historical facts, or rather historical not-facts. She authenticated the not-facts by simply repeating that they had happened. For example, she wanted people to believe—she wanted to believe herself—that she had been intimate with Chawdron for years and years, from childhood, from the time of her birth. The fact that he had known her since she was 'so high' would explain and justify her present relationship with him. The scandalmongers would have no excuse for talking. So she proceeded bit by bit to fabricate a lifelong intimacy, even a bit of an actual kinship, with her Uncle Benny. I told you that that was what she called him, didn't I? That nickname had its significance; it planted him at once in the table of consanguinity and so disinfected their relations, so to speak, automatically made them innocent."

"Or incestuous," I added.

"Or incestuous. Quite. But she didn't consider the D'Annunzioesque refinements. When she gave him that name, she promoted Chawdron to the rank of a dear old kinsman, or at least a dear old family friend. Sometimes she even called him 'Nunky Benny,' so as to show that she had known him from the cradle—had lisped of nunkies, for the nunkies came. But that wasn't enough. The evidence had to be fuller, more circumstantial. So she invented it— romps with Nunky in the hay, visits to the pantomime with him, a whole outfit of childish memories."

"But what about Chawdron?" I asked. "Did he share the invented memories?"

Tilney nodded. "But for him, of course, they *were* invented. Other people, however, accepted them as facts. Her reminiscences were so detailed and circumstantial that, unless you *knew* she was a liar, you simply had to accept them. With Chawdron himself she couldn't, of course, pretend that she'd known him, literally and historically, all those years. Not at first, in any case. The lifelong intimacy started by being figurative and spiritual. 'I feel as though I'd known my Uncle Benny ever since I was a tiny baby,' she said to me in his presence, quite soon after she'd first got to know him; and as always, on such occasions, she made her voice even more whiningly babyish than usual. Dreadful that voice was— so whiney-piney, so falsely sweet. 'Ever since I was a teeny, tiny baby. Don't you feel like that, Uncle Benny?' And Chawdron heartily agreed; of course he felt like that. From that time forward she began to expatiate on the incidents which ought to have occurred in that far-off childhood with darling Nunky. They were the same incidents, of course, as those which she actually remembered when she was talking to strangers and he wasn't there. She made him give her old photographs of himself—visions of him in high collars and frock-coats, in queer-looking Norfolk jackets, in a top-hat sitting in a victoria. They helped her to make her fancies real. With their aid and the aid of his reminiscences she constructed a whole life in common with him. 'Do you remember, Uncle Benny, the time we went to Cowes on your yacht and I fell into the sea?' she'd ask. And Chawdron, who thoroughly entered into the game, would answer: 'Of course I remember. And when we'd fished you out, we had to wrap you in hot blankets and give you warm rum and milk. And you got quite drunk.' 'Was I funny when I was drunk, Uncle

Benny?' And Chawdron would rather lamely and
ponderously invent a few quaintnesses which were
then incorporated in the history. So that on a future
occasion the Fairy could begin: 'Nunky Benny, do
you remember those ridiculous things I said when
you made me drunk with rum and hot milk that time
I fell into the sea at Cowes?' And so on. Chawdron
loved the game, thought it simply too sweet and
whimsical and touching—positively like something
out of Barrie or A. A. Milne—and was never tired
of playing it. As for the Fairy—for her it wasn't a
game at all. The not-facts had been repeated till
they became facts. 'But, come, Miss Spindell,' I said
to her once, when she'd been telling me—*me!*—about
some adventure she'd had with Uncle Benny when
she was a toddler, 'come, come, Miss Spindell' (I
always called her that, though she longed to be my
Fairy as well as Chawdron's and would have called
me Uncle Ted, if I'd given her the smallest encouragement; but I took a firm line; she was always Miss
Spindell for me), 'come,' I said, 'you seem to forget
that it's only just over a year since you saw Mr.
Chawdron for the first time.' She looked at me quite
blankly for a moment without saying anything. 'You
can't seriously expect me to forget too,' I added.
Poor Fairy! The blankness suddenly gave place to
a painful, blushing embarrassment. 'Oh, of course,'
she began, and laughed nervously. 'It's as though
I'd known him for ever. My imagination . . .' She
trailed off into silence, and a minute later made an

excuse to leave me. I could see she was upset, physically upset, as though she'd been woken up too
suddenly out of a sound sleep, jolted out of one
world into another moving in a different direction.
But when I saw her the next day, she seemed to be
quite herself again. She had suggested herself back
into the dream world; from the other end of the
table, at lunch, I heard her talking to an American
business acquaintance of Chawdron's about the fun
she and Uncle Benny used to have on his grouse
moor in Scotland. But from that time forth, I noticed, she never talked to me about her apocryphal
childhood again. A curious incident; it made me look
at her hypocrisy in another light. It was then I began to realize that the lie in her soul was mainly an
unconscious lie, the product of pathology and a lack
of talent. Mainly; but sometimes, on the contrary,
the lie was only too conscious and deliberate. The
most extraordinary of them was the lie at the bottom
of the great Affair of the Stigmata."

"The stigmata?" I echoed. "A pious lie, then."

"Pious." He nodded. "That was how she justified
it to herself. Though, of course, in her eyes, all her
lies were pious lies. Pious, because they served *her*
purposes and she was a saint; her cause was sacred.
And afterwards, of course, when she'd treated the lies
to her process of imaginative disinfection, they
ceased to be lies and fluttered away as snow-white
pious truths. But to start with they were undoubt-
edly pious lies, even for her. The Affair of the Stig-

mata made that quite clear. I caught her in the act. It all began with a boil that developed on Chawdron's foot."

"Curious place to have a boil."

"Not common," he agreed. "I once had one there myself, when I was a boy. Most unpleasant, I can assure you. Well, the same thing happened to Chawdron. He and I were down at his country place, playing golf and in the intervals concocting the *Autobiography*. We'd settle down with brandy and cigars and I'd gently question him. Left to himself, he was apt to wander and become incoherent and unchronological. I had to canalize his narrative, so to speak. Remarkably frank he was. I learnt some curious things about the business world, I can tell you. Needless to say, they're not in the *Autobiography*. I'm reserving them for the *Life*. Which means, alas, that nobody will ever know them. Well, as I say, we were down there in the country for a long week-end, Friday to Tuesday. The Fairy had stayed in London. Periodically she took her librarianship very seriously and protested that she simply had to get on with the catalogue. 'I have my duties,' she said when Chawdron suggested that she should come down to the country with us. 'You must let me get on with my duties. I don't think one ought to be just frivolous; do you Uncle Benny? Besides, I really love my work.' God, how she enraged me with that whiney-piney talk! But Chawdron, of course, was touched and enchanted. 'What an extraordinary little person she is!' he said to me as we left the house together. Even more extraordinary than you suppose, I thought. He went on rhapsodizing as far as Watford. But in a way, I could see, when we arrived, in a way he was quite pleased she hadn't come. It was a relief to him to be having a little masculine holiday. She had the wit to see that he needed these refreshments from time to time. Well, we duly played our golf, with the result that by Sunday morning poor Chawdron's boil, which had been a negligible little spot on the Friday, had swollen up with the chafing and the exercise into a massive red hemisphere that made walking an agony. Unpleasant, no doubt; but nothing, for any ordinary person, to get seriously upset about. Chawdron, however, wasn't an ordinary person where boils were concerned. He had a carbuncle-complex, a boilophobia. Excusably, perhaps; for it seems that his brother had died of some awful kind of gangrene that had started, to all appearances harmlessly, in a spot on his cheek. Chawdron couldn't develop a pimple without imagining that he'd caught his brother's disease. This affair on his foot scared him out of his wits. He saw the bone infected, the whole leg rotting away, amputations, death. I offered what comfort and encouragement I could and sent for the local doctor. He came at once and turned out to be a young man, very determined and efficient and confidence-inspiring. The boil was anaesthetized, lanced, cleaned out, tied up. Chawdron was promised there'd be no complications. And there weren't. The thing healed up quite normally. Chawdron decided to go back to town on the Tuesday, as he'd arranged. 'I wouldn't like to disappoint Fairy,' he explained. 'She'd be so sad if I didn't come back when I'd promised. Besides, she might be nervous. You've no idea what an intuition that little girl has—almost uncanny, like second sight. She'd guess something was wrong and be upset; and you know how bad it is for her to be upset.' I did indeed; those mystic headaches of hers were the bane of my life. No, no, I agreed. She mustn't be upset. So it was decided that the Fairy should be kept in blissful ignorance of the boil until Chawdron had actually arrived. But the question then arose: how should he arrive? We had gone down into the country in Chawdron's Bugatti. He had a weakness for speed. But it wasn't the car for an invalid. It was arranged that the chauffeur should drive the Bugatti up to town and come back with the Rolls. In the unlikely event of his seeing Miss Spindell, he was not to tell her why he had been sent to town. Those were his orders. The man went and duly returned with the Rolls. Chawdron was installed, almost as though he were in an ambulance, and we rolled majestically up to London. What a homecoming! In anticipation of the sympathy he would get from the Fairy, Chawdron began to have a slight relapse as we approached the house. 'I feel it throbbing,' he assured me; and when he got out of the car, what a limp! As though he'd lost a leg at Gallipoli.

Really heroic. The butler had to support him up to the drawing-room. He was lowered onto the sofa. 'Is Miss Spindell in her room?' The butler thought so. 'Then ask her to come down here at once.' The man went out; Chawdron closed his eyes—wearily, like a very sick man. He was preparing to get all the sympathy he could and, I could see, luxuriously relishing it in advance. 'Still throbbing?' I asked, rather irreverently. He nodded, without opening his eyes. 'Still throbbing.' The manner was grave and sepulchral. I had to make an effort not to laugh. There was a silence; we waited. And then the door opened. The Fairy appeared. But a maimed Fairy. One foot in a high-heeled shoe, the other in a slipper. Such a limp! 'Another leg lost at Gallipoli,' thought I. When he heard the door open, Chawdron shut his eyes tighter than ever and turned his face to the wall, or at any rate the back of the sofa. I could see that this rather embarrassed the Fairy. Her entrance had been dramatic; she had meant him to see her disablement at once; hadn't counted on finding a death-bed scene. She had hastily to improvise another piece of stage business, a new set of lines; the scene she had prepared wouldn't do. Which was the more embarrassing for her as I was there, looking on—a very cool spectator, as she knew; not in the least a Maggie Spindell fan. She hesitated a second near the door, hoping Chawdron would look round; but he kept his eyes resolutely shut and his face averted. He'd evidently decided to play the moribund part for all it was worth. So, after one rather nervous glance at me, she limped across the room to the sofa. 'Uncle Benny!' He gave a great start, as though he hadn't known she was there. 'Is that you, Fairy?' This was *pianissimo, con espressione*. Then, *molto agitato* from the Fairy: 'What is it, Nunky Benny? What is it? Oh, tell me.' She was close enough now to lay a hand on his shoulder. 'Tell me.' He turned his face towards her—the tenderly transfigured burglar. His heart overflowed—'Fairy!'—a slop of hog-wash. 'But what's the matter, Nunky Benny?' 'Nothing, Fairy.' The tone implied that it was a heroic understatement in the manner of Sir Philip Sidney. 'Only my foot.' 'Your foot!' The Fairy registered such astonishment that we both fairly jumped. 'Something wrong with your foot?' 'Yes, why not?' Chawdron was rather annoyed; he wasn't getting the kind of sympathy he'd looked forward to. She turned to me. 'But when did it happen, Mr. Tilney?' I was breezy. 'A nasty boil,' I explained. 'Walking round the course did it no good. It had to be lanced on Sunday.' 'At about half-past eleven on Sunday morning?' 'Yes, I suppose it was about half-past eleven,' I said, thinking the question was an odd one. 'It was just half-past eleven when *this* happened,' she said dramatically, pointing to her slippered foot. 'What's "this"?' asked Chawdron crossly. He was thoroughly annoyed at being swindled out of sympathy. I took pity on the Fairy; things seemed to be going so badly for her. I could see that she had prepared a coup and that it hadn't come off. 'Miss Spindell also seems to have hurt her foot,' I explained. 'You didn't see how she limped.' 'How did you hurt it?' asked Chawdron. He was still very grumpy. 'I was sitting quietly in the library, working at the catalogue,' she began: and I guessed, by the way the phrases came rolling out, that she was at last being able to make use of the material she had prepared, 'when suddenly, almost exactly at half-past eleven (I remember looking at the clock), I felt a terrible pain in my foot. As though some one were driving a sharp, sharp knife into it. It was so intense that I nearly fainted.' She paused for a moment, expecting appropriate comment. But Chawdron wouldn't make it. So I put in a polite 'Dear me, most extraordinary!' with which she had to be content. 'When I got up,' she continued, 'I could hardly stand, my foot hurt me so; and I've been limping ever since. And the most extraordinary thing is that there's a red mark on my foot, like a scar.' Another expectant pause. But still no word from Chawdron. He sat there with his mouth tight shut and the lines that divided his cheeks from that wide simian upper lip of his were as though engraved in stone. The Fairy looked at him and saw that she had taken hopelessly the wrong line. Was it too late to remedy the mistake? She put the new plan of campaign into immediate execution. 'But you poor Nunky Benny!' she began in the sort of tone in which you'd talk to a sick dog. 'How selfish of me to talk about my ailments, when you're lying there with your poor foot bandaged up!' The dog began to wag his tail at once. The beatific look returned to his face. He took her hand. I couldn't stand it. 'I think I'd better be going,' I said; and I went."

"But the foot?" I asked. "The stabbing pain at exactly half-past eleven?"

"You may well ask. As Chawdron himself remarked, when next I saw him, 'There are more things in heaven and earth, Horatio, than are dreamt of in your philosophy.' " Tilney laughed. "The Fairy had triumphed. After he'd had his dose of mother love and Christian charity and kittenish sympathy, he'd been ready, I suppose, to listen to *her* story. The stabbing pain at eleven-thirty, the red scar. Strange, mysterious, unaccountable. He discussed it all with me, very gravely and judiciously. We talked of spiritualism and telepathy. We distinguished carefully between the miraculous and the super-normal. 'As you know,' he told me, 'I've been a good Presbyterian all my life, and as such have been inclined to dismiss as mere fabrications all the stories of the Romish saints. I never believed in the story of St. Francis's stigmata, for example. But now I accept it!' Solemn and tremendous pause. 'Now I *know* it's true.' I just bowed my head in silence. But the next time I saw M'Crea, the chauffeur, I asked a few questions. Yes, he *had* seen Miss Spindell that day he drove the Bugatti up to London and came back with the Rolls. He'd gone into the secretaries' office to see if there were any letters to take down for Mr. Chawdron, and Miss Spindell had run into him as he came out. She'd asked him what he was doing in London and he hadn't been able to think of anything to answer, in spite of Mr. Chawdron's orders, except the truth. It had been on his conscience ever since; he hoped it hadn't done any harm. 'On the contrary,' I assured him, and that I certainly wouldn't tell Mr. Chawdron. Which I never did. I thought . . . But good heavens!" he interrupted himself; "what's this?" It was Hawtrey, who had come in to lay the table for lunch. She ignored us, actively. It was not only as though we didn't exist; it was as though we also had no right to exist. Tilney took out his watch. "Twenty past one. God almighty! Do you mean to say I've been talking here the whole morning since breakfast?"

"So it appears," I answered.

He groaned. "You see," he said, "you see what it is to have a gift of the gab. A whole precious morning utterly wasted."

"Not for me," I said.

He shrugged his shoulders. "Perhaps not. But then for you the story was new and curious. Whereas for me it's known, it's stale."

"But for Shakespeare so was the story of Othello, even before he started to write it."

"Yes, but he *wrote*, he didn't talk. There was something to show for the time he'd spent. His Othello didn't just disappear into thin air, like my poor Chawdron." He sighed and was silent. Stone-faced and grim, Hawtrey went rustling starchily round the table; there was a clinking of steel and silver as she laid the places. I waited till she had left the room before I spoke again. When one's servants are more respectable than one is oneself (and nowadays they generally are), one cannot be too careful.

"And how did it end?" I asked.

"How did it end?" he repeated in a voice that had suddenly gone flat and dull; he was bored with his story, wanted to think of something else. "It ended, so far as I was concerned, with my finishing the *Autobiography* and getting tired of its subject. I gradually faded out of Chawdron's existence. Like the Cheshire Cat."

"And the Fairy?"

"Faded out of life about a year after the Affair of the Stigmata. She retired to her mystic death-bed once too often. Her pretending came true at last; it was always the risk with her. She really did die."

The door opened; Hawtrey re-entered the room, carrying a dish.

"And Chawdron, I suppose, was inconsolable?" Inconsolability is, happily, a respectable subject.

Tilney nodded. "Took to spiritualism, of course. Nemesis again."

Hawtrey raised the lid of the dish; a smell of fried sole escaped into the air. "Luncheon is served," she said with what seemed to me an ill-concealed contempt and disapproval.

"Luncheon is served," Tilney echoed, moving towards his place. He sat down and opened his napkin. "One meal after another, punctually, day after day, day after day. Such is life. Which would be tolerable enough if something ever got done between meals. But in my case nothing does. Meal after meal, and between meals a vacuum, a kind of . . ." Hawtrey, who had been offering him the *sauce tartare* for the past several seconds, here gave him the discreetest nudge. Tilney turned his head. "Ah, thank you," he said, and helped himself.

THE REST CURE

SHE was a tiny woman, dark-haired and with grey-blue eyes, very large and arresting in a small pale face. A little girl's face, with small, delicate features, but worn—prematurely; for Mrs. Tarwin was only twenty-eight; and the big, wide-open eyes were restless and unquietly bright. "Moira's got nerves," her husband would explain when people enquired why she wasn't with him. Nerves that couldn't stand the strain of London or New York. She had to take things quietly in Florence. A sort of rest cure. "Poor darling!" he would add in a voice that had suddenly become furry with sentiment; and he would illuminate his ordinarily rather blankly intelligent face with one of those lightning smiles of his—so wistful and tender and charming. Almost too charming, one felt uncomfortably. He turned on the charm and the wistfulness like electricity. Click! his face was briefly illumined. And then, click! the light went out again and he was once more the blankly intelligent research. student. Cancer was his subject.

Poor Moira! Those nerves of hers! She was full of

caprices and obsessions. For example, when she leased the villa on the slopes of Bellosguardo, she wanted to be allowed to cut down the cypresses at the end of the garden. "So terribly like a cemetery," she kept repeating to old Signor Bargioni. Old Bargioni was charming, but firm. He had no intention of sacrificing his cypresses. They gave the finishing touch of perfection to the loveliest view in all Florence; from the best bedroom window you saw the dome and Giotto's tower framed between their dark columns. Inexhaustibly loquacious, he tried to persuade her that cypresses weren't really at all funereal. For the Etruscans, on the contrary (he invented this little piece of archæology on the spur of the moment) the cypress was a symbol of joy; the feasts of the vernal equinox concluded with dances round the sacred tree. Boecklin, it was true, had planted cypresses on his Island of the Dead. But then Boecklin, after all . . . And if she really found the trees depressing, she could plant nasturtiums to climb up them. Or roses. Roses, which the Greeks . . .

"All right, all right," said Moira Tarwin hastily. "Let's leave the cypresses."

That voice, that endless flow of culture and foreign English! Old Bargioni was really terrible. She would have screamed if she had had to listen a moment longer. She yielded in mere self-defence.

"*E la Tarwinnè?*" questioned Signora Bargioni when her husband came home.

He shrugged his shoulders. *"Una donnina piuttosto sciocca,"* was his verdict.

Rather silly. Old Bargioni was not the only man
who had thought so. But he was one of the not so
many who regarded her silliness as a fault. Most of
the men who knew her were charmed by it; they
adored while they smiled. In conjunction with that
tiny stature, those eyes, that delicate childish face,
her silliness inspired avuncular devotions and protective loves. She had a faculty for making men feel,
by contrast, agreeably large, superior and intelligent.
And as luck, or perhaps as ill luck, would have it,
Moira had passed her life among men who were really
intelligent and what is called superior. Old Sir Watney Croker, her grandfather, with whom she had lived
ever since she was five (for her father and mother had
both died young) was one of the most eminent physi-
cians of his day. His early monograph on duodenal
ulcers remains even now the classical work on the
subject. Between one duodenal ulcer and another Sir
Watney found leisure to adore and indulge and spoil
his little granddaughter. Along with fly-fishing and
metaphysics she was his hobby. Time passed; Moira
grew up, chronologically; but Sir Watney went on
treating her as a spoilt child, went on being enchanted
by her birdy chirrupings and ingenuousnesses and
impertinent *enfant-terrible-isms*. He encouraged, he
almost compelled her to preserve her childishness.
Keeping her a baby in spite of her age amused him.
He loved her babyish and could only love her so. All

those duodenal ulcers—perhaps they had done something to his sensibility, warped it a little, kept it somehow stunted and un-adult, like Moira herself. In the
depths of his unspecialized, unprofessional being Sir
Watney was a bit of a baby himself. Too much preoccupation with the duodenum had prevented this
neglected instinctive part of him from fully growing
up. Like gravitates to like; old baby Watney loved
the baby in Moira and wanted to keep the young
woman permanently childish. Most of his friends
shared Sir Watney's tastes. Doctors, judges, professors, civil servants—every member of Sir Watney's
circle was professionally eminent, a veteran specialist.
To be asked to one of his dinner parties was a privilege. On these august occasions Moira had always,
from the age of seventeen, been present, the only
woman at the table. Not really a woman, Sir Watney explained; a child. The veteran specialists were
all her indulgent uncles. The more childish she was,
the better they liked her. Moira gave them pet names.
Professor Stagg, for example, the neo-Hegelian, was
Uncle Bonzo; Mr. Justice Gidley was Giddy Goat.
And so on. When they teased, she answered back im-
pertinently. How they laughed! When they started
to discuss the Absolute or Britain's Industrial Future, she interjected some deliciously irrelevant re-
mark that made them laugh even more heartily. Exquisite! And the next day the story would be told to
colleagues in the law courts or the hospital, to cronies
at the Athenæum. In learned and professional circles

Moira enjoyed a real celebrity. In the end she had ceased not only to be a woman; she had almost ceased to be a child. She was hardly more than their mascot.

At half-past nine she left the dining-room, and the talk would come back to ulcers and Reality and Emergent Evolution.

"One would like to keep her as a pet," John Tarwin had said as the door closed behind her on that first occasion he dined at Sir Watney's.

Professor Broadwater agreed. There was a little silence. It was Tarwin who broke it.

"What's your feeling," he asked, leaning forward with that expression of blank intelligence on his eager, sharp-featured face, "what's *your* feeling about the validity of experiments with artificially grafted tumours as opposed to natural tumours?"

Tarwin was only thirty-three and looked even younger among Sir Watney's veterans. He had already done good work, Sir Watney explained to his assembled guests before the young man's arrival, and might be expected to do much more. An interesting fellow too. Had been all over the place—tropical Africa, India, North and South America. Well off. Not tied to an academic job to earn his living. Had worked here in London, in Germany, at the Rockefeller Institute in New York, in Japan. Enviable opportunities. A great deal to be said for a private income. "Ah, here you are, Tarwin. Good evening. No, not at all late. This is Mr. Justice Gidley, Professor Broadwater, Professor Stagg and—bless me! I hadn't noticed you, Moira; you're really too ultra-microscopic—my granddaughter." Tarwin smiled down at her. She was really ravishing.

Well, now they had been married five years, Moira was thinking, as she powdered her face in front of the looking-glass. Tonino was coming to tea; she had been changing her frock. Through the window behind the mirror one looked down between the cypress trees on to Florence—a jumble of brown roofs, and above them, in the midst, the marble tower and the huge, up-leaping, airy dome. Five years. It was John's photograph in the leather travelling-frame that made her think of their marriage. Why did she keep it there on the dressing-table? Force of habit, she supposed. It wasn't as though the photograph reminded her of days that had been particularly happy. On the contrary. There was something, she now felt, slightly dishonest about keeping it there. Pretending to love him when she didn't. . . . She looked at it again. The profile was sharp and eager. The keen young research student intently focused on a tumour. She really liked him better as a research student than when he was having a soul, or being a poet or a lover. It seemed a dreadful thing to say—but there it was: the research student was of better quality than the human being.

She had always known it—or, rather, not known, felt it. The human being had always made her rather uncomfortable. The more human, the more uncomfortable. She oughtn't ever to have married him, of course. But he asked so persistently; and then he had so much vitality; everybody spoke so well of him; she rather liked his looks; and he seemed to lead such a jolly life, travelling about the world; and she was tired of being a mascot for her grandfather's veterans. There were any number of such little reasons. Added together, she had fancied they would be the equivalent of the one big, cogent reason. But they weren't; she had made a mistake.

Yes, the more human, the more uncomfortable. The disturbing way he turned on the beautiful illumination of his smile! Turned it on suddenly, only to switch it off again with as little warning when something really serious, like cancer or philosophy, had to be discussed. And then his voice, when he was talking about Nature, or Love, or God, or something of that sort—furry with feeling! The quite unnecessarily moved and tremulous way he said good-bye! "Like a Landseer dog," she told him once, before they were married, laughing and giving a ludicrous imitation of his too heart-felt "Good-bye, Moira." The mockery hurt him. John prided himself as much on his soul and his feelings as upon his intellect; as much on his appreciation of Nature and his poetical love-longings as upon his knowledge of tumours. Goethe was his favourite literary and historical character. Poet and man of science, deep thinker and ardent lover, artist in thought and in life—John saw himself in the rich part. He made her read *Faust* and *Wilhelm Meister*.

Moira did her best to feign the enthusiasm she did not feel. Privately she thought Goethe a humbug.

"I oughtn't to have married him," she said to her image in the glass, and shook her head.

John was the pet-fancier as well as the loving educator. There were times when Moira's childishnesses delighted him as much as they had delighted Sir Watney and his veterans, when he laughed at every naïveté or impertinence she uttered, as though it were a piece of the most exquisite wit; and not only laughed, but drew public attention to it, led her on into fresh infantilities and repeated the stories of her exploits to any one who was prepared to listen to them. He was less enthusiastic, however, when Moira had been childish at his expense, when her silliness had in any way compromised *his* dignity or interests. On these occasions he lost his temper, called her a fool, told her she ought to be ashamed of herself. After which, controlling himself, he would become grave, paternal, pedagogic. Moira would be made to feel, miserably, that she wasn't worthy of him. And finally he switched on the smile and made it all up with caresses that left her like a stone.

"And to think," she reflected, putting away her powder-puff, "to think of my spending all that time and energy trying to keep up with him."

All those scientific papers she had read, those outlines of medicine and physiology, those text-books of something or other (she couldn't even remember the name of the science), to say nothing of all that dreary stuff by Goethe! And then all the going out when she had a headache or was tired! All the meeting of people who bored her, but who were really, according to John, so interesting and important! All the travelling, the terribly strenuous sight-seeing, the calling on distinguished foreigners and their generally less distinguished wives! It was difficult for her to keep up even physically—her legs were so short and John was always in such a hurry. Mentally, in spite of all her efforts, she was always a hundred miles behind.

"Awful!" she said aloud.

Her whole marriage had really been awful. From that awful honeymoon at Capri, when he had made her walk too far, too fast, uphill, only to read her extracts from Wordsworth when they reached the *Aussichtspunkt;* when he had talked to her about love and made it, much too frequently, and told her the Latin names of the plants and butterflies—from that awful honeymoon to the time when, four months ago, her nerves had gone all to pieces and the doctor had said that she must take things quietly, apart from John. Awful! The life had nearly killed her. And it wasn't (she had come at last to realize) it wasn't really a life at all. It was just a galvanic activity, like the twitching of a dead frog's leg when you touch the nerve with an electrified wire. Not life, just galvanized death.

She remembered the last of their quarrels, just before the doctor had told her to go away. John had been sitting at her feet, with his head against her knee. And his head was beginning to go bald! She could hardly bear to look at those long hairs plastered across the scalp. And because he was tired with all that microscope work, tired and at the same time (not having made love to her, thank goodness! for more than a fortnight) amorous, as she could tell by the look in his eyes, he was being very sentimental and talking in his furriest voice about Love and Beauty and the necessity for being like Goethe. Talking till she felt like screaming aloud. And at last she could bear it no longer.

"For goodness sake, John," she said in a voice that was on the shrill verge of being out of control, "be quiet!"

"What *is* the matter?" He looked up at her questioningly, pained.

"Talking like that!" She was indignant. "But you've never loved anybody, outside yourself. Nor felt the beauty of anything. Any more than that old humbug Goethe. You know what you *ought* to feel when there's a woman about, or a landscape; you know what the best people feel. And you deliberately set yourself to feel the same, out of your head."

John was wounded to the quick of his vanity. "How can you say that?"

"Because it's true, it's true. You only live out of your head. And it's a bald head too," she added, and began to laugh, uncontrollably.

What a scene there had been! She went on laughing all the time he raged at her; she couldn't stop.

"You're hysterical," he said at last; and then he

calmed down. The poor child was ill. With an effort
he switched on the expression of paternal tenderness
and went to fetch the sal volatile.

One last dab at her lips, and there! she was ready.
She went downstairs to the drawing-room, to find
that Tonino had already arrived—he was always
early—and was waiting. He rose as she entered,
bowed over her outstretched hand and kissed it. Moira
was always charmed by his florid, rather excessive
Southern good manners. John was always too busy
being the keen research student or the furry-voiced
poet to have good manners. He didn't think politeness
particularly important. It was the same with clothes.
He was chronically ill-dressed. Tonino, on the other
hand, was a model of dapper elegance. That pale grey
suit, that lavender-coloured tie, those piebald shoes of
white kid and patent leather—marvellous!

One of the pleasures or dangers of foreign travel
is that you lose your class-consciousness. At home
you can never, with the best will in the world, forget
it. Habit has rendered your own people as immediately legible as your own language. A word, a gesture is sufficient; your man is placed. But in foreign
parts your fellows are unreadable. The less obvious
products of upbringing—all the subtler refinements,
the finer shades of vulgarity—escape your notice. The
accent, the inflexion of voice, the vocabulary, the
gestures tell you nothing. Between the duke and the
insurance clerk, the profiteer and the country gentleman, your inexperienced eye and ear detect no differ-

ence. For Moira, Tonino seemed the characteristic flower of Italian gentility. She knew, of course, that he wasn't well off; but then, plenty of the nicest people are poor. She saw in him the equivalent of one of those younger sons of impoverished English squires —the sort of young man who advertises for work in the Agony Column of the *Times*. "Public School education, sporting tastes; would accept any well-paid position of trust and confidence." She would have been pained, indignant, and surprised to hear old Bargioni describing him, after their first meeting, as "*il tipo del parruchiere napoletano*"—the typical Neapolitan barber. Signora Bargioni shook her head over the approaching scandal and was secretly delighted.

As a matter of actual fact Tonino was not a barber. He was the son of a capitalist—on a rather small scale, no doubt; but still a genuine capitalist. Vasari senior owned a restaurant at Pozzuoli and was ambitious to start a hotel. Tonino had been sent to study the tourist industry with a family friend who was the manager of one of the best establishments in Florence. When he had learnt all the secrets, he was to return to Pozzuoli and be the managing director of the rejuvenated boarding-house which his father was modestly proposing to rechristen the Grand Hotel Ritz-Carlton. Meanwhile, he was an underworked lounger in Florence. He had made Mrs. Tarwin's acquaintance romantically, on the highway. Driving, as was her custom, alone, Moira had run

over a nail. A puncture. Nothing is easier than changing wheels—nothing, that is to say, if you have sufficient muscular strength to undo the nuts which hold
the punctured wheel to its axle. Moira had not. When
Tonino came upon her, ten minutes after the mishap,
she was sitting on the running-board of the car,
flushed and dishevelled with her efforts, and in tears.

"*Una signora forestiera.*" At the café that evening Tonino recounted his adventure with a certain
rather fatuous self-satisfaction. In the small bourgeoisie in which he had been brought up, a Foreign
Lady was an almost fabulous creature, a being of
legendary wealth, eccentricity, independence. "*In-
glese,*" he specified. "*Giovane,*" and "*bella, bellis-
sima.*" His auditors were incredulous; beauty, for
some reason, is not common among the specimens of
English womanhood seen in foreign parts. "*Ricca,*"
he added. That sounded less intrinsically improbable;
foreign ladies were all rich, almost by definition.
Juicily, and with unction, Tonino described the car
she drove, the luxurious villa she inhabited.

Acquaintance had ripened quickly into friendship.
This was the fourth or fifth time in a fortnight that
he had come to the house.

"A few poor flowers," said the young man in a
tone of soft, ingratiating apology; and he brought
forward his left hand, which he had been hiding behind his back. It held a bouquet of white roses.

"But how kind of you!" she cried in her bad Italian.
"How lovely!" John never brought flowers to any

one; he regarded that sort of thing as rather non-sensical. She smiled at Tonino over the blossoms. "Thank you a thousand times."

Making a deprecating gesture, he returned her smile. His teeth flashed pearly and even. His large eyes were bright, dark, liquid, and rather expressionless, like a gazelle's. He was exceedingly good-looking. "White roses for the white rose," he said.

Moira laughed. The compliment was ridiculous, but it pleased her all the same.

Paying compliments was not the only thing Tonino could do. He knew how to be useful. When, a few days later, Moira decided to have the rather dingy hall and dining-room redistempered, he was invaluable. It was he who haggled with the decorator, he who made scenes when there were delays, he who interpreted Moira's rather special notions about colours to the workmen, he who superintended their activities.

"If it hadn't been for you," said Moira gratefully, when the work was finished, "I'd have been hopelessly swindled and they wouldn't have done anything properly."

It was such a comfort, she reflected, having a man about the place who didn't always have something more important to do and think about; a man who could spend his time being useful and a help. Such a comfort! And such a change! When she was with John, it was she who had to do all the tiresome, practical things. John always had his work, and his work took precedence of everything, including her convenience. Tonino was just an ordinary man, with nothing in the least superhuman about either himself or his functions. It was a great relief.

Little by little Moira came to rely on him for everything. He made himself universally useful. The fuses blew out; it was Tonino who replaced them. The hornets nested in the drawing-room chimney; heroically Tonino stank them out with sulphur. But his speciality was domestic economy. Brought up in a restaurant, he knew everything there was to be known about food and drink and prices. When the meat was unsatisfactory, he went to the butcher and threw the tough beefsteak in his teeth, almost literally. He beat down the extortionate charges of the green-grocer. With a man at the fish market he made a friendly arrangement whereby Moira was to have the pick of the soles and the red mullet. He bought her wine for her, her oil—wholesale, in huge glass demijohns; and Moira, who since Sir Watney's death could have afforded to drink nothing cheaper than Pol Roger 1911 and do her cooking in imported yak's butter, exulted with him in long domestic conversations over economies of a farthing a quart or a shilling or two on a hundredweight. For Tonino the price and the quality of victuals and drink were matters of gravest importance. To secure a flask of Chianti for five lire ninety instead of six lire was, in his eyes, a real victory; and the victory became a triumph if it could be proved that the Chianti was fully three years old and had an alcohol content of more than fourteen per cent. By nature Moira was neither greedy nor avaricious. Her upbringing had confirmed her in her natural tendencies. She had the disinterestedness of those who have never known a shortage of cash; and her abstemious indifference to the pleasures of the table had never been tempered by the housewife's preoccupation with other people's appetites and digestions. Never; for Sir Watney had kept a professional housekeeper, and with John Tarwin, who anyhow hardly noticed what he ate, and thought that women ought to spend their time doing more important and intellectual things than presiding over kitchens, she had lived for the greater part of their married life in hotels or service flats, or else in furnished rooms and in a chronic state of picnic. Tonino revealed to her the world of markets and the kitchen. Still accustomed to thinking, with John, that ordinary domestic life wasn't good enough, she laughed at first at his earnest preoccupation with meat and halfpence. But after a little she began to be infected by his almost religious enthusiasm for housekeeping; she began to discover that meat and halfpence were interesting after all, that they were real and important—much more real and important, for example, than reading Goethe when one found him a bore and a humbug. Tenderly brooded over by the most competent of solicitors and brokers, the late Sir Watney's fortune was bringing in a steady five per cent. free of tax. But in Tonino's company Moira could forget her bank balance. De-

scending from the financial Sinai on which she had
been lifted so high above the common earth, she discovered, with him, the preoccupations of poverty.
They were curiously interesting and exciting.

"The prices they ask for fish in Florence!" said
Tonino, after a silence, when he had exhausted the
subject of white roses. "When I think how little we
pay for octopus at Naples! It's scandalous."

"Scandalous!" echoed Moira with an indignation
as genuine as his own. They talked, interminably.

Next day the sky was no longer blue, but opaquely
white. There was no sunshine, only a diffused glare
that threw no shadows. The landscape lay utterly
lifeless under the dead and fishy stare of heaven. It
was very hot, there was no wind, the air was hardly
breathable and as though woolly. Moira woke up with
a headache, and her nerves seemed to have an uneasy
life of their own, apart from hers. Like caged birds
they were, fluttering and starting and twittering at
every alarm; and her aching, tired body was their
aviary. Quite against her own wish and intention she
found herself in a temper with the maid and saying
the unkindest things. She had to give her a pair of
stockings to make up for it. When she was dressed,
she wanted to write some letters; but her fountain-
pen made a stain on her fingers and she was so furious
that she threw the beastly thing out of the window. It
broke to pieces on the flagstones below. She had nothing to write with; it was too exasperating. She washed
the ink off her hands and took out her embroidery

frame. But her fingers were all thumbs. And then she pricked herself with the needle. Oh, so painfully! The tears came into her eyes; she began to cry. And having begun, she couldn't stop. Assunta came in five minutes later and found her sobbing. "But what is it, signora?" she asked, made most affectionately solicitous by the gift of the stockings. Moira shook her head. "Go away," she said brokenly. The girl was insistent. "Go away," Moira repeated. How could she explain what was the matter when the only thing that had happened was that she had pricked her finger? Nothing was the matter. And yet everything was the matter, everything.

The everything that was the matter resolved itself finally into the weather. Even in the best of health Moira had always been painfully conscious of the approach of thunder. Her jangled nerves were more than ordinarily sensitive. The tears and furies and despairs of this horrible day had a purely meteorological cause. But they were none the less violent and agonizing for that. The hours passed dismally. Thickened by huge black clouds, the twilight came on in a sultry and expectant silence, and it was prematurely night. The reflection of distant lightnings, flashing far away below the horizon, illuminated the eastern sky. The peaks and ridges of the Apennines stood out black against the momentary pale expanses of silvered vapour and disappeared again in silence; the attentive hush was still unbroken. With a kind of sinking apprehension—for she was terrified of storms

—Moira sat at her window, watching the black hills leap out against the silver and die again, leap out and die. The flashes brightened; and then, for the first time, she heard the approaching thunder, far off and faint like the whisper of the sea in a shell. Moira shuddered. The clock in the hall struck nine, and, as though the sound were a signal prearranged, a gust of wind suddenly shook the magnolia tree that stood at the crossing of the paths in the garden below. Its long stiff leaves rattled together like scales of horn. There was another flash. In the brief white glare she could see the two funereal cypresses writhing and tossing as though in the desperate agitation of pain. And then all at once the storm burst catastrophically, it seemed directly overhead. At the savage violence of that icy downpour Moira shrank back and shut the window. A streak of white fire zig-zagged fearfully just behind the cypresses. The immediate thunder was like the splitting and fall of a solid vault. Moira rushed away from the window and threw herself on the bed. She covered her face with her hands. Through the continuous roaring of the rain the thunder crashed and reverberated, crashed again and sent the fragments of sound rolling unevenly in all directions through the night. The whole house trembled. In the window-frames the shaken glasses rattled like the panes of an old omnibus rolling across the cobbles.

"Oh God, Oh God," Moira kept repeating. In the enormous tumult her voice was small and, as it were, naked, utterly abject.

"But it's too stupid to be frightened." She remembered John's voice, his brightly encouraging, superior manner. "The chances are thousands to one against your being struck. And anyhow, hiding your head won't prevent the lightning from . . ."

How she hated him for being so reasonable and right! "Oh God!" There was another. "God, God, God. . . ."

And then suddenly a terrible thing happened; the light went out. Through her closed eyelids she saw no longer the red of translucent blood, but utter blackness. Uncovering her face, she opened her eyes and anxiously looked round—on blackness again. She fumbled for the switch by her bed, found it, turned and turned; the darkness remained impenetrable.

"Assunta!" she called.

And all at once the square of the window was a suddenly uncovered picture of the garden, seen against a background of mauve-white sky and shining, downpouring rain.

"Assunta!" Her voice was drowned in a crash that seemed to have exploded in the very roof. "Assunta, Assunta!" In a panic she stumbled across the grave-dark room to the door. Another flash revealed the handle. She opened. "Assunta!"

Her voice was hollow above the black gulf of the stairs. The thunder exploded again above her. With a crash and a tinkle of broken glass one of the windows in her room burst open. A blast of cold wind lifted her hair. A flight of papers rose from her writing-table and whirled with crackling wings through the darkness. One touched her cheek like a living thing and was gone. She screamed aloud. The door slammed behind her. She ran down the stairs in terror, as though the fiend were at her heels. In the hall she met Assunta and the cook coming towards her, lighting matches as they came.

"Assunta, the lights!" She clutched the girl's arm.

Only the thunder answered. When the noise subsided Assunta explained that the fuses had all blown out and that there wasn't a candle in the house. Not a single candle, and only one more box of matches.

"But then we shall be left in the dark," said Moira hysterically.

Through the three blackly reflecting windows of the hall three separate pictures of the streaming garden revealed themselves and vanished. The old Venetian mirrors on the walls blinked for an instant into life, like dead eyes briefly opened.

"In the dark," she repeated with an almost mad insistence.

"Aie!" cried Assunta, and dropped the match that had begun to burn her fingers. The thunder fell on them out of a darkness made denser and more hopeless by the loss of light.

When the telephone bell rang, Tonino was sitting in the managerial room of his hotel, playing cards with the proprietor's two sons and another friend. "Someone to speak to you, Signor Tonino," said the underporter, looking in. "A lady." He grinned significantly.

Tonino put on a dignified air and left the room. When he returned a few minutes later, he held his hat in one hand and was buttoning up his rain-coat with the other.

"Sorry," he said. "I've got to go out."

"Go out?" exclaimed the others incredulously. Beyond the shuttered windows the storm roared like a cataract and savagely exploded. "But where?" they asked. "Why? Are you mad?"

Tonino shrugged his shoulders, as though it were nothing to go out into a tornado, as though he were used to it. The *signora forestiera*, he explained, hating them for their inquisitiveness; the Tarwin—she had asked him to go up to Bellosguardo at once. The fuses . . . not a candle in the house . . . utterly in the dark . . . very agitated . . . nerves. . . .

"But on a night like this. . . . But you're not the electrician." The two sons of the proprietor spoke in chorus. They felt, indignantly, that Tonino was letting himself be exploited.

But the third young man leaned back in his chair and laughed. "*Vai, caro, vai,*" he said, and then, shaking his finger at Tonino knowingly, "*Ma fatti pagare per il tuo lavoro,*" he added. "Get yourself paid for your trouble." Berto was notoriously the lady-killer, the tried specialist in amorous strategy, the acknowledged expert. "Take the opportunity."

The others joined in his rather unpleasant laughter. Tonino also grinned and nodded.

The taxi rushed splashing through the wet deserted streets like a travelling fountain. Tonino sat in the darkness of the cab ruminating Berto's advice. She was pretty, certainly. But somehow—why was it?—it had hardly occurred to him to think of her as a possible mistress. He had been politely gallant with her—on principle almost, and by force of habit —but without really wanting to succeed; and when she had shown herself unresponsive, he hadn't cared. But perhaps he ought to have cared, perhaps he ought to have tried harder. In Berto's world it was a sporting duty to do one's best to seduce every woman one could. The most admirable man was the man with the greatest number of women to his credit. Really lovely, Tonino went on to himself, trying to work up an enthusiasm for the sport. It would be a triumph to be proud of. The more so as she was a foreigner. And very rich. He thought with inward satisfaction of that big car, of the house, the servants, the silver. "*Certo,*" he said to himself complacently, "*mi vuol bene.*" She liked him; there was no doubt of it. Meditatively he stroked his smooth face; the muscles stirred a little under his fingers. He was smiling to himself in the darkness; naïvely, an ingenuous prostitute's smile. "*Moira,*" he said aloud. "*Moira. Strano, quel nome. Piuttosto ridicolo.*"

It was Moira who opened the door for him. She

had been standing at the window, looking out, waiting and waiting.

"Tonino!" She held out both her hands to him; she had never felt so glad to see any one.

The sky went momentarily whitish-mauve behind him as he stood there in the open doorway. The skirts of his rain-coat fluttered in the wind; a wet gust blew past him, chilling her face. The sky went black again. He slammed the door behind him. They were in utter darkness.

"Tonino, it was too sweet of you to have come. Really too . . ."

The thunder that interrupted her was like the end of the world. Moira shuddered. "Oh God!" she whimpered; and then suddenly she was pressing her face against his waistcoat and crying, and Tonino was holding her and stroking her hair. The next flash showed him the position of the sofa. In the ensuing darkness he carried her across the room, sat down and began to kiss her tear-wet face. She lay quite still in his arms, relaxed, like a frightened child that has at last found comfort. Tonino held her, kissing her softly again and again. "*Ti amo, Moira.*" he whispered. And it was true. Holding her, touching her in the dark he did love her. "*Ti amo.*" How profoundly! "*Ti voglio un bene immenso,*" he went on, with a passion, a deep warm tenderness born almost suddenly of darkness and soft blind contact. Heavy and warm with life, she lay pressed against him. Her body curved and was solid under his hands, her cheeks were rounded and cool, her eyelids rounded and tremulous and tear-wet, her mouth so soft, so soft under his touching lips. "*Ti amo, ti amo.*" He was breathless with love, and it was as though there were a hollowness at the center of his being, a void of desiring tenderness that longed to be filled, that could only be filled by her, an emptiness that drew her towards him, into him, that drank her as an empty vessel eagerly drinks the water. Still, with closed eyes, quite still she lay there in his arms, suffering herself to be drunk up by his tenderness, to be drawn into the yearning vacancy of his heart, happy in being passive, in yielding herself to his soft insistent passion.

"*Fatti pagare, fatti pagare.*" The memory of Berto's words transformed him suddenly from a lover into an amorous sportsman with a reputation to keep up and records to break. "*Fatti pagare.*" He risked a more intimate caress. But Moira winced so shudderingly at the touch that he desisted, ashamed of himself.

"*Ebbene,*" asked Berto when, an hour later, he returned, "did you mend the fuses?"

"Yes, I mended the fuses."

"And did you get yourself paid?"

Tonino smiled an amorous sportsman's smile. "A little on account," he answered, and at once disliked himself for having spoken the words, disliked the others for laughing at them. Why did he go out of his way to spoil something which had been so beautiful? Pretexting a headache, he went upstairs to his bedroom. The storm had passed on, the moon was shining now out of a clear sky. He opened the window and looked out. A river of ink and quicksilver, the Arno flowed whispering past. In the street below the puddles shone like living eyes. The ghost of Caruso was singing from a gramophone, far away on the other side of the water. "*Stretti, stretti, nell' estasi d'amor.* . . ." Tonino was profoundly moved.

The sky was blue next morning, the sunlight glittered on the shiny leaves of the magnolia tree, the air was demurely windless. Sitting at her dressing-table, Moira looked out and wondered incredulously if such things as storms were possible. But the plants were broken and prostrate in their beds; the paths were strewn with scattered leaves and petals. In spite of the soft air and the sunlight, last night's horrors had been more than a bad dream.

Moira sighed and began to brush her hair. Set in its leather frame, John Tarwin's profile confronted her, brightly focused on imaginary tumours. Her eyes fixed on it, Moira went on mechanically brushing her hair. Then, suddenly, interrupting the rhythm of her movements, she got up, took the leather frame and, walking across the room, threw it up, out of sight, on to the top of the high wardrobe. There! She returned to her seat and, filled with a kind of frightened elation, went on with her interrupted brushing.

When she was dressed, she drove down to the town and spent an hour at Settepassi's, the jewellers. When she left, she was bowed out on to the Lungarno like a princess.

"No, don't smoke those," she said to Tonino that afternoon as he reached for a cigarette in the silver box that stood on the drawing-room mantelpiece. "I've got a few of those Egyptian ones you like. Got them specially for you." And, smiling, she handed him a little parcel.

Tonino thanked her profusely—too profusely, as was his custom. But when he had stripped away the paper and saw the polished gold of a large cigarette-case, he could only look at her in an embarrassed and enquiring amazement.

"Don't you think it's rather pretty?" she asked.

"Marvellous! But is it . . ." He hesitated. "Is it for me?"

Moira laughed with pleasure at his embarrassment. She had never seen him embarrassed before. He was always the self-possessed young man of the world, secure and impregnable within his armour of Southern good manners. She admired that elegant carapace. But it amused her for once to take him without it, to see him at a loss, blushing and stammering like a little boy. It amused and it pleased her; she liked him all the more for being the little boy as well as the polished and socially competent young man.

"For me?" she mimicked, laughing. "Do you like it?" Her tone changed; she became grave. "I wanted you to have something to remind you of last night." Tonino took her hands and silently kissed them. She

had received him with such off-handed gaiety, so non-
chalantly, as though nothing had happened, that the
tender references to last night's happenings (so carefully prepared as he walked up the hill) had remained
unspoken. He had been afraid of saying the wrong
thing and offending her. But now the spell was broken
—and by Moira herself. "One oughtn't to forget one's
good actions," Moira went on, abandoning him her
hands. "Each time you take a cigarette out of this
case, will you remember how kind and good you were
to a silly ridiculous little fool?"

Tonino had had time to recover his manners. "I
shall remember the most adorable, the most beautiful. . ." Still holding her hands, he looked at her for
a moment in silence, eloquently. Moira smiled back at
him. "Moira!" And she was in his arms. She shut her
eyes and was passive in the strong circle of his arms,
soft and passive against his firm body. "I love you,
Moira." The breath of his whispering was warm on
her cheek. "*Ti amo.*" And suddenly his lips were on
hers again, violently, impatiently kissing. Between
the kisses his whispered words came passionate to her
ears. "*Ti amo pazzamente . . . piccina . . . tesoro
. . . amore . . . cuore . . .*" Uttered in Italian, his
love seemed somehow specially strong and deep.
Things described in a strange language themselves
take on a certain strangeness. "*Amami, Moira,
amami. Mi ami un po?*" He was insistent. "A little,
Moira—do you love me a little?"

She opened her eyes and looked at him. Then, with

a quick movement, she took his face between her two hands, drew it down and kissed him on the mouth. "Yes," she whispered, "I love you." And then, gently, she pushed him away. Tonino wanted to kiss her again. But Moira shook her head and slipped away from him. "No, no," she said with a kind of peremptory entreaty. "Don't spoil it all now."

The days passed, hot and golden. Summer approached. The nightingales sang unseen in the cool of the evening.

"*L'ussignuolo*," Moira whispered softly to herself, as she listened to the singing. "*L'ussignuolo*." Even the nightingales were subtly better in Italian. The sun had set. They were sitting in the little summer-house at the end of the garden, looking out over the darkening landscape. The white-walled farms and villas on the slope below stood out almost startlingly clear against the twilight of the olive trees, as though charged with some strange and novel significance. Moira sighed. "I'm so happy," she said; Tonino took her hand. "Ridiculously happy." For, after all, she was thinking, it *was* rather ridiculous to be so happy for no valid reason. John Tarwin had taught her to imagine that one could only be happy when one was doing something "interesting" (as he put it), or associating with people who were "worth while." Tonino was nobody in particular, thank goodness! And going for picnics wasn't exactly "interesting" in John's sense of the word; nor was talking about the respective merits of different brands of car; nor teaching

him to drive; nor going shopping; nor discussing the
problem of new curtains for the drawing-room; nor,
for that matter, sitting in the summer-house and saying nothing. In spite of which, or because of which,
she was happy with an unprecedented happiness.
"Ridiculously happy," she repeated.

Tonino kissed her hand. "So am I," he said. And
he was not merely being polite. In his own way he
was genuinely happy with her. People envied him
sitting in that magnificent yellow car at her side. She
was so pretty and elegant, so foreign too; he was
proud to be seen about with her. And then the cigarette case, the gold-mounted, agate-handled cane she
had given him for his birthday. . . . Besides, he was
really very fond of her, really, in an obscure way,
in love with her. It was not for nothing that he had
held and caressed her in the darkness of that night of
thunder. Something of that deep and passionate tenderness, born suddenly of the night and their warm
sightless contact, still remained in him—still remained even after the physical longings she then inspired had been vicariously satisfied. (And under
Berto's knowing guidance they *had* been satisfied,
frequently.) If it hadn't been for Berto's satirical
comments on the still platonic nature of his attach-
ment, he would have been perfectly content.

"*Alle donne,*" Berto sententiously generalized,
"*piace sempre la violenza.* They long to be raped.
You don't know how to make love, my poor boy."
And he would hold up his own achievements as ex-

amples to be followed. For Berto, love was a kind of salacious vengeance on women for the crime of their purity.

Spurred on by his friend's mockeries, Tonino made another attempt to exact full payment for his mending of the fuses on the night of the storm. But his face was so soundly slapped, and the tone in which Moira threatened never to see him again unless he behaved himself was so convincingly stern, that he did not renew his attack. He contented himself with looking sad and complaining of her cruelty.

But in spite of his occasionally long face, he was happy with her. Happy like a fireside cat. The car, the house, her elegant foreign prettiness, the marvellous presents she gave him, kept him happily purring.

The days passed and the weeks. Moira would have liked life to flow on like this for ever, a gay bright stream with occasional reaches of calm sentimentality but never dangerously deep or turbulent, without fall or whirl or rapid. She wanted her existence to remain for ever what it was at this moment—a kind of game with a pleasant and emotionally exciting companion, a playing at living and loving. If only this happy play-time could last for ever!

It was John Tarwin who decreed that it should not. "ATTENDING CYTOLOGICAL CONGRESS ROME WILL STOP FEW DAYS ON WAY ARRIVING THURSDAY LOVE JOHN." That was the text of the telegram Moira found awaiting her on her return to the villa one evening. She read it and felt suddenly depressed and apprehensive. Why did he want to come? He would spoil everything. The bright evening went dead before her eyes; the happiness with which she had been brimming when she returned with Tonino from that marvellous drive among the Apennines was drained out of her. Her gloom retrospectively darkened the blue and golden beauty of the mountains, put out the bright flowers, dimmed the day's laughter and talk. "Why does he want to come?" Miserably and resentfully, she wondered. "And what's going to happen, what's going to happen?" She felt cold and rather breathless and almost sick with the questioning apprehension.

John's face, when he saw her standing there at the station, lit up instantaneously with all its hundred-candle-power tenderness and charm.

"My darling!" His voice was furry and tremulous. He leaned towards her; stiffening, Moira suffered herself to be kissed. His nails, she noticed disgustedly, were dirty.

The prospect of a meal alone with John had appalled her; she had asked Tonino to dinner. Besides, she wanted John to meet him. To have kept Tonino's existence a secret from John would have been to admit that there was something wrong in her relations with him. And there wasn't. She wanted John to meet him just like that, naturally, as a matter of course. Whether he'd like Tonino when he'd met him was another question. Moira had her doubts. They were justified by the event. John had begun by protesting when he heard that she had invited a guest. Their first evening—how could she? The voice trembled—fur in a breeze. She had to listen to out-pourings of sentiment. But finally, when dinner-time arrived, he switched off the pathos and became once more the research student. Brightly enquiring, blankly intelligent, John cross-questioned his guest about all the interesting and important things that were happening in Italy. What was the real political situation? How did the new educational system work? What did people think of the reformed penal code? On all these matters Tonino was, of course, far less well-informed than his interrogator. The Italy he knew was the Italy of his friends and his family, of shops and cafés and girls and the daily fight for money. All that historical, impersonal Italy, of which John so intelligently read in the high-class reviews, was utterly unknown to him. His answers to John's questions were childishly silly. Moira sat listening, dumb with misery.

"What *do* you find in that fellow?" her husband asked, when Tonino had taken his leave. "He struck me as quite particularly uninteresting."

Moira did not answer. There was a silence. John suddenly switched on his tenderly, protectively, yearningly marital smile. "Time to go to bed, my sweetheart," he said. Moira looked up at him and saw in his eyes that expression she knew so well and dreaded. "My sweetheart," he repeated, and the

Landseer dog was also amorous. He put his arms round her and bent to kiss her face. Moira shuddered —but helplessly, dumbly, not knowing how to escape. He led her away.

When John had left her, she lay awake far into the night, remembering his ardours and his sentimentalities with a horror that the passage of time seemed actually to increase. Sleep came at last to deliver her.

Being an archæologist, old Signor Bargioni was decidedly "interesting."

"But he bores me to death," said Moira when, next day, her husband suggested that they should go to see him. "That voice! And the way he goes on and on! And that beard! And his wife!"

John flushed with anger. "Don't be childish," he snapped out, forgetting how much he enjoyed her childishness when it didn't interfere with his amusements or his business. "After all," he insisted, "there's probably no man living who knows more about Tuscany in the Dark Ages."

Nevertheless, in spite of darkest Tuscany, John had to pay his call without her. He spent a most improving hour, chatting about Romanesque architecture and the Lombard kings. But just before he left, the conversation somehow took another turn; casually, as though by chance, Tonino's name was mentioned. It was the *signora* who had insisted that it should be mentioned. Ignorance, her husband protested, is bliss. But Signora Bargioni loved scandal, and being middle-aged, ugly, envious, and malicious, was full of righteous indignation against the young wife and of hypocritical sympathy for the possibly injured husband. Poor Tarwin, she insisted—he ought to be warned. And so, tactfully, without seeming to say anything in particular, the old man dropped his hints.

Walking back to Bellosguardo, John was uneasily pensive. It was not that he imagined that Moira had been, or was likely to prove, unfaithful. Such things really didn't happen to oneself. Moira obviously liked the uninteresting young man; but, after all, and in spite of her childishness, Moira was a civilized human being. She had been too well brought up to do anything stupid. Besides, he reflected, remembering the previous evening, remembering all the years of their marriage, she had no temperament; she didn't know what passion was, she was utterly without sensuality. Her native childishness would reinforce her principles. Infants may be relied on to be pure; but not (and this was what troubled John Tarwin) worldly-wise. Moira wouldn't allow herself to be made love to; but she might easily let herself be swindled. Old Bargioni had been very discreet and non-committal; but it was obvious that he regarded this young fellow as an adventurer, out for what he could get. John frowned as he walked, and bit his lip.

He came home to find Moira and Tonino superintending the fitting of the new cretonne covers for the drawing-room chairs.

"Carefully, carefully," Moira was saying to the upholsterer as he came in. She turned at the sound of his footsteps. A cloud seemed to obscure the brightness of her face when she saw him; but she made an effort to keep up her gaiety. "Come and look, John," she called. "It's like getting a very fat old lady into a very tight dress. Too ridiculous!"

But John did not smile with her; his face was a mask of stony gravity. He stalked up to the chair, nodded curtly to Tonino, curtly to the upholsterer, and stood there watching the work as though he were a stranger, a hostile stranger at that. The sight of Moira and Tonino laughing and talking together had roused in him a sudden and violent fury. "Disgusting little adventurer," he said to himself ferociously behind his mask.

"It's a pretty stuff, don't you think?" said Moira. He only grunted.

"Very modern too," added Tonino. "The shops are very modern here," he went on, speaking with all the rather touchy insistence on up-to-dateness which characterizes the inhabitants of an under-bathroomed and over-monumented country.

"Indeed?" said John sarcastically.

Moira frowned. "You've no idea how helpful Tonino has been," she said with a certain warmth.

Effusively Tonino began to deny that she had any obligation towards him. John Tarwin interrupted him. "Oh, I've no doubt he was helpful," he said in the same sarcastic tone and with a little smile of contempt.

There was an uncomfortable silence. Then Tonino took his leave. The moment he was gone, Moira turned on her husband. Her face was pale, her lips trembled.

"How dare you speak to one of my friends like that?" she asked in a voice unsteady with anger.

John flared up. "Because I wanted to get rid of the fellow," he answered; and the mask was off, his face was nakedly furious. "It's disgusting to see a man like that hanging round the house. An adventurer. Exploiting your silliness. Sponging on you."

"Tonino doesn't sponge on me. And anyhow, what do you know about it?"

He shrugged his shoulders. "One hears things."

"Oh, it's those old beasts, is it?" She hated the Bargionis, *hated* them. "Instead of being grateful to Tonino for helping me! Which is more than you've ever done, John. You, with your beastly tumours and your rotten old *Faust!*" The contempt in her voice was blasting. "Just leaving me to sink or swim. And when somebody comes along and is just humanly decent to me, you insult him. And you fly into a rage of jealousy because I'm normally grateful to him."

John had had time to readjust his mask. "I don't fly into any sort of rage," he said, bottling his anger and speaking slowly and coldly. "I just don't want you to be preyed upon by handsome, black-haired young pimps from the slums of Naples."

"John!"

"Even if the preying *is* done platonically," he went on. "Which I'm sure it is. But I don't want to have even a platonic pimp about." He spoke coldly, slowly, with the deliberate intention of hurting her as much as he could. "How much has he got out of you so far?"

Moira did not answer, but turned and hurried from the room.

Tonino had just got to the bottom of the hill, when a loud insistent hooting made him turn round. A big yellow car was close at his heels.

"Moira!" he called in astonishment. The car came to a halt beside him.

"Get in," she commanded almost fiercely, as though she were angry with him. He did as he was told.

"But where did you think of going?" he asked.

"I don't know. Anywhere. Let's take the Bologna road into the mountains."

"But you've got no hat," he objected, "no coat."

She only laughed and, throwing the car into gear, drove off at full speed. John spent his evening in solitude. He began by reproaching himself. "I oughtn't to have spoken so brutally," he thought, when he heard of Moira's precipitate departure. What tender, charming things he would say, when she came back, to make up for his hard words! And then, when she'd made peace, he would talk to her gently, paternally about the dangers of having bad friends. Even the anticipation of what he would say to her caused his face to light up with a beautiful smile. But when, three-quarters of an hour after dinner-time, he sat down to a lonely and overcooked meal, his mood had changed. "If she wants to sulk," he said to himself, "why, let her sulk." And as the hours passed, his heart grew harder. Midnight struck. His anger began to be tempered by a certain apprehension. Could anything have happened to her? He was anxious. But all the same he went to bed, on principle, firmly. Twenty minutes later he heard Moira's step on the stairs and then the closing of her door. She was back; nothing had happened; perversely, he felt all the more exasperated with her for being safe. Would she come and say good-night? He waited.

Absently, meanwhile, mechanically, Moira had undressed. She was thinking of all that had happened in the eternity since she had left the house. That marvellous sunset in the mountains! Every westward slope was rosily gilded; below them lay a gulf of blue shadow. They had stood in silence, gazing.

"Kiss me, Tonino," she had suddenly whispered, and the touch of his lips had sent a kind of delicious apprehension fluttering under her skin. She pressed herself against him; his body was firm and solid within her clasp. She could feel the throb of his heart against her cheek, like something separately alive. Beat, beat, beat—and the throbbing life was not the life of the Tonino she knew, the Tonino who laughed

and paid compliments and brought flowers; it was the
life of some mysterious and separate power. A power
with which the familiar individual Tonino happened
to be connected, but almost irrelevantly. She shuddered a little. Mysterious and terrifying. But the
terror was somehow attractive, like a dark precipice
that allures. "Kiss me, Tonino, kiss me." The light
faded; the hills died away into featureless flat shapes
against the sky. "I'm cold," she said at last, shivering.
"Let's go." They dined at a little inn, high up between the two passes. When they drove away, it was
night. He put his arm round her and kissed her neck,
at the nape, where the cropped hair was harsh against
his mouth. "You'll make me drive into the ditch," she
laughed. But there was no laughter for Tonino.
"Moira, Moira," he repeated; and there was something like agony in his voice. "Moira." And finally,
at his suffering entreaty, she stopped the car. They
got out. Under the chestnut trees, what utter darkness!

Moira slipped off her last garment and, naked before the mirror, looked at her image. It seemed the
same as ever, her pale body; but in reality it was
different, it was new, it had only just been born.

John still waited, but his wife did not come. "All
right then," he said to himself, with a spiteful little
anger that disguised itself as a god-like and impersonal serenity of justice; "let her sulk if she wants
to. She only punishes herself." He turned out the
light and composed himself to sleep. Next morning

he left for Rome and the Cytological Congress without saying good-bye; that would teach her. But "Thank goodness!" was Moira's first reflection when she heard that he had gone. And then, suddenly, she felt rather sorry for him. Poor John! Like a dead frog, galvanized; twitching, but never alive. He was pathetic really. She was so rich in happiness, that she could afford to be sorry for him. And in a way she was even grateful to him. If he hadn't come, if he hadn't behaved so unforgivably, nothing would have happened between Tonino and herself. Poor John! But all the same he was hopeless.

Day followed bright serene day. But Moira's life no longer flowed like the clear and shallow stream it had been before John's coming. It was turbulent now, there were depths and darknesses. And love was no longer a game with a pleasant companion; it was violent, all-absorbing, even rather terrible. Tonino became for her a kind of obsession. She was haunted by him—by his face, by his white teeth and his dark hair, by his hands and limbs and body. She wanted to be with him, to feel his nearness, to touch him. She would spend whole hours stroking his hair, ruffling it up, rearranging it fantastically, on end, like a golliwog's, or with hanging fringes, or with the locks twisted up into horns. And when she had contrived some specially ludicrous effect, she clapped her hands and laughed, laughed, till the tears ran down her cheeks. "If you could see yourself now!" she cried. Offended by her laughter, "You play with me as

though I were a doll," Tonino would protest with a
rather ludicrous expression of angry dignity. The
laughter would go out of Moira's face and with a
seriousness that was fierce, almost cruel, she would
lean forward and kiss him, silently, violently, again
and again.

Absent, he was still unescapably with her, like a
guilty conscience. Her solitudes were endless medita-
tions on the theme of him. Sometimes the longing for
his tangible presence was too achingly painful to be
borne. Disobeying all his injunctions, breaking all
her promises, she would telephone for him to come
to her, she would drive off in search of him. Once, at
about midnight, Tonino was called down from his
room at the hotel by a message that a lady wanted to
speak to him. He found her sitting in the car. "But
I couldn't help it. I simply couldn't help it!" she
cried to excuse herself and mollify his anger. Tonino
refused to be propitiated. Coming like this in the
middle of the night! It was madness, it was scandalous! She sat there, listening, pale and with trembling
lips and the tears in her eyes. He was silent at last.
"But if you knew, Tonino," she whispered, "if you
only knew . . ." She took his hand and kissed it,
humbly.

Berto, when he heard the good news (for Tonino
proudly told him at once) was curious to know
whether the *signora forestiera* was as cold as northern
ladies were proverbially supposed to be.

"*Macchè!*" Tonino protested vigorously. On the

contrary. For a long time the two young sportsmen discussed the question of amorous temperatures, discussed it technically, professionally.

Tonino's raptures were not so extravagant as Moira's. So far as he was concerned, this sort of thing had happened before. Passion with Moira was not diminished by satisfaction, but rather, since the satisfaction was for her so novel, so intrinsically apocalyptic, increased. But that which caused her passion to increase produced in his a waning. He had got what he wanted; his night-begotten, touch-born longing for her (dulled in the interval and diminished by all the sporting love-hunts undertaken with Berto) had been fulfilled. She was no longer the desired and unobtainable, but the possessed, the known. By her surrender she had lowered herself to the level of all the other women he had ever made love to; she was just another item in the sportsman's grand total.

His attitude towards her underwent a change. Familiarity began to blunt his courtesy; his manner became offhandedly marital. When he saw her after an absence, *"Ebbene, tesoro,"* he would say in a genially unromantic tone, and pat her once or twice on the back or shoulder, as one might pat a horse. He permitted her to run her own errands and even his. Moira was happy to be his servant. Her love for him was, in one at least of its aspects, almost abject. She was dog-like in her devotion. Tonino found her adoration very agreeable so long as it expressed itself in fetching and carrying, in falling in with his suggestions, and in making him presents. "But you mustn't, my darling, you shouldn't," he protested each time she gave him something. Nevertheless, he accepted a pearl tie-pin, a pair of diamond and enamel links, a half-hunter on a gold and platinum chain. But Moira's devotion expressed itself also in other ways. Love demands as much as it gives. She wanted so much—his heart, his physical presence, his caresses, his confidences, his time, his fidelity. She was tyrannous in her adoring abjection. She pestered him with devotion. Tonino was bored and irritated by her excessive love. The omniscient Berto, to whom he carried his troubles, advised him to take a strong line. Women, he pronounced, must be kept in their places, firmly. They love one all the better if they are a little maltreated.

Tonino followed his advice and, pretexting work and social engagements, reduced the number of his visits. What a relief to be free of her importunity! Disquieted, Moira presented him with an amber cigar-holder. He protested, accepted it, but gave her no more of his company in return. A set of diamond studs produced no better effect. He talked vaguely and magniloquently about his career and the necessity for unremitting labour; that was his excuse for not coming more often to see her. It was on the tip of her tongue, one afternoon, to say that *she* would be his career, would give him anything he wanted, if only . . . But the memory of John's hateful words made her check herself. She was terrified lest he might make no difficulties about accepting her offer. "Stay with me this evening," she begged, throwing her arms round his neck. He suffered himself to be kissed.

"I wish I could stay," he said hypocritically. "But I have some important business this evening." The important business was playing billiards with Berto.

Moira looked at him for a moment in silence; then, dropping her hands from his shoulders, turned away. She had seen in his eyes a weariness that was almost a horror.

Summer drew on; but in Moira's soul there was no inward brightness to match the sunshine. She passed her days in a misery that was alternately restless and apathetic. Her nerves began once more to lead their own irresponsible life apart from hers. For no sufficient cause and against her will, she would find herself uncontrollably in a fury, or crying, or laughing. When Tonino came to see her, she was almost always, in spite of all her resolutions, bitterly angry or hysterically tearful. "But why do I behave like this?" she would ask herself despairingly. "Why do I say such things? I'm making him hate me." But the next time he came, she would act in precisely the same way. It was as though she were possessed by a devil. And it was not her mind only that was sick. When she ran too quickly upstairs, her heart seemed to stop beating for a moment and there was a whirling darkness before her eyes. She had an almost daily headache, lost appetite, could not digest what she ate. In her thin sallow face her eyes became enormous.

Looking into the glass, she found herself hideous, old repulsive. "No wonder he hates me," she thought, and she would brood, brood for hours over the idea that she had become physically disgusting to him, disgusting to look at, to touch, tainting the air with her breath. The idea became an obsession, indescribably painful and humiliating.

"Questa donna!" Tonino would complain with a sigh, when he came back from seeing her. Why didn't he leave her, then? Berto was all for strong measures. Tonino protested that he hadn't the courage; the poor woman would be too unhappy. But he also enjoyed a good dinner and going for drives in an expensive car and receiving sumptuous additions to his wardrobe. He contented himself with complaining and being a Christian martyr. One evening his old friend Carlo Menardi introduced him to his sister. After that he bore his martyrdom with even less patience than before. Luisa Menardi was only seventeen, fresh, healthy, provocatively pretty, with rolling black eyes that said all sorts of things and an impertinent tongue. Tonino's business appointments became more numerous than ever. Moira was left to brood in solitude on the dreadful theme of her own repulsiveness.

Then, quite suddenly, Tonino's manner towards her underwent another change. He became once more assiduously tender, thoughtful, affectionate. Instead of hardening himself with a shrug of indifference against her tears, instead of returning anger for hysterical anger, he was patient with her, was lovingly and cheerfully gentle. Gradually, by a kind of spiritual infection, she too became loving and gentle. Almost reluctantly—for the devil in her was the enemy of life and happiness—she came up again into the light.

"My dear son," Vasari senior had written in that eloquent and disquieting letter, "I am not one to complain feebly of Destiny; my whole life has been one long act of Faith and unshatterable Will. But there are blows under which even the strongest man must stagger—blows which . . ." The letter rambled on for pages in the same style. The hard unpleasant fact that emerged from under the eloquence was that Tonino's father had been speculating on the Naples stock exchange, speculating unsuccessfully. On the first of the next month he would be required to pay out some fifty thousand francs more than he could lay his hands on. The Grand Hotel Ritz-Carlton was doomed; he might even have to sell the restaurant. Was there anything Tonino could do?

"Is it possible?" said Moira with a sigh of happiness. "It seems too good to be true." She leaned against him; Tonino kissed her eyes and spoke caressing words. There was no moon; the dark-blue sky was thickly constellated; and, like another starry universe gone deliriously mad, the fire-flies darted, alternately eclipsed and shining, among the olive trees. "Darling," he said aloud and wondered if this would be a propitious moment to speak. "*Piccina mia.*" In the end he decided to postpone matters for another day or two. In another day or two, he calculated, she wouldn't be able to refuse him anything.

Tonino's calculations were correct. She let him have the money, not only without hesitation, but eagerly, joyfully. The reluctance was all on his side, in the receiving. He was almost in tears as he took the cheque, and the tears were tears of genuine emotion. "You're an angel," he said, and his voice trembled. "You've saved us all." Moira cried outright as she kissed him. How could John have said those things? She cried and was happy. A pair of silver-backed hair brushes accompanied the cheque—just to show that the money had made no difference to their relationship. Tonino recognized the delicacy of her intention and was touched. "You're too good to me," he insisted, "too good." He felt rather ashamed.

"Let's go for a long drive to-morrow," she suggested.

Tonino had arranged to go with Luisa and her brother to Prato. But so strong was his emotion, that he was on the point of accepting Moira's invitation and sacrificing Luisa.

"All right," he began, and then suddenly thought better of it. After all, he could go out with Moira any day. It was seldom that he had a chance of jaunting with Luisa. He struck his forehead, he made a despairing face. "But what am I thinking of!" he cried. "To-morrow's the day we're expecting the manager of the hotel company from Milan."

"But must you be there to see him?"

"Alas."

It was too sad. Just how sad Moira only fully realized the next day. She had never felt so lonely, never longed so ardently for his presence and affection. Unsatisfied, her longings were an unbearable restlessness. Hoping to escape from the loneliness and ennui with which she had filled the house, the garden, the landscape, she took out the car and drove away at random, not knowing whither. An hour later she found herself at Pistoia, and Pistoia was as hateful as every other place; she headed the car homewards. At Prato there was a fair. The road was crowded; the air was rich with a haze of dust and the noise of brazen music. In a field near the entrance to the town, the merry-go-round revolved with a glitter in the sunlight. A plunging horse held up the traffic. Moira stopped the car and looked about her at the crowd, at the swings, at the whirling roundabouts, looked with a cold hostility and distaste. Hateful! And suddenly there was Tonino sitting on a swan in the nearest merry-go-round, with a girl in pink muslin sitting in front of him between the white wings and the arching neck. Rising and falling as it went, the swan turned away out of sight. The music played on. *But poor poppa, poor poppa, he's got nothin' at all.* The swan reappeared. The girl in pink was looking back over her shoulder, smiling. She was very young, vulgarly pretty, shining and plumped with health. Tonino's lips moved; behind

the wall of noise what was he saying? All that Moira
knew was that the girl laughed; her laughter was like
an explosion of sensual young life. Tonino raised his
hand and took hold of her bare brown arm. Like an
undulating planet, the swan once more wheeled away
out of sight. Meanwhile, the plunging horse had been
quieted, the traffic had begun to move forward. Behind her a horn hooted insistently. But Moira did not
stir. Something in her soul desired that the agony
should be repeated and prolonged. Hoot, hoot, hoot!
She paid no attention. Rising and falling, the swan
emerged once more from eclipse. This time Tonino
saw her. Their eyes met; the laughter suddenly went
out of his face. *"Porco madonna!"* shouted the infuri-
ated motorist behind her. "Can't you move on?"
Moira threw the car into gear and shot forward along
the dusty road.

The cheque was in the post; there was still time,
Tonino reflected, to stop the payment of it.

"You're very silent," said Luisa teasingly, as they
drove back towards Florence. Her brother was sitting
in front, at the wheel; he had no eyes at the back of
his head. But Tonino sat beside her like a dummy.

"Why are you so silent?"

He looked at her, and his face was grave and
stonily unresponsive to her bright and dimpling pro-
vocations. He sighed; then, making an effort, he
smiled, rather wanly. Her hand was lying on her
knee, palm upwards, with a pathetic look of being

unemployed. Dutifully doing what was expected of him, Tonino reached out and took it.

At half-past six he was leaning his borrowed motor-cycle against the wall of Moira's villa. Feeling like a man who is about to undergo a dangerous operation, he rang the bell.

Moira was lying on her bed, had lain there ever since she came in; she was still wearing her dust-coat, she had not even taken off her shoes. Affecting an easy cheerfulness, as though nothing unusual had happened, Tonino entered almost jauntily.

"Lying down?" he said in a tone of surprised solicitude. "You haven't got a headache, have you?" His words fell, trivial and ridiculous, into abysses of significant silence. With a sinking of the heart, he sat down on the edge of the bed, he laid a hand on her knee. Moira did not stir, but lay with averted face, remote and unmoving. "What is it, my darling?" He patted her soothingly. "You're not upset because I went to Prato, are you?" he went on, in the incredulous voice of a man who is certain of a negative answer to his question. Still she said nothing. This silence was almost worse than the outcry he had anticipated. Desperately, knowing it was no good, he went on to talk about his old friend, Carlo Menardi, who had come round in his car to call for him; and as the director of the hotel company had left immediately after luncheon—most unexpectedly—and as he'd thought Moira was certain to be out, he had finally yielded and gone along with Carlo and his party. Of course, if he'd realized that Moira hadn't gone out, he'd have asked her to join them. For his own sake her company would have made all the difference.

His voice was sweet, ingratiating, apologetic. "A black-haired pimp from the slums of Naples." John's words reverberated in her memory. And so Tonino had never cared for her at all, only for her money. That other woman . . . She saw again that pink dress, lighter in tone than the sleek, sunburnt skin; Tonino's hand on the bare brown arm; that flash of eyes and laughing teeth. And meanwhile he was talking on and on, ingratiatingly; his very voice was a lie.

"Go away," she said at last, without looking at him.

"But, my darling . . ." Bending over her, he tried to kiss her averted cheek. She turned and, with all her might, struck him in the face.

"You little devil!" he cried, made furious by the pain of the blow. He pulled out his handkerchief and held it to his bleeding lip. "Very well, then." His voice trembled with anger. "If you want me to go, I'll go. With pleasure." He walked heavily away. The door slammed behind him.

But perhaps, thought Moira, as she listened to the sound of his footsteps receding on the stairs, perhaps it hadn't really been as bad as it looked; perhaps she had misjudged him. She sat up; on the yellow counterpane was a little circular red stain—a drop of his blood. And it was she who had struck him.

"Tonino!" she called; but the house was silent. "Tonino!" Still calling, she hurried downstairs, through the hall, out on to the porch. She was just in time to see him riding off through the gate on his motor-cycle. He was steering with one hand; the other still pressed a handkerchief to his mouth.

"Tonino, Tonino!" But either he didn't, or else he wouldn't hear her. The motor-cycle disappeared from view. And because he had gone, because he was angry, because of his bleeding lip, Moira was suddenly convinced that she had been accusing him falsely, that the wrong was all on her side. In a state of painful, uncontrollable agitation she ran to the garage. It was essential that she should catch him, speak to him, beg his pardon, implore him to come back. She started the car and drove out.

"One of these days," John had warned her, "you'll go over the edge of the bank, if you're not careful. It's a horrible turning."

Coming out of the garage door, she pulled the wheel hard over as usual. But too impatient to be with Tonino, she pressed the accelerator at the same time. John's prophecy was fulfilled. The car came too close to the edge of the bank; the dry earth crumbled and slid under its outer wheels. It tilted horribly, tottered for a long instant on the balancing point, and went over.

But for the ilex tree, it would have gone crashing down the slope. As it was, the machine fell only a foot or so and came to rest, leaning drunkenly sideways with its flank against the bole of the tree. Shaken, but quite unhurt, Moira climbed over the edge of the car and dropped to the ground. "Assunta! Giovanni!" The maids, the gardener came running. When they saw what had happened, there was a small babel of exclamations, questions, comments.

"But can't you get it on to the drive again?" Moira insisted to the gardener; because it was necessary, absolutely necessary, that she should see Tonino at once.

Giovanni shook his head. It would take at least four men with levers and a pair of horses. . . .

"Telephone for a taxi, then," she ordered Assunta and hurried into the house. If she remained any longer with those chattering people, she'd begin to scream. Her nerves had come to a separate life again; clenching her fists, she tried to fight them down.

Going up to her room, she sat down before the mirror and began, methodically and with deliberation (it was her will imposing itself on her nerves) to make up her face. She rubbed a little red on to her pale cheeks, painted her lips, dabbed on the powder. "I must look presentable," she thought and put on her smartest hat. But would the taxi never come? She struggled with her impatience. "My purse," she said to herself. "I shall need some money for the cab." She was pleased with herself for being so full of foresight, so coolly practical in spite of her nerves. "Yes, of course; my purse."

But where was the purse? She remembered so

clearly having thrown it on to the bed when she came
in from her drive. It was not there. She looked under
the pillow, lifted the counterpane. Or perhaps it had
fallen on the floor. She looked under the bed; the
purse wasn't there. Was it possible that she hadn't
put it on the bed at all? But it wasn't on her dressing-
table, or on the mantelpiece, or on any of the shelves,
or in any of the drawers of her wardrobe. Where,
where, where? And suddenly a terrible thought occurred to her. Tonino. . . . Was it possible? The
seconds passed. The possibility became a dreadful
certainty. A thief as well as . . . John's words echoed
in her head. "Black-haired pimp from the slums of
Naples, black-haired pimp from the slums. . . ."
And a thief as well. The bag was made of gold chain-
work; there were more than four thousand lire in it.
A thief, a thief. . . . She stood quite still, strained,
rigid, her eyes staring. Then something broke, something seemed to collapse within her. She cried aloud
as though under a sudden intolerable pain.

The sound of the shot brought them running upstairs. They found her lying face downwards across
the bed, still faintly breathing. But she was dead
before the doctor could come up from the town. On a
bed standing, as hers stood, in an alcove, it was difficult to lay out the body. When they moved it out of
its recess, there was the sound of a hard, rather metal-
lic fall. Assunta bent down to see what had dropped.

"It's her purse," she said. "It must have got stuck
between the bed and the wall."

THE CLAXTONS

In their little house on the common, how beautifully the Claxtons lived, how spiritually! Even the cat was a vegetarian—at any rate officially—even the cat. Which made little Sylvia's behaviour really quite inexcusable. For after all little Sylvia was human and six years old, whereas Pussy was only four and an animal. If Pussy could be content with greens and potatoes and milk and an occasional lump of nut butter, as a treat—Pussy, who had a tiger in her blood—surely Sylvia might be expected to refrain from surreptitious bacon-eating. Particularly in somebody else's house. What made the incident so specially painful to the Claxtons was that it had occurred under Judith's roof. It was the first time they had stayed with Judith since their marriage. Martha Claxton was rather afraid of her sister, afraid of her sharp tongue and her laughter and her scarifying irreverence. And on her own husband's account she was a little jealous of Judith's husband. Jack Bamborough's books were not only esteemed; they also brought in money. Whereas poor Herbert. . . .

"Herbert's art is too *inward*," his wife used to explain, "too spiritual for most people to understand." She resented Jack Bamborough's success; it was too complete. She wouldn't have minded so much if he had made pots of money in the teeth of critical contempt; or if the critics had approved and he had made nothing. But to earn praise *and* a thousand a year—that was too much. A man had no right to make the best of both worlds like that, when Herbert never sold anything and was utterly ignored. In spite of all which she had at last accepted Judith's often repeated invitation. After all, one ought to love one's sister and one's sister's husband. Also all the chimneys in the house on the common needed sweeping, and the roof would have to be repaired where the rain was coming in. Judith's invitation arrived most conveniently. Martha accepted it. And then Sylvia went and did that really inexcusable thing. Coming down to breakfast before the others she stole a rasher from the dish of bacon with which her aunt and uncle unregenerately began the day. Her mother's arrival prevented her from eating it on the spot; she had to hide it. Weeks later when Judith was looking for something in the inlaid Italian cabinet, a little pool of dried grease in one of the drawers bore eloquent witness to the crime. The day passed; but Sylvia found no opportunity to consummate the outrage she had begun. It was only in the evening, while her little brother Paul was being given his bath, that she was able to retrieve the now stiff and clammy-cold rasher. With guilty speed she hurried upstairs with it and hid it under her pillow. When the lights were turned out she ate it. In the morning, the grease stains and a piece of gnawed rind betrayed her. Judith went into fits of inextinguishable laughter.

"It's like the Garden of Eden," she gasped between the explosions of her mirth. "The meat of the Pig of the Knowledge of Good and Evil. But if you *will* surround bacon with categorical imperatives and mystery, what can you expect, my dear Martha?"

Martha went on smiling her habitual smile of sweet forgiving benevolence. But inside she felt extremely angry; the child had made a fool of them all in front of Judith and Jack. She would have liked to give her a good smacking. Instead of which—for one must never be rough with a child, one must never let it see that one is annoyed—she reasoned with Sylvia, she explained, she appealed, more in sorrow than in anger, to her better feelings.

"Your daddy and I don't think it's right to make animals suffer when we can eat vegetables which don't suffer anything."

"How do you know they don't?" asked Sylvia, shooting out the question malignantly. Her face was ugly with sullen ill-temper.

"We don't think it right, darling," Mrs. Claxton went on, ignoring the interruption. "And I'm sure you wouldn't either, if you realized. Think, my pet; to make that bacon, a poor little pig had to be killed.

To be *killed*, Sylvia. Think of that. A poor innocent little pig that hadn't done anybody any harm."

"But I hate pigs," cried Sylvia. Her sullenness flared up into sudden ferocity; her eyes that had been fixed and glassy with a dull resentment, darkly flashed. "I hate them, hate them, *hate* them."

"Quite right," said Aunt Judith, who had come in most inopportunely in the middle of the lecture. "Quite right. Pigs *are* disgusting. That's why people called them pigs."

Martha was glad to get back to the little house on the common and their beautiful life, happy to escape from Judith's irreverent laughter and the standing reproach of Jack's success. On the common she ruled, she was the mistress of the family destinies. To the friends who came to visit them there she was fond of saying, with that smile of hers, "I feel that, in our way and on a tiny scale, we've built Jerusalem in England's green and pleasant land."

It was Martha's great-grandfather who started the brewery business. Postgate's Entire was a household word in Cheshire and Derbyshire. Martha's share of the family fortune was about seven hundred a year. The Claxtons' spirituality and disinterestedness were the flowers of an economic plant whose roots were bathed in beer. But for the thirst of British workmen, Herbert would have had to spend his time and energies profitably doing instead of beautifully being. Beer and the fact that he had married Martha permitted him to cultivate the arts and the religions, to distinguish himself in a gross world as an apostle of idealism.

"It's what's called the division of labour," Judith would laughingly say. "Other people drink. Martha and I think. Or at any rate we think we think."

Herbert was one of those men who are never without a knapsack on their backs. Even in Bond Street, on the rare occasions when he went to London, Herbert looked as though he were just about to ascend Mont Blanc. The rücksack is a badge of spirituality. For the modern high-thinking, pure-hearted Teuton or Anglo-Saxon the scandal of the rücksack is what the scandal of the cross was to the Franciscans. When Herbert passed, long-legged and knickerbockered, his fair beard like a windy explosion round his face, his rücksack overflowing with the leeks and cabbages required in such profusion to support a purely graminivorous family, the street-boys yelled, the flappers whooped with laughter. Herbert ignored them, or else smiled through his beard forgivingly and with a rather studied humorousness. We all have our little rücksack to bear. Herbert bore his not merely with resignation, but boldly, provocatively, flauntingly in the faces of men; and along with the rücksack the other symbols of difference, of separation from ordinary, gross humanity—the concealing beard, the knickerbockers, the Byronic shirt. He was proud of his difference.

"Oh, I know you think us ridiculous," he would

say to his friends of the crass materialistic world, "I know you laugh at us for a set of cranks."

"But we don't, we don't," the friends would answer, politely lying.

"And yet, if it hadn't been for the cranks," Herbert pursued, "where would you be now, what would you be doing? You'd be beating children, and torturing animals and hanging people for stealing a shilling, and doing all the other horrible things they did in the good old days."

He was proud, proud; he knew himself superior. So did Martha. In spite of her beautiful Christian smile, she too was certain of her superiority. That smile of hers—it was the hall-mark of her spirituality. A more benevolent version of Mona Lisa's smile, it kept her rather thin, bloodless lips almost chronically curved into a crescent of sweet and forgiving charitableness, it surcharged the natural sullenness of her face with a kind of irrelevant sweetness. It was the product of long years of wilful self-denial, of stubborn aspirations towards the highest, of conscious and determined love for humanity and her enemies. (And for Martha the terms were really identical; humanity, though she didn't of course admit it, *was* her enemy, she felt it hostile and *therefore* loved it, consciously and conscientiously; loved it because she really hated it.)

In the end habit had fixed the smile undetachably to her face. It remained there permanently shining, like the head-lamps of a motor-car inadvertently

turned on and left to burn, unnecessarily, in the day-
light. Even when she was put out or downright angry,
even when she was stubbornly, mulishly fighting
to have her own will, the smile persisted. Framed
between its pre-Raphaelitic loops of mouse-coloured
hair the heavy, sullen-featured, rather unwholesomely
pallid face continued to shine incongruously with
forgiving love for the whole of hateful, hostile humanity; only in the grey eyes was there any trace of
the emotions which Martha so carefully repressed.

It was her great-grandfather and her grandfather who had made the money. Her father was
already by birth and upbringing the landed gentleman. Brewing was only the dim but profitable background to more distinguished activities as a sportsman, an agriculturist, a breeder of horses and
rhododendrons, a member of Parliament and the best
London clubs.

The fourth generation was obviously ripe for Art
and Higher Thought. And duly, punctually, the adolescent Martha discovered William Morris and Mrs.
Besant, discovered Tolstoy and Rodin and Folk
Dancing and Lao-Tzse. Stubbornly, with all the
force of her heavy will, she addressed herself to the
conquest of spirituality, to the siege and capture of
the Highest. And no less punctually than her sister,
the adolescent Judith discovered French literature
and was lightly enthusiastic (for it was in her nature
to be light and gay) about Manet and Daumier, even,
in due course, about Matisse and Cézanne. In the long

run brewing almost infallibly leads to impressionism or theosophy or communism. But there are other roads to the spiritual heights; it was by one of these other roads that Herbert had travelled. There were no brewers among Herbert's ancestors. He came from a lower, at any rate a poorer, stratum of society. His father kept a drapery shop at Nantwich. Mr. Claxton was a thin, feeble man with a taste for argumentation and pickled onions. Indigestion had spoilt his temper and the chronic consciousness of inferiority had made him a revolutionary and a domestic bully. In the intervals of work he read the literature of socialism and unbelief and nagged at his wife, who took refuge in non-conformist piety. Herbert was a clever boy with a knack for passing examinations. He did well at school. They were very proud of him at home, for he was an only child.

"You mark my words," his father would say, prophetically glowing in that quarter of an hour of beatitude which intervened between the eating of his dinner and the beginning of his dyspepsia, "that boy'll do something remarkable."

A few minutes later, with the first rumblings and convulsions of indigestion, he would be shouting at him in fury, cuffing him, sending him out of the room.

Being no good at games Herbert revenged himself on his more athletic rivals by reading. Those afternoons in the public library instead of on the football field, or at home with one of his father's revolutionary volumes, were the beginning of his difference and superiority. It was, when Martha first knew him, a political difference, an anti-Christian superiority. Her superiority was mainly artistic and spiritual. Martha's was the stronger character; in a little while Herbert's interest in socialism was entirely secondary to his interest in art, his anti-clericalism was tinctured by Oriental religiosity. It was only to be expected.

What was not to be expected was that they should have married at all, that they should ever even have met. It was not easy for the children of land-owning brewers and shop-owning drapers to meet and marry.

Morris-dancing accomplished the miracle. They came together in a certain garden in the suburbs of Nantwich where Mr. Winslow, the Extension Lecturer, presided over the rather solemn stampings and prancings of all that was earnestly best among the youth of eastern Cheshire. To that suburban garden Martha drove in from the country, Herbert cycled out from the High Street. They met; love did the rest.

Martha was at that time twenty-four and, in her heavy, pallid style, not unhandsome. Herbert was a year older, and tall, a disproportionately narrow young man, with a face strong-featured and aquiline, yet singularly mild ("a sheep in eagle's clothing" was how Judith had once described him) and very fair hair. Beard at that time he had none. Economic necessity still prevented him from advertising the fact of his difference and superiority. In the auctioneer's office, where Herbert worked as a clerk, a beard would have been as utterly inadmissible as knickerbockers, an open shirt, and that outward and visible symbol of inward grace, the rücksack. For Herbert these things only became possible when marriage and Martha's seven hundred yearly pounds had lifted him clear of the ineluctable workings of economic law. In those Nantwich days the most he could permit himself was a red tie and some private opinions.

It was Martha who did most of the loving. Dumbly, with a passion that was almost grim in its stubborn intensity, she adored him—his frail body, his long-fingered, delicate hands, the aquiline face with its, for other eyes, rather spurious air of distinction and intelligence, all of him, all. "He has read William Morris and Tolstoy," she wrote in her diary; "he's one of the very few people I've met who feel *responsible* about things. Every one else is so terribly frivolous and self-centred and indifferent. Like Nero fiddling while Rome was burning. He isn't like that. He's conscious, he's aware, he accepts the burden. That's why I like him." That was why, at any rate, she thought she liked him. But her passion was really for the physical Herbert Claxton. Heavily, like a dark cloud charged with thunder, she hung over him with a kind of menace, ready to break out on him with the lightnings of passions and domineering will. Herbert was charged with some of the electricity of passion which he had called out of her. Because she loved, he loved her in return. His vanity, too, was flattered; it was only theoretically that he despised class-distinctions and wealth.

The land-owning brewers were horrified when they heard from Martha that she was proposing to marry the son of a shopkeeper. Their objections only intensified Martha's stubborn determination to have her own way. Even if she hadn't loved him, she would have married him on principle, just because his father *was* a draper and because all this class business was an irrelevant nonsense. Besides, Herbert had talents. What sort of talents it was rather hard to specify. But whatever the talents might be, they were being smothered in the auctioneer's office. Her seven hundred a year would give them scope. It was practically a duty to marry him.

"A man's a man for all that," she said to her father, quoting, in the hope of persuading him, from his favourite poet; she herself found Burns too gross and unspiritual.

"And a sheep's a sheep," retorted Mr. Postgate, "and a woodlouse is a woodlouse—for all that and all that."

Martha flushed darkly and turned away without saying anything more. Three weeks later she and the almost passive Herbert were married.

Well, now Sylvia was six years old and a handful, and little Paul, who was whiny and had adenoids, was just on five, and Herbert, under his wife's influence, had discovered unexpectedly enough that his talents were really artistic and was by this time a painter with an established reputation for lifeless ineptitude. With every reaffirmation of his lack of success he flaunted more defiantly than ever the scandal of the rücksack, the scandals of the knicker-bockers and beard. Martha, meanwhile, talked about the inwardness of Herbert's art. They were able to persuade themselves that it was their superiority which prevented them from getting the recognition they deserved. Herbert's lack of success was even a proof (though not perhaps the most satisfactory kind of proof) of that superiority.

"But Herbert's time will come," Martha would affirm prophetically. "It's bound to come."

Meanwhile the little house on the Surrey common was overflowing with unsold pictures. Allegorical they were, painted very flatly in a style that was Early Indian tempered, wherever the Oriental originals ran too luxuriantly to breasts and wasp-waists and moon-like haunches, by the dreary respect-ability of Puvis de Chavannes.

"And let me beg you, Herbert"—those had been Judith's parting words of advice as they stood on the platform waiting for the train to take them back again to their house on the common—"let me implore you: try to be a little more *indecent* in your paintings. Not so shockingly pure. You don't know how happy you'd make me if you could really be obscene for once. Really obscene."

It was a comfort, thought Martha, to be getting away from that sort of thing. Judith was really too . . . Her lips smiled, her hand waved good-bye.

"Isn't it lovely to come back to our own dear little house!" she cried, as the station taxi drove them bumpily over the track that led across the common to the garden gate. "Isn't it lovely?"

"Lovely!" said Herbert dutifully echoing her rather forced rapture.

"Lovely!" repeated little Paul, rather thickly through his adenoids. He was a sweet child, when he wasn't whining, and always did and said what was expected of him.

Through the window of the cab Sylvia looked critically at the long low house among the trees. "I think Aunt Judith's house is nicer," she concluded with decision.

Martha turned upon her the sweet illumination of her smile. "Aunt Judith's house is bigger," she said, "and much grander. But this is Home, my sweet. Our very own Home."

"All the same," persisted Sylvia, "I like Aunt Judith's house better."

Martha smiled at her forgivingly and shook her head. "You'll understand what I mean when you're older," she said. A strange child, she was thinking, a difficult child. Not like Paul, who was so easy. Too easy. Paul fell in with suggestions, did what he was

told, took his colour from the spiritual environment.
Not Sylvia. She had her own will. Paul was like his
father. In the girl Martha saw something of her own
stubbornness and passion and determination. If the
will could be well directed. . . . But the trouble was
that it was so often hostile, resistant, contrary.
Martha thought of that deplorable occasion, only
a few months before, when Sylvia, in a fit of rage at
not being allowed to do something she wanted to do,
had spat in her father's face. Herbert and Martha
had agreed that she ought to be punished. But how?
Not smacked, of course; smacking was out of the
question. The important thing was to make the child
realize the heinousness of what she had done. In the
end they decided that the best thing would be for
Herbert to talk to her very seriously (but very
gently, of course), and then leave her to choose her
own punishment. Let her conscience decide. It
seemed an excellent idea.

"I want to tell you a story, Sylvia," said Herbert
that evening, taking the child on to his knees. "About
a little girl, who had a daddy who loved her so much,
so much." Sylvia looked at him suspiciously, but
said nothing. "And one day that little girl, who was
sometimes rather a thoughtless little girl, though I
don't believe she was really naughty, was doing
something that it wasn't right or good for her to do.
And her daddy told her not to. And what do you
think that little girl did? She spat in her daddy's
face. And her daddy was very very sad. Because

what his little girl did was wrong, wasn't it?" Sylvia nodded a brief defiant assent. "And when one has done something wrong, one must be punished, mustn't one?" The child nodded again. Herbert was pleased; his words had had their effect; her conscience was being touched. Over the child's head he exchanged a glance with Martha. "If you had been that daddy," he went on, "and the little girl you loved so much had spat in your face, what would you have done, Sylvia?"

"Spat back," Sylvia answered fiercely and without hesitation.

At the recollection of the scene Martha sighed. Sylvia was difficult, Sylvia was decidedly a problem. The cab drew up at the gate; the Claxtons unpacked themselves and their luggage. Inadequately tipped, the driver made his usual scene. Bearing his rücksack, Herbert turned away with a dignified patience. He was used to this sort of thing; it was a chronic martyrdom. The unpleasant duty of paying was always his. Martha only provided the cash. With what extreme and yearly growing reluctance! He was always between the devil of the undertipped and the deep sea of Martha's avarice.

"Four miles' drive and a tuppenny tip!" shouted the cab driver at Herbert's receding and rücksacked back.

Martha grudged him even the twopence. But convention demanded that something should be given. Conventions are stupid things; but even the **Children** of the Spirit must make some compromise with the World. In this case Martha was ready to compromise with the World to the extent of twopence. But no more. Herbert knew that she would have been very angry if he had given more. Not openly, of course; not explicitly. She never visibly lost her temper or her smile. But her forgiving disapproval would have weighed heavily on him for days. And for days she would have found excuses for economizing in order to make up for the wanton extravagance of a sixpenny instead of a twopenny tip. Her economies were mostly on the food, and their justification was always spiritual. Eating was gross; high living was incompatible with high thinking; it was dreadful to think of the poor going hungry while you yourself were living in luxurious gluttony. There would be a cutting down of butter and Brazil nuts, of the more palatable vegetables and the choicer fruits. Meals would come to consist more and more exclusively of porridge, potatoes, cabbages, bread. Only when the original extravagance had been made up several hundred times would Martha begin to relax her asceticism. Herbert never ventured to complain. After one of these bouts of plain living he would for a long time be very careful to avoid other extravagances, even when, as in this case, his economies brought him into painful and humiliating conflict with those on whom they were practiced.

"Next time," the taxi driver was shouting, "I'll charge extra for the whiskers."

Herbert passed over the threshold and closed the door behind him. Safe! He took off his rücksack and deposited it carefully on a chair. Gross, vulgar brute! But anyhow he had taken himself off with the twopence. Martha would have no cause to complain or cut down the supply of peas and beans. In a mild and spiritual way Herbert was very fond of his food. So was Martha—darkly and violently fond of it. That was why she had become a vegetarian, why her economies were always at the expense of the stomach —precisely because she liked food so much. She suffered when she deprived herself of some delicious morsel. But there was a sense in which she loved her suffering more than the morsel. Denying herself, she felt her whole being irradiated by a glow of power; suffering, she was strengthened, her will was wound up, her energy enhanced. The dammed-up instincts rose and rose behind the wall of voluntary mortification, deep and heavy with potentialities of force. In the struggle between the instincts Martha's love of power was generally strong enough to overcome her greed; among the hierarchy of pleasures, the joy of exerting the personal conscious will was more intense than the joy of eating even Turkish delight or strawberries and cream. Not always, however; for there were occasions when, overcome by a sudden irresistible desire, Martha would buy and, in a single day, secretly consume a whole pound of chocolate creams, throwing herself upon the sweets with the same heavy violence as had characterized her first passion for

Herbert. With the passage of time and the waning, after the birth of her two children, of her physical passion for her husband, Martha's orgies among the chocolates became more frequent. It was as though her vital energies were being forced, by the closing of the sexual channel, to find explosive outlet in gluttony. After one of these orgies Martha always tended to become more than ordinarily strict in her ascetic spirituality.

Three weeks after the Claxtons' return to their little house on the common, the War broke out.

"It's changed most people," Judith remarked in the third year, "it's altered some out of all recognition. Not Herbert and Martha, though. It's just made them more so—more like themselves than they were before. Curious." She shook her head. "Very curious."

But it wasn't really curious at all; it was inevitable. The War could not help intensifying all that was characteristically Herbertian and Martha-ish in Herbert and Martha. It heightened their sense of remote superiority by separating them still further from the ordinary herd. For while ordinary people believed in the war, fought and worked to win, Herbert and Martha utterly disapproved and, on grounds that were partly Buddhistic, partly Socialist-International, partly Tolstoyan, refused to have anything to do with the accursed thing. In the midst of universal madness they almost alone were sane. And their superiority was proved and divinely

hallowed by persecution. Unofficial disapproval was
succeeded, after the passing of the Conscription Act,
by official repression. Herbert pleaded a conscientious
objection. He was sent to work on the land in Dorset,
a martyr, a different and spiritually higher being.
The act of a brutal War Office had definitely promoted him out of the ranks of common humanity. In
this promotion Martha vicariously participated. But
what most powerfully stimulated her spirituality was
not War-time persecution so much as War-time financial instability, War-time increase in prices. In the
first weeks of confusion she had been panic-stricken;
she imagined that all her money was lost, she saw
herself with Herbert and the children, hungry and
houseless, begging from door to door. She immediately dismissed her two servants, she reduced the
family food supply to a prison ration. Time passed
and her money came in very much as usual. But Martha was so much delighted with the economies she had
made that she would not revert to the old mode of
life.

"After all," she argued, "it's really not pleasant to
have strangers in the house to serve you. And then,
why should they serve us? They who are just as good
as we are." It was a hypocritical tribute to Christian
doctrine; they were really immeasurably inferior.
"Just because we happen to be able to pay them—
that's why they have to serve us. It's always made
me feel uncomfortable and ashamed. Hasn't it you,
Herbert?"

"Always," said Herbert, who always agreed with his wife.

"Besides," she went on, "I think one ought to do one's own work. One oughtn't to get out of touch with the humble small realities of life. I've felt really happier since I've been doing the housework, haven't you?"

Herbert nodded.

"And it's so good for the children. It teaches them humility and service. . . ."

Doing without servants saved a clear hundred and fifty a year. But the economies she made on food were soon counterbalanced by the results of scarcity and inflation. With every rise in prices Martha's enthusiasm for ascetic spirituality became more than ever fervid and profound. So too did her conviction that the children would be spoilt and turned into worldlings if she sent them to an expensive boarding-school. "Herbert and I believe very strongly in home education, don't we, Herbert?" And Herbert would agree that they believed in it very strongly indeed. Home education without a governess, insisted Martha. Why should one let one's children be influenced by strangers? Perhaps badly influenced. Anyhow, not influenced in exactly the way one would influence them oneself. People hired governesses because they dreaded the hard work of educating their children. And of course it *was* hard work—the harder, the higher your ideals. But wasn't it worth making sacrifices for one's children? With the uplifting questions,

Martha's smile curved itself into a crescent of more than ordinary soulfulness. Of course it was worth it. The work was an incessant delight—wasn't it, Herbert? For what could be more delightful, more profoundly soul-satisfying than to help your own children to grow up beautifully, to guide them, to mould their characters into ideal forms, to lead their thoughts and desires into the noblest channels? Not by any system of compulsion, of course; children must never be compelled; the art of education was persuading children to mould themselves in the most ideal forms, was showing them how to be the makers of their own higher selves, was firing them with enthusiasm for what Martha felicitously described as "self-sculpture."

On Sylvia, her mother had to admit to herself, this art of education was hard to practise. Sylvia didn't want to sculpture herself, at any rate into the forms which Martha and Herbert found most beautiful. She was quite discouragingly without that sense of moral beauty on which the Claxtons relied as a means of education. It was ugly, they told her, to be rough, to disobey, to say rude things and tell lies. It was beautiful to be gentle and polite, obedient and truthful. "But I don't mind being ugly," Sylvia would retort. There was no possible answer, except a spanking; and spanking was against the Claxtons' principles.

Aesthetic and intellectual beauty seemed to mean as little to Sylvia as moral beauty. What difficulties they had to make her take an interest in the piano! This was the more extraordinary, her mother considered, as Sylvia was obviously musical; when she was two and a half she had already been able to sing "Three Blind Mice" in tune. But she didn't want to learn her scales. Her mother talked to her about a wonderful little boy called Mozart. Sylvia hated Mozart. "No, no!" she would shout, whenever her mother mentioned the abhorred name. "I don't want to hear." And to make sure of not hearing, she would put her fingers in her ears. Nevertheless, by the time she was nine she could play "The Merry Peasant" from beginning to end without a mistake. Martha still had hopes of turning her into the musician of the family. Paul, meanwhile, was the future Giotto; it had been decided that he inherited his father's talents. He accepted his career as docilely as he had consented to learn his letters. Sylvia, on the other hand, simply refused to read.

"But think," said Martha ecstatically, "how *wonderful* it will be when you can open any book and read all the *beautiful* things people have written!" Her coaxing was ineffective.

"I like playing better," said Sylvia obstinately, with that expression of sullen bad temper which was threatening to become as chronic as her mother's smile. True to their principles, Herbert and Martha let her play; but it was a grief to them.

"You make your daddy and mummy so sad," they said, trying to appeal to her better feelings. "So sad.

Won't you try to read to make your daddy and mummy happy?" The child confronted them with an expression of sullen, stubborn wretchedness, and shook her head. "Just to please us," they wheedled. "You make us *so* sad." Sylvia looked from one mournfully forgiving face to the other and burst into tears.

"Naughty," she sobbed incoherently. "Naughty. Go away." She hated them for being sad, for making her sad. "No, go away, go away," she screamed when they tried to comfort her. She cried inconsolably; but still, she wouldn't read.

Paul, on the other hand, was beautifully teachable and plastic. Slowly (for, with his adenoids, he was not a very intelligent boy) but with all the docility that could be desired, he learnt to read about the lass on the ass in the grass and other such matters. "Hear how beautifully Paul reads," Martha would say, in the hope of rousing Sylvia to emulation. But Sylvia would only make a contemptuous face and walk out of the room. In the end she taught herself to read secretly, in a couple of weeks. Her parents' pride in the achievement was tempered when they discovered her motives for making the extraordinary effort.

"But what is this dreadful little book?" asked Martha holding up the copy of "Nick Carter and the Michigan Boulevard Murderers" which she had discovered carefully hidden under Sylvia's winter underclothing. On the cover was a picture of a man being thrown off the roof of a skyscraper by a gorilla.

The child snatched it from her. "It's a lovely book," she retorted, flushing darkly with an anger that was intensified by her sense of guilt.

"Darling," said Martha, beautifully smiling on the surface of her annoyance. "You mustn't snatch like that. Snatching's *ugly*." "Don't care." "Let me look at it please." Martha held out her hand. She smiled, but her pale face was heavily determined, her eyes commanded.

Sylvia confronted her, stubbornly she shook her head. "No, I don't want you to."

"Please," begged her mother, more forgivingly and more commandingly than ever, "please." And in the end, with a sudden outburst of tearful rage, Sylvia handed over the book and ran off into the garden. "Sylvia, Sylvia!" her mother called. But the child would not come back. To have stood by while her mother violated the secrets of her private world would have been unbearable.

Owing to his adenoids Paul looked and almost was an imbecile. Without being a Christian Scientist, Martha disbelieved in doctors; more particularly she disliked surgeons, perhaps because they were so expensive. She left Paul's adenoids unextirpated; they grew and festered in his throat. From November to May he was never without a cold, a quinsy, an ear-ache. The winter of 1921 was a particularly bad one for Paul. He began by getting influenza which turned into pneumonia, caught measles during his convalescence and developed at the New Year an infection of the middle ear which threatened to leave him permanently deaf. The doctor peremptorily advised an operation, treatment, a convalescence in Switzerland, at an altitude and in the sun. Martha hesitated to follow his advice. She had come to be so firmly convinced of her poverty that she did not see how she could possibly afford to do what the doctor ordered. In her perplexity she wrote to Judith. Two days later Judith arrived in person.

"But do you want to kill the boy?" she asked her sister fiercely. "Why didn't you get him out of this filthy dank hole weeks ago?"

In a few hours she had arranged everything. Herbert and Martha were to start at once with the boy. They were to travel direct to Lausanne by sleeper. "But surely a sleeper's hardly necessary," objected Martha. "You forget" (she beautifully smiled) "we're simple folk." "I only remember you've got a sick child with you," said Judith, and the sleeper was booked. At Lausanne he was to be operated. (Expensive reply-paid telegram to the clinic; poor Martha suffered.) And when he was well enough he was to go to a sanatorium at Leysin. (Another telegram, for which Judith paid, however. Martha forgot to give the money back.) Martha and Herbert, meanwhile, were to find a good hotel, where Paul would join them as soon as his treatment was over. And they were to stay at least six months and preferably a year. Sylvia, meanwhile, was to stay with her aunt in England; that would save Martha a lot of money. Judith would try to find a tenant for the house on the common.

"Talk of savages!" said Judith to her husband. "I've never seen such a little cannibal as Sylvia." "It's what comes of having vegetarian parents, I suppose."

"Poor little creature!" Judith went on with an indignant pity. "There are times when I'd like to drown Martha, she's such a criminal fool. Bringing those children up without ever letting them go near another child of their own age! It's scandalous! And then talking to them about spirituality and Jesus and *ahimsa* and beauty and goodness knows what! And not wanting them to play stupid games, but be artistic! And always being sweet, even when she's furious! It's dreadful, really dreadful! And so silly. Can't she see that the best way of turning a child into a devil is to try to bring it up as an angel? Ah well. . . ." She sighed and was silent, pensively; she herself had had no children and, if the doctors were right, never would have children.

The weeks passed and gradually the little savage was civilized. Her first lessons were lessons in the art of moderation. The food, which at the Bamboroughs house was good and plentiful, was at the beginning a terrible temptation to a child accustomed to the austerities of the spiritual life.

"There'll be more to-morrow," Judith would say,

when the child asked for yet another helping of pudding. "You're not a snake, you know; you can't store up to-day's overeating for next week's dinners. The only thing you can do with too much food is to be sick with it."

At first Sylvia would insist, would wheedle and whine for more. But luckily, as Judith remarked to her husband, luckily she had a delicate liver. Her aunt's prophecies were only too punctually realized. After three or four bilious attacks Sylvia learned to control her greed. Her next lesson was in obedience. The obedience she was accustomed to give her parents was slow and grudging. Herbert and Martha never on principle, commanded, but only suggested. It was a system that had almost forced upon the child a habit of saying no, automatically to whatever proposition was made to her. "No, no, no!" she regularly began and then gradually suffered herself to be persuaded, reasoned, or moved by the expression of her parents' sadness into a belated and generally grudging acquiescence. Obeying at long last, she felt an obscure resentment against those who had not compelled her to obey at once. Like most children, she would have liked to be relieved compulsorily of responsibility for her own actions; she was angry with her father and mother for forcing her to expend so much will in resisting them, such a quantity of painful emotion in finally letting her will be overcome. It would have been so much simpler if they had insisted from the first, had compelled her to obey at once and so spared her all her spiritual effort and pain. Darkly and bitterly did she resent the incessant appeal they made to her better feelings. It wasn't fair, it wasn't fair. They had no right to smile and forgive and make her feel a beast, to fill her with sadness by being sad themselves. She felt that they were somehow taking a cruel advantage of her. And perversely, just because she hated their being sad, she deliberately went out of her way to say and do the things that would most sorely distress them. One of her favourite tricks was to threaten to "go and walk across the plank over the sluice." Between the smooth pond and the shallow rippling of the stream, the gentle water became for a moment terrible. Pent in a narrow channel of oozy brickwork six feet of cataract tumbled with unceasing clamour into a black and heaving pool. It was a horrible place. How often her parents had begged her not to play near the sluice! Her threat would make them repeat their recommendations; they would implore her to be reasonable. "No, I won't be reasonable," Sylvia would shout and run off towards the sluice. If, in fact, she never ventured within five yards of the roaring gulf, that was because she was much more terrified for herself than her parents were for her. But she would go as near as she dared for the pleasure (the pleasure which she hated) of hearing her mother mournfully express her sadness at having a little girl so disobedient, so selfishly reckless of danger. She tried the same trick with her Aunt Judith. "I shall go into the woods by myself," she menaced one day, scowling. To her great surprise, instead of begging her to be reasonable and not to distress the grown-ups by disobediently running into danger, Judith only shrugged her shoulders. "Trot along then, if you want to be a little fool," she said without looking up from her letter. Indignantly, Sylvia trotted; but she was frightened of being alone in the huge wood. Only pride kept her from returning at once. Damp, dirty, tear-stained, and scratched, she was brought back two hours later by a gamekeeper.

"What luck," said Judith to her husband, "what enormous luck that the little idiot should have gone and got herself lost." The scheme of things was marshalled against the child's delinquency. But Judith did not rely exclusively on the scheme of things to enforce her code; she provided her own sanctions. Obedience had to be prompt, or else there were prompt reprisals. Once Sylvia succeeded in provoking her aunt to real anger. The scene made a profound impression on her. An hour later she crept diffidently and humbly to where her aunt was sitting. "I'm sorry, Aunt Judith," she said, "I'm sorry," and burst into tears. It was the first time she had ever spontaneously asked for forgiveness.

The lessons which profited Sylvia most were those which she learned from other children. After a certain number of rather unsuccessful and occasionally painful experiments she learned to play, to behave as an equal among equals. Hitherto she had lived almost exclusively as a chronological inferior among grown-ups, in a state of unceasing rebellion and guerilla warfare. Her life had been one long *risorgimento* against forgiving Austrians and all too gentle, beautifully smiling Bourbons. With the little Carters from down the road, the little Holmeses from over the way, she was now suddenly required to adapt herself to democracy and parliamentary government. There were difficulties at first; but when in the end the little bandit had acquired the arts of civility, she was unprecedentedly happy. The grown-ups exploited the childish sociability for their own educational ends. Judith got up amateur theatricals; there was a juvenile performance of the *Midsummer Night's Dream*. Mrs. Holmes, who was musical, organized the children's enthusiasm for making a noise into part singing. Mrs. Carter taught them country dances. In a few months Sylvia had acquired all that passion for the higher life which her mother had been trying to cultivate for years, always in vain. She loved poetry, she loved music, she loved dancing —rather platonically, it was true; for Sylvia was one of those congenitally clumsy and æsthetically insensitive natures whose earnest passion for the arts is always destined to remain unconsummated. She loved ardently, but hopelessly; yet not unhappily, for she was not yet, perhaps, never would be, conscious of the hopelessness of her passion. She even loved the arithmetic and geography, the English history and French grammar, which Judith had arranged that

she should imbibe, along with the little Carters, from
the little Carters' formidable governess.

"Do you remember what she was like when she
arrived?" said Judith one day to her husband.

He nodded, comparing in his mind the sullen little
savage of nine months before with the gravely,
earnestly radiant child who had just left the room.

"I feel like a lion tamer," Judith went on with a
little laugh that covered a great love and a great
pride. "But what does one do, Jack, when the lion
takes to high Anglicanism? Dolly Carter's being prepared for confirmation and Sylvia's caught the infection." Judith sighed. "I suppose she's already
thinking we're both damned."

"She'd be damned herself if she didn't," Jack
answered philosophically. "Much more seriously
damned, what's more, because she'd be damned in
this world. It would be a terrible flaw in her character if she didn't believe in some sort of rigmarole
at this age."

"But suppose," said Judith, "she were to go on
believing in it?"

* * * * * *

Martha, meanwhile, had not been liking Switzerland, perhaps because it suited her, physically, too
well. There was something, she felt, rather indecent
about enjoying such perfect health as she enjoyed
at Leysin. It was difficult when one was feeling so
full of animal spirits, to think very solicitously about

suffering humanity and God, about Buddha and the higher life and what not. She resented the genial care-free selfishness of her own healthy body. Waking periodically to conscience-stricken realizations that she had been thinking of nothing for hours and even days together but the pleasure of sitting in the sun, of breathing the aromatic air beneath the pines, of walking in the high meadows picking flowers and looking at the view, she would launch a campaign of intensive spirituality; but after a little while the sun and the bright eager air were too much for her and she would relapse once more into a shamefully irresponsible state of mere well-being.

"I shall be glad," she kept saying, "when Paul is quite well again and we can go back to England."

And Herbert would agree with her, partly on principle, because, being resigned to his economic and moral inferiority, he always agreed with her, and partly because he too, though unprecedentedly healthy, found Switzerland spiritually unsatisfying. In a country where everybody wore knickerbockers, an open shirt and a rücksack there was no superiority, no distinction in being so attired. The scandal of the top hat would have been the equivalent at Leysin of the scandal of the cross; he felt himself undistinguishedly orthodox.

Fifteen months after their departure the Claxtons were back again in the house on the common. Martha had a cold and a touch of lumbago; deprived of mountain exercise, Herbert was already succumbing to the attacks of his old enemy, chronic constipation. They overflowed with spirituality.

Sylvia also returned to the house on the common and, for the first weeks, it was Aunt Judith here and Aunt Judith there, at Aunt Judith's we did this, Aunt Judith never made me do that. Beautifully smiling, but with unacknowledged resentment at her heart, "Dearest," Martha would say, "I'm not Aunt Judith." She really hated her sister for having succeeded where she herself had failed. "You've done wonders with Sylvia," she wrote to Judith, "and Herbert and I can never be sufficiently grateful." And she would say the same in conversation to friends. "We can never be grateful enough to her, can we, Herbert?" And Herbert would punctually agree that they could never be grateful enough. But the more grateful to her sister she dutifully and even supererogatively was, the more Martha hated her, the more she resented Judith's success and her influence over the child. True, the influence had been unequivocally good; but it was precisely because it had been so good that Martha resented it. It was unbearable to her that frivolous, unspiritual Judith should have been able to influence the child more happily than she had ever done. She had left Sylvia sullenly ill-mannered and disobedient, full of rebellious hatred for all the things which her parents admired; she returned to find her well behaved, obliging, passionately interested in music and poetry, earnestly preoccupied with the newly discovered prob-

lems of religion. It was unbearable. Patiently Martha
set to work to undermine her sister's influence on the
child. Judith's own work had made the task more easy
for her. For thanks to Judith, Sylvia was now mal-
leable. Contact with children of her own age had
warmed and softened and sensitized her, had miti-
gated her savage egotism and opened her up towards
external influences. The appeal to her better feelings
could now be made with the certainty of evoking a
positive, instead of a rebelliously negative, response.
Martha made the appeal constantly and with skill.
She harped (with a beautiful resignation, of course)
on the family's poverty. If Aunt Judith did and permitted many things which were not done and permitted in the house on the common, that was because
Aunt Judith was so much better off. She could afford
many luxuries which the Claxtons had to do without.
"Not that your father and I mind doing without,"
Martha insisted. "On the contrary. It's really rather
a blessing not to be rich. You remember what Jesus
said about rich people." Sylvia remembered and was
thoughtful. Martha would develop her theme; being
able to afford luxuries and actually indulging in them
had a certain coarsening, despiritualizing effect. It
was so easy to become worldly. The implication, of
course, was that Aunt Judith and Uncle Jack had
been tainted by worldliness. Poverty had happily preserved the Claxtons from the danger—poverty and
also, Martha insisted, their own meritorious wish. For
of course they could have afforded to keep at least

one servant, even in these difficult times; but they had preferred to do without, "because, you see, serving is better than being served." Jesus had said that the way of Mary was better than the way of Martha. "But I'm a Martha," said Martha Claxton, "who tries her best to be a Mary too. Martha *and* Mary— that's the best way of all. Practical service *and* contemplation. Your father isn't one of those artists who selfishly detach themselves from all contact with the humble facts of life. He is a creator, but he is not too proud to do the humblest service." Poor Herbert! he couldn't have refused to do the humblest service, if Martha had commanded. Some artists, Martha continued, thought only of immediate success, worked only with an eye to profits and applause. But Sylvia's father, on the contrary was one who worked without thought of the public, only for the sake of creating truth and beauty.

On Sylvia's mind, these and similar discourses, constantly repeated with variations and in every emotional key, had a profound effect. With all the earnestness of puberty she desired to be good and spiritual and disinterested, she longed to sacrifice herself, it hardly mattered to what so long as the cause was noble. Her mother had now provided her with the cause. She gave herself up to it with all the stubborn energy of her nature. How fiercely she practised her piano! With what determination she read through even the dreariest books! She kept a notebook in which she copied out the most inspiring passages of her daily reading; and another in which she recorded her good resolutions and with them, in an agonized and chronically remorseful diary, her failures to abide by the resolutions, her lapses from grace. "Greed. Promised I'd eat only one greengage. Took four at lunch. None to-morrow. O.G.H.M.T.-B.G."

"What does O.G.H.M.T.B.G. mean?" asked Paul maliciously one day.

Sylvia flushed darkly. "You've been reading my diary!" she said. "Oh, you beast, you little beast." And suddenly she threw herself on her brother like a fury. His nose was bleeding when he got away from her. "If you ever look at it again, I'll kill you." And standing there with her clenched teeth and quivering nostrils, her hair flying loose around her pale face, she looked as though she meant it. "I'll kill you," she repeated. Her rage was justified; O.G.H.-M.T.B.G. meant "O God, help me to be good."

That evening she came to Paul and asked his pardon.

. . . . .

Aunt Judith and Uncle Jack had been in America for the best part of a year.

"Yes, go; go by all means," Martha had said when Judith's letter came, inviting Sylvia to spend a few days with them in London. "You mustn't miss such a chance of going to the opera and all those lovely concerts."

"But is it quite fair, mother?" said Sylvia hesitatingly. "I mean, I don't want to go and enjoy myself all alone. It seems somehow . . ."

"But you ought to go," Martha interrupted her. She felt so certain of Sylvia now that she had no fears of Judith. "For a musician like you it's a necessity to hear *Parsifal* and the *Magic Flute*. I was meaning to take you myself next year; but now the opportunity has turned up this year, you must take it. Gratefully," she added, with a sweetening of her smile.

Sylvia went. *Parsifal* was like going to church, but much more so. Sylvia listened with a reverent excitement that was, however, interrupted from time to time by the consciousness, irrelevant, ignoble even, but oh, how painful! that her frock, her stockings, her shoes were dreadfully different from those worn by that young girl of her own age, whom she had noticed in the row behind as she came in. And the girl, it had seemed to her, had returned her gaze derisively. Round the Holy Grail there was an explosion of bells and harmonious roaring. She felt ashamed of herself for thinking of such unworthy things in the presence of the mystery. And when, in the entr'acte, Aunt Judith offered her an ice, she refused almost indignantly.

Aunt Judith was surprised. "But you used to love ices so much."

"But not now, Aunt Judith. Not now." An ice in church—what sacrilege! She tried to think about the Grail. A vision of green satin shoes and a lovely mauve artificial flower floated up before her inward eye.

Next day they went shopping. It was a bright cloudless morning of early summer. The windows of the drapers' shops in Oxford Street had blossomed with bright pale colours. The waxen dummies were all preparing to go to Ascot, to Henley, were already thinking of the Eton and Harrow match. The pavements were crowded; an immense blurred noise filled the air like a mist. The scarlet and golden buses looked regal and the sunlight glittered with a rich and oily radiance on the polished flanks of the passing limousines. A little procession of unemployed slouched past with a brass band at their head making joyful music, as though they were only too happy to be unemployed, as though it were a real pleasure to be hungry.

Sylvia had not been in London for nearly two years, and these crowds, this noise, this innumerable wealth of curious and lovely things in every shining window went to her head. She felt even more excited than she had felt at *Parsifal*.

For an hour they wandered through Selfridge's. "And now, Sylvia," said Aunt Judith, when at last she had ticked off every item on her long list, "now you can choose whichever of these frocks you like best." She waved her hand. A display of Summer Modes for Misses surrounded them on every side. Lilac and lavender, primrose and pink and green, blue and mauve, white, flowery, spotted—a sort of herbaceous border of young frocks. "Whichever you like," Aunt Judith repeated. "Or if you'd prefer a frock for the evening. . . ."

Green satin shoes and a big mauve flower. The girl had looked derisively. It was unworthy, unworthy.

"No, really, Aunt Judith." She blushed, she stammered. "Really, I don't need a frock. Really."

"All the more reason for having it if you don't need it. Which one?"

"No, really. I don't, I can't. . . ." And suddenly, to Aunt Judith's uncomprehending astonishment, she burst into tears.

·　　　·　　　·　　　·　　　·　　　·

The year was 1924. The house on the common basked in the soft late-April sunshine. Through the open windows of the drawing-room came the sound of Sylvia's practising. Stubbornly, with a kind of fixed determined fury, she was trying to master Chopin's Valse in D flat. Under her conscientious and insensitive fingers the lilt and languor of the dance rhythm was laboriously sentimental, like the rendering on the piano of a cornet solo outside a public house; and the quick flutter of semi-quavers in the contrasting passages was a flutter, when Sylvia played, of mechanical butterflies, a beating of nickel-plated wings. Again and again she played, again and again. In the little copse on the other side of the stream at the bottom of the garden the birds went about their business undisturbed. On the trees the new small leaves were like the spirits of leaves, almost immaterial, but vivid like little flames at the tip of every twig. Herbert was sitting on a tree stump in the middle of the wood doing those yoga breathing exercises, accompanied by auto-suggestion, which he found so good for his constipation. Closing his right nostril with a long fore-finger, he breathed in deeply through his left—in, in, deeply, while he counted four heart beats. Then through sixteen beats he held his breath and between each beat he said to himself very quickly, "I'm not constipated, I'm not constipated." When he had made the affirmation sixteen times, he closed his left nostril and breathed out, while he counted eight, through his right. After which he began again. The left nostril was the more favoured; for it breathed in with the air a faint cool sweetness of primroses and leaves and damp earth. Near him, on a camp stool, Paul was making a drawing of an oak tree. Art at all costs; beautiful, uplifting, disinterested Art. Paul was bored. Rotten old tree—what was the point of drawing it? All round him the sharp green spikes of the wild hyacinths came thrusting out of the dark mould. One had pierced through a dead leaf and lifted it, transfixed, into the air. A few more days of sunshine and every spike would break out into a blue flower. Next time his mother sent him into Godalming on his bicycle, Paul was thinking, he'd see if he couldn't overcharge her two shillings on the shopping instead of one, as he had done last time. Then he'd be able to buy some chocolate

as well as go to the cinema; and perhaps even some
cigarettes, though that might be dangerous. . . .

"Well, Paul," said his father, who had taken a
sufficient dose of his mystical equivalent of Cascara,
"how are you getting on?" He got up from his tree
stump and walked across the glade to where the boy
was sitting. The passage of time had altered Herbert
very little; his explosive beard was still as blond as
it had always been, he was as thin as ever, his head
showed no signs of going bald. Only his teeth had
visibly aged; his smile was discoloured and broken.

"But he really ought to go to a dentist," Judith
had insistently urged on her sister, the last time they
met.

"He doesn't want to," Martha had replied. "He
doesn't really believe in them." But perhaps her own
reluctance to part with the necessary number of
guineas had something to do with Herbert's lack of
faith in dentists. "Besides," she went on, "Herbert
hardly notices such merely material, physical things.
He lives so much in the noumenal world that he's
hardly aware of the phenomenal. Really not aware."

"Well, he jolly well ought to be aware," Judith
answered, "that's all I can say." She was indignant.

"How are you getting on?" Herbert repeated and
laid his hand on the boy's shoulder.

"The bark's most horribly difficult to get right,"
Paul answered in a complainingly angry voice.

"That makes it all the more worth while to get
right," said Herbert. "Patience and work—they're

the only things. Do you know how a great man once
defined genius?" Paul knew very well how a great
man had once defined genius; but the definition
seemed to him so stupid and such a personal insult
to himself, that he did not answer, only grunted. His
father bored him, maddeningly. "Genius," Herbert
went on, answering his own question, "genius is an
infinite capacity for taking pains." At that moment
Paul detested his father.

"One-and two-and three-and, One-and two-and
three-and . . ." Under Sylvia's fingers the mechanical
butterflies continued to flap their metal wings. Her
face was set, determined, angry; Herbert's great man
would have found genius in her. Behind her stiff determined back her mother came and went with a
feather brush in her hand, dusting. Time had thickened and coarsened her; she walked heavily. Her hair
had begun to go grey. When she had finished dusting, or rather when she was tired of it, she sat down.
Sylvia was laboriously cornet-soloing through the
dance rhythm. Martha closed her eyes. "Beautiful,
beautiful!" she said and smiled her most beautiful
smile. "You play it beautifully, my darling." She was
proud of her daughter. Not merely as a musician; as
a human being too. When she thought what trouble
she had had with Sylvia in the old days. . . . "Beautifully." She rose at last and went upstairs to her
bedroom. Unlocking a cupboard, she took out a box
of candied fruits and ate several cherries, a plum,
and three apricots. Herbert had gone back to his

studio and his unfinished picture of "Europe and America at the feet of Mother India." Paul pulled a catapult out of his pocket, fitted a buckshot into the leather pouch and let fly at a nuthatch that was running like a mouse up the oak tree on the other side of the glade. "Hell!" he said as the bird flew away unharmed. But the next shot was more fortunate. There was a spurt of flying feathers, there were two or three little squeaks. Running up Paul found a hen chaffinch lying in the grass. There was blood on the feathers. Thrilling with a kind of disgusted excitement Paul picked up the little body. How warm. It was the first time he had ever killed anything. What a good shot! But there was nobody he could talk to about it. Sylvia was no good: she was almost worse than mother about some things. With a fallen branch he scratched a hole and buried the little corpse, for fear somebody might find it and wonder how it had been killed. They'd be furious if they knew! He went into lunch feeling tremendously pleased with himself. But his face fell as he looked round the table. "Only this beastly cold stuff?"

"Paul, Paul," said his father reproachfully.

"Where's mother?"

"She's not eating to-day," Herbert answered.

"All the same," Paul grumbled under his breath, "she really might have taken the trouble to make something hot for us."

Sylvia meanwhile sat without raising her eyes from her plate of potato salad, eating in silence.

AFTER THE FIREWORKS

I

"LATE as usual. Late." Judd's voice was censorious. The words fell sharp, like beak-blows. "As though I were a nut," Miles Fanning thought resentfully, "and he were a woodpecker. And yet he's devotion itself, he'd do anything for me. Which is why, I suppose, he feels entitled to crack my shell each time he sees me." And he came to the conclusion, as he had so often come before, that he really didn't like Colin Judd at all. "My oldest friend, whom I quite definitely don't like. Still . . ." Still, Judd was an asset, Judd was worth it.

"Here are your letters," the sharp voice continued.

Fanning groaned as he took them. "Can't one ever escape from letters? Even here, in Rome? They seem to get through everything. Like filter-passing bacteria. Those blessed days before post offices!" Sipping, he examined over the rim of his coffee cup the addresses on the envelopes.

"You'd be the first to complain if people didn't

write," Judd rapped out. "Here's your egg. Boiled for three minutes exactly. I saw to it myself."

Taking his egg, "On the contrary," Fanning answered, "I'd be the first to rejoice. If people write, it means they exist; and all I ask for is to be able to pretend that the world doesn't exist. The wicked flee when no man pursueth. How well I understand them! But letters don't allow you to be an ostrich. The Freudians say . . ." He broke off suddenly. After all he was talking to Colin—to *Colin*. The confessional, self-accusatory manner was wholly misplaced. Pointless to give Colin the excuse to say something disagreeable. But what he had been going to say about the Freudians was amusing. "The Freudians," he began again.

But taking advantage of forty years of intimacy Judd had already started to be disagreeable. "But you'd be miserable," he was saying, "if the post didn't bring you your regular dose of praise and admiration and sympathy and . . ."

"And humiliation," added Fanning, who had opened one of the envelopes and was looking at the letter within. "Listen to this. From my American publishers. Sales and Publicity Department. 'My dear Mr. Fanning.' *My* dear, mark you. Wilbur F. Schmalz's dear. 'My dear Mr. Fanning,—Won't you take us into your confidence with regard to your plans for the Summer Vacation? What aspect of the Great Outdoors are you favouring this year? Ocean or Mountain, Woodland or purling Lake? I would

esteem it a great privilege if you would inform me,
as I am preparing a series of notes for the Literary
Editors of our leading journals, who are, as I have
often found in the past, exceedingly receptive to
such personal material, particularly when accompanied by well-chosen snapshots. So won't you co-
operate with us in providing this service? Very cor-
dially yours, Wilbur F. Schmalz.' Well, what do
you think of that?"

"I think you'll answer him," said Judd. "Charm-
ingly," he added, envenoming his malice. Fanning
gave a laugh, whose very ease and heartiness betrayed his discomfort. "And you'll even send him a
snapshot."

Contemptuously—too contemptuously (he felt it
at the time)—Fanning crumpled up the letter and
threw it into the fireplace. The really humiliating
thing, he reflected, was that Judd was quite right:
he *would* write to Mr. Schmalz about the Great Outdoors, he *would* send the first snapshot anybody took
of him. There was a silence. Fanning ate two or three
spoonfuls of egg. Perfectly boiled, for once. But
still, what a relief that Colin was going away! After
all, he reflected, there's a great deal to be said for a
friend who has a house in Rome and who invites you
to stay, even when he isn't there. To such a man
much must be forgiven—even his infernal habit of
being a woodpecker. He opened another envelope
and began to read.

Possessive and preoccupied, like an anxious

mother, Judd watched him. With all his talents and intelligence, Miles wasn't fit to face the world alone. Judd had told him so (peck, peck!) again and again. "You're a child!" He had said it a thousand times. "You ought to have somebody to look after you." But if any one other than himself offered to do it, how bitterly jealous and resentful he became! And the trouble was that there were always so many applicants for the post of Fanning's bear-leader. Foolish men or, worse and more frequently, foolish women, attracted to him by his reputation and then conquered by his charm. Judd hated and professed to be loftily contemptuous of them. And the more Fanning liked his admiring bear-leaders, the loftier Judd's contempt became. For that was the bitter and unforgivable thing: Fanning manifestly preferred their bear-leading to Judd's. They flattered the bear, they caressed and even worshipped him; and the bear, of course, was charming to them, until such time as he growled, or bit, or, more often, quietly slunk away. Then they were surprised, they were pained. Because, as Judd would say with a grim satisfaction, they didn't know what Fanning was *really* like. Whereas he did know and had known since they were schoolboys together, nearly forty years before. Therefore he had a right to like him—a right and, at the same time, a duty to tell him all the reasons why he ought not to like him. Fanning didn't much enjoy listening to these reasons; he preferred to go where the bear was a sacred animal. With that air, which seemed so natural on his grey sharp face, of being dispassionately impersonal, "You're afraid of healthy criticism," Judd would tell him. "You always were, even as a boy."

"He's Jehovah," Fanning would complain. "Life with Judd is one long Old Testament. Being one of the Chosen People must have been bad enough. But to be *the* Chosen Person, in the singular . . ." And he would shake his head. "Terrible!"

And yet he had never seriously quarrelled with Colin Judd. Active unpleasantness was something which Fanning avoided as much as possible. He had never even made any determined attempt to fade out of Judd's existence as he had faded, at one time or another, out of the existence of so many once intimate bear-leaders. The habit of their intimacy was of too long standing and, besides, old Colin was so useful, so bottomlessly reliable. So Judd remained for him the Oldest Friend whom one definitely dislikes; while for Judd, he was the Oldest Friend whom one adores and at the same time hates for not adoring back, the Oldest Friend whom one never sees enough of, but whom, when he *is* there, one finds insufferably exasperating, the Oldest Friend whom, in spite of all one's efforts, one is always getting on the nerves of.

"If only," Judd was thinking, "he could have faith!" The Catholic Church was there to help him. (Judd himself was a convert of more than twenty years' standing.) But the trouble was that Fanning didn't want to be helped by the Church; he could only see the comic side of Judd's religion. Judd was reserving his missionary efforts till his Friend should be old or ill. But if only, meanwhile, if only, by some miracle of grace. . . . So thought the good Catholic; but it was the jealous friend who felt and who obscurely schemed. Converted, Miles Fanning would be separated from his other friends and brought, Judd realized, nearer to himself.

Watching him, as he read his letter, Judd noticed, all at once, that Fanning's lips were twitching involuntarily into a smile. They were full lips, well cut, sensitive and sensual; his smiles were a little crooked. A dark fury suddenly fell on Colin Judd.

"Telling *me* that you'd like to get no letters!" he said with an icy vehemence. "When you sit there grinning to yourself over some silly woman's flatteries."

Amazed, amused, "But what an outburst!" said Fanning, looking up from his letter.

Judd swallowed his rage; he had made a fool of himself. It was in a tone of calm dispassionate flatness that he spoke. Only his eyes remained angry. "Was I right?" he asked.

"So far as the woman was concerned," Fanning answered. "But wrong about the flattery. Women have no time nowadays to talk about anything except themselves."

"Which is only another way of flattering," said Judd obstinately. "They confide in you, because they think you'll like being treated as a person who understands."

"Which is what, after all, I am. By profession even." Fanning spoke with an exasperating mildness. "What *is* a novelist, unless he's a person who understands?" He paused; but Judd made no answer, for the only words he could have uttered would have been whirling words of rage and jealousy. He was jealous not only of the friends, the lovers, the admiring correspondents; he was jealous of a part of Fanning himself, of the artist, the public personage; for the artist, the public personage seemed so often to stand between his friend and himself. He hated, while he gloried in them.

Fanning looked at him for a moment, expectantly; but the other kept his mouth tight shut, his eyes averted. In the same exasperatingly gentle tone, "And flattery or no flattery," Fanning went on, "this is a charming letter. And the girl's adorable."

He was having his revenge. Nothing upset poor Colin Judd so much as having to listen to talk about women or love. He had a horror of anything connected with the act, the mere thought, of sex. Fanning called it his perversion. "You're one of those unspeakable chastity-perverts," he would say, when he wanted to get his own back after a bout of pecking. "If I had children, I'd never allow them to frequent your company. Too dangerous." When he spoke of the forbidden subject, Judd would either writhe, a martyr, or else unchristianly explode. On

this occasion he writhed and was silent. "Adorable,"
Fanning repeated, provocatively. "A ravishing little
creature. Though of course she *may* be a huge great
camel. That's the danger of unknown correspondents. The best letter-writers are often camels. It's a
piece of natural history I've learned by the bitterest
experience." Looking back at the letter, "All the
same," he went on, "when a young girl writes to one
that she's sure one's the only person in the world
who can tell her exactly who and what (both heavily
underlined) she is—well, one's rather tempted, I
must confess, to try yet once more. Because even if
she were a camel she'd be a very young one. Twenty-
one—isn't that what she says?" He turned over a
page of the letter. "Yes; twenty-one. Also she writes
in orange ink. And doesn't like the Botticellis at
the Uffizi. But I hadn't told you; she's at Florence.
This letter has been to London and back. We're
practically neighbours. And here's something that's
really rather good. Listen. 'What I like about the
Italian women is that they don't seem to be rather
ashamed of being women, like so many English girls
are, because English girls seem to go about apolo-
gizing for their figures, as though they were punctured, the way they hold themselves—it's really
rather abject. But here they're all pleased and proud
and not a bit apologetic or punctured, but just the
opposite, which I really like, don't you?' Yes I do,"
Fanning answered looking up from the letter. "I like
it very much indeed. I've always been opposed to

these modern *Ars est celare arsem* fashions. I like unpuncturedness and I'm charmed by the letter. Yes, charmed. Aren't you?"

In a voice that trembled with hardly restrained indignation, "No, I'm not!" Judd answered; and without looking at Fanning, he got up and walked quickly out of the room.

II

Judd had gone to stay with his old Aunt Caroline at Montreux. It was an annual affair; for Judd lived chronometrically. Most of June and the first half of July were always devoted to Aunt Caroline and devoted, invariably, at Montreux. On the fifteenth of July, Aunt Caroline was rejoined by her friend Miss Gaskin and Judd was free to proceed to England. In England he stayed till September the thirtieth, when he returned to Rome—"for the praying season," as Fanning irreverently put it. The beautiful regularity of poor Colin's existence was a source of endless amusement to his friend. Fanning never had any plans. "I just accept what turns up," he would explain. "Heads or tails—it's the only rational way of living. Chance generally knows so much better than we do. The Greeks elected most of their officials by lot—how wisely! Why shouldn't we toss up for Prime Ministers? We'd be much better governed. Or a sort of Calcutta Sweep for all the responsible posts in Church and State. The only horror would be if one were to win the sweep oneself. Imagine drawing the Permanent Under-Secretaryship for Education! Or the Archbishopric of Canterbury! Or the Viceroyalty of India! One would just have to drink weed-killer. But as things are, luckily . . ."

Luckily, he was at liberty, under the present dispensation, to stroll, very slowly, in a suit of cream-coloured silk, down the shady side of the Via Condotti towards the Spanish Steps. Slowly, slowly. The air was streaked with invisible bars of heat and cold. Coolness came flowing out of shadowed doorways, and at every transverse street the sun breathed fiercely. Like walking through the ghost of a zebra, he thought.

Three beautiful young women passed him, talking and laughing together. Like laughing flowers, like deer, like little horses. And of course absolutely unpunctured, unapologetic. He smiled to himself, thinking of the letter and also of his own reply to it.

A pair of pink and white monsters loomed up, as though from behind the glass of an aquarium. But not speechless. For *"Grossartig!"* fell enthusiastically on Fanning's ear as they passed, and *"Fabelhaft!"* These Nordics! He shook his head. Time they were put a stop to.

In the looking-glasses of a milliner's window a tall man in creamy-white walked slowly to meet him, hat in hand. The face was aquiline and eager, brown with much exposure to the sun. The waved, rather wiry hair was dark almost to blackness. It grew thickly, and the height of the forehead owed nothing to the approach of baldness. But what pleased Fanning most was the slimness and straightness of the tall figure. Those sedentary men of letters, with their sagging tremulous paunches—they were enough to make one hate the very thought of literature. What had been Fanning's horror when, a year before, he had realized that his own paunch was showing the first preliminary signs of sagging! But Mr. Hornibrooke's exercises had been wonderful. "The Culture of the Abdomen." So much more important, as he had remarked in the course of the last few months at so many dinner tables, than the culture of the mind! For of course he had taken everybody into his confidence about the paunch. He took everybody into his confidence about almost everything. About his love-affairs and his literary projects; about his illnesses and his philosophy; his vices and his bank balance. He lived a rich and variegated private life in public; it was one of the secrets of his charm. To the indignant protests of poor jealous Colin, who reproached him with being an exhibitionist, shameless, a self-exploiter, "You take everything so moralistically," he had answered. "You seem to imagine people do everything on purpose. But people do hardly anything on purpose. They behave as they do because they can't help it; that's what they happen to be like. 'I am that I am'; Jehovah's is the last word in realistic psychology. I am what *I* am—a sort of soft transparent jelly-fish. While you're what *you* are—very tightly shut, opaque, heavily ar-

moured: in a word, a giant clam. Morality doesn't
enter; it's a case for scientific classification. You
should be more of a Linnæus, Colin, and less the
Samuel Smiles." Judd had been reduced to a grum-
bling silence. What he really resented was the fact
that Fanning's confidences were given to upstart
friends, to strangers even, before they were given to
him. It was only to be expected. The clam's shell
keeps the outside things out as effectually as it keeps
the inside things in. In Judd's case, moreover, the
shell served as an instrument of reproachful pinching.

From his cool street Fanning emerged into the
Piazza di Spagna. The sunlight was stinging hot
and dazzling. The flower vendors on the steps sat in
the midst of great explosions of colour. He bought a
gardenia from one of them and stuck it in his buttonhole. From the windows of the English bookshop
"The Return of Eurydice, by Miles Fanning"
stared at him again and again. They were making a
regular display of his latest volume in Tauchnitz.
Satisfactory, no doubt; but also, of course, rather
ridiculous and even humiliating, when one reflected
that the book would be read by people like that es-
timable upper middle-class couple there, with their
noses at the next window—that Civil Servant, he
guessed, with the sweet little artistic wife and the
artistic little house on Campden Hill—would be
read by them dutifully (for of course they worked
hard to keep abreast of everything) and discussed

at their charming little dinner parties and finally condemned as "extraordinarily brilliant, but . . ." Yes, but, but, but. For they were obviously regular subscribers to *Punch*, were vertebrae in the backbone of England, were upholders of all that was depressingly finest, all that was lifelessly and genteelly best in the English upper-class tradition. And when they recognized him (as it was obvious to Fanning, in spite of their discreet politeness, that they did) his vanity, instead of being flattered, was hurt. Being recognized by people like that—such was fame! What a humiliation, what a personal insult!

At Cook's, where he now went to draw some money on his letter of credit, Fame still pursued him, trumpeting. From behind the brass bars of his cage the cashier smiled knowingly as he counted out the banknotes.

"Of course your name's very familiar to me, Mr. Fanning," he said; and his tone was at once ingratiating and self-satisfied; the compliment to Fanning was at the same time a compliment to himself. "And if I may be permitted to say so," he went on, pushing the money through the bars, as one might offer a piece of bread to an ape, "gratters on your last book. Gratters," he repeated, evidently delighted with his very public-schooly colloquialism.

"All gratitude for gratters," Fanning answered and turned away. He was half amused, half annoyed. Amused by the absurdity of those more than Etonian congratulations, annoyed at the damned impertinence of the congratulator. So intolerably patronizing! he grumbled to himself. But most admirers were like that; they thought they were doing you an enormous favour by admiring you. And how much more they admired themselves for being capable of appreciating than they admired the object of their appreciation! And then there were the earnest ones who thanked you for giving such a perfect expression to their ideas and sentiments. They were the worst of all. For, after all, what were they thanking you for? For being *their* interpreter, *their* dragoman, for playing John the Baptist to *their* Messiah. Damn their impertinence! Yes, damn their impertinence!

"Mr. Fanning." A hand touched his elbow.

Still indignant with the thought of damned impertinences, Fanning turned round with an expression of such ferocity on his face, that the young woman who had addressed him involuntarily fell back.

"Oh . . . I'm so sorry," she stammered; and her face, which had been bright, deliberately, with just such an impertinence as Fanning was damning, was discomposed into a child-like embarrassment. The blood tingled painfully in her cheeks. Oh, what a fool, she thought, what a fool she was making of herself! This idiotic blushing! But the way he had turned round on her, as if he were going to bite. . . . Still, even that was no excuse for blushing and saying she was sorry, as though she were still at school

and he were Miss Huss. Idiot! she inwardly shouted
at herself. And making an enormous effort, she re-
adjusted her still scarlet face, giving it as good an
expression of smiling nonchalance as she could sum-
mon up. "I'm sorry," she repeated, in a voice that
was meant to be light, easy, ironically polite, but
which came out (oh, idiot, idiot!) nervously shaky
and uneven. "I'm afraid I disturbed you. But I just
wanted to introduce . . . I mean, as you were
passing . . ."

"But how charming of you!" said Fanning, who
had had time to realize that this latest piece of impertinence was one to be blessed, not damned.
"Charming!" Yes, charming it was, that young face
with the grey eyes and the little straight nose, like
a cat's, and the rather short upper lip. And the
heroic way she had tried, through all her blushes, to
be the accomplished woman of the world—that too
was charming. And touchingly charming even were
those rather red, large-wristed English hands, which
she wasn't yet old enough to have learnt the importance of tending into whiteness and softness.
They were still the hands of a child, a tomboy. He
gave her one of those quick, those brilliantly and yet
mysteriously significant smiles of his; those smiles
that were still so youthfully beautiful when they
came spontaneously. But they could also be put on;
he knew how to exploit their fabricated charm, deliberately. To a sensitive eye, the beauty of his expression was, on these occasions, subtly repulsive.

Reassured, "I'm Pamela Tarn," said the young girl, feeling warm with gratitude for the smile. He was handsomer, she was thinking, than in his photographs. And much more fascinating. It was a face that had to be seen in movement.

"Pamela Tarn?" he repeated questioningly.

"The one who wrote you a letter." Her blush began to deepen again. "You answered so nicely. I mean, it was so kind . . . I thought . . ."

"But of course!" he cried, so loudly, that people looked round, startled. "Of course!" He took her hand and held it, shaking it from time to time, for what seemed to Pamela hours. "The most enchanting letter. Only I'm so bad at names. So you're Pamela Tarn." He looked at her appraisingly. She returned his look for a moment, then flinched away in confusion from his bright dark eyes.

"Excuse me," said a chilly voice; and a very large suit of plus fours edged past them to the door.

"I like you," Fanning concluded, ignoring the plus fours; she uttered an embarrassed little laugh. "But then, I liked you before. You don't know how pleased I was with what you said about the difference between English and Italian women." The colour rose once more into Pamela's cheeks. She had only written those sentences after long hesitation and had written them then recklessly, dashing them down with a kind of anger, just because Miss Huss would have been horrified by their unwomanliness, just because Aunt Edith would have found them so distressing, just because they had, when she spoke them aloud one day in the streets of Florence, so shocked the two schoolmistresses from Boston whom she had met at the pension and was doing the sights with. Fanning's mention of them pleased her and at the same time made her feel dreadfully guilty. She hoped he wouldn't be too specific about those differences; it seemed to her that every one was listening. "So profound," he went on in his musical ringing voice. "But out of the mouths of babes, with all due respect." He smiled again, "And 'punctured' —that was really the *mot juste*. I shall steal it and use it as my own."

"*Permesso*." This time it was a spotted muslin and brown arms and a whiff of synthetic carnations.

"I think we're rather in the way," said Pamela, who was becoming more and more uncomfortably aware of being conspicuous. And the spirit presences of Miss Huss, of Aunt Edith, of the two American ladies at Florence seemed to hang about her, hauntingly. "Perhaps we'd better . . . I mean . . ." And, turning, she almost ran to the door.

"Punctured, punctured," repeated his pursuing voice behind her. "Punctured with the shame of being warm-blooded mammals. Like those poor lank creatures that were standing at the counter in there," he added, coming abreast with her, as they stepped over the threshold into the heat and glare. "Did you see them? So pathetic. But, oh dear!" he shook his head. "Oh dear, oh dear!"

She looked up at him and Fanning saw in her face a new expression, an expression of mischief and laughing malice and youthful impertinence. Even her breasts he now noticed with an amused appreciation, even her breasts were impertinent. Small, but beneath the pale blue stuff of her dress, pointed, firm, almost comically insistent. No ashamed deflation here.

"Pathetic," she mockingly echoed, "but, oh dear, how horrible, how disgusting! Because they *are* disgusting," she added defiantly, in answer to his look of humorous protest. Here in the sunlight and with the noise of the town isolating her from every one except Fanning, she had lost her embarrassment and her sense of guilt. The spiritual presences had evaporated. Pamela was annoyed with herself for having felt so uncomfortable among those awful old English cats at Cook's. She thought of her mother; her mother had never been embarrassed, or at any rate she had always managed to turn her embarrassment into something else. Which was what Pamela was doing now. "Really disgusting," she almost truculently insisted. She was reasserting herself, she was taking a revenge.

"You're very ruthless to the poor old things," said Fanning. "So worthy in spite of their mangy dimness, so obviously good."

"I hate goodness," said Pamela with decision, speeding the parting ghosts of Miss Huss and Aunt Edith and the two ladies from Boston.

Fanning laughed aloud. "Ah, if only we all had the courage to say so, like you, my child!" And with a familiar affectionate gesture, as though she were indeed a child and he had known her from the cradle, he dropped a hand on her shoulder. "To say so and to act up to our beliefs. As you do, I'm sure." And he gave the slim hard little shoulder a pat. "A world without goodness—it'd be Paradise."

They walked some steps in silence. His hand lay heavy and strong on her shoulder, and a strange warmth that was somehow intenser than the warmth of mere flesh and blood seemed to radiate through her whole body. Her heart quickened its beating; an anxiety oppressed her lungs; her very mind was as though breathless.

"Putting his hand on my shoulder like that!" she was thinking. "It would have been cheek if some one else . . . Perhaps I ought to have been angry, perhaps . . ." No, that would have been silly. "It's silly to take things like that too seriously, as though one were Aunt Edith." But meanwhile his hand lay heavy on her shoulder, broodingly hot, its weight, its warmth insistently present in her consciousness.

She remembered characters in his books. Her namesake Pamela in *Pastures New*. Pamela the cold, but for that very reason an experimenter with passion; cold and therefore dangerous, full of power, fatal. Was she like Pamela? She had often thought so. But more recently she had often thought she was like Joan in *The Return of Eurydice*—Joan, who had emerged from the wintry dark underworld of an unawakened life with her husband (that awful, good, disinterested husband—so like Aunt Edith) into the warmth and brilliance of that transfiguring passion for Walter, for the adorable Walter whom she had always imagined must be so like Miles Fanning himself. She was sure of it now. But what of her own identity? Was she Joan, or was she Pamela? And which of the two would it be nicer to be? Warm Joan, with her happiness—but at the price of surrender? Or the cold, the unhappy, but conquering, dangerous Pamela? Or wouldn't it perhaps be best to be a little of both at once? Or first one and then the other? And in any case there was to be no goodness in the Aunt Edith style; he had been sure she wasn't good.

In her memory the voice of Aunt Edith sounded, as it had actually sounded, only a few weeks before, in disapproving comment on her reference to the passionless, experimental Pamela of *Pastures New*. "It's a book I don't like. A most unnecessary book." And then, laying her hand on Pamela's, "Dear child," she had added, with that earnest, that dutifully willed affectionateness, which Pamela so bitterly resented, "I'd rather you didn't read any of Miles Fanning's books."

"Mother never objected to my reading them. So I don't see . . ." The triumphant consciousness of having at this very moment the hand that had written those unnecessary books upon her shoulder was promising to enrich her share of the remembered dialogue with a lofty impertinence which the original had hardly possessed. "I don't see that you have the smallest right. . . ."

Fanning's voice fell startlingly across the eloquent silence. "A penny for your thoughts, Miss Pamela," it said.

He had been for some obscure reason suddenly depressed by his own last words. "A world without goodness—it'd be Paradise." But it wouldn't, no more than now. The only paradises were fool's paradises, ostrich's paradises. It was as though he had suddenly lifted his head out of the sand and seen time bleeding away—like the stabbed bull at the end of a bull-fight, swaying on his legs and soundlessly spouting the red blood from his nostrils—bleeding, bleeding away stanchlessly into the darkness. And it was all, even the loveliness and the laughter and the sunlight, finally pointless. This young girl at his side, this beautiful pointless creature pointlessly walking down the Via del Babuino. . . . The feelings crystallized themselves, as usual, into whole phrases in his mind, and suddenly the phrases were metrical.

Pointless and arm in arm with pointlessness,
I pace and pace the Street of the Baboon.

Imbecile! Annoyed with himself, he tried to shake off his mood of maudlin depression, he tried to force his spirit back into the ridiculous and charming universe it had inhabited, on the whole so happily, all the morning.

"A penny for your thoughts," he said, with a certain rather forced jocularity, giving her shoulder a little clap. "Or forty centesimi, if you prefer them." And, dropping his hand to his side, "In Germany," he went on, "just after the War one could afford to be more munificent. There was a time when I regularly offered a hundred and ninety million marks for a thought—yes, and gained on the exchange. But now . . ."

"Well, if you really want to know," said Pamela, deciding to be bold, "I was thinking how much my Aunt Edith disapproved of your books."

"Did she? I suppose it was only to be expected. Seeing that I don't write for aunts—at any rate, not for aunts in their specifically auntly capacity. Though of course, when they're off duty . . ."

"Aunt Edith's never off duty."

"And I'm never on. So you see." He shrugged his shoulders. "But I'm sure," he added, "you never paid much attention to her disapproval."

"None," she answered, playing the un-good part for all it was worth. "I read Freud this spring," she boasted, "and Gide's autobiography, and Krafft-Ebbing. . . ."

"Which is more than I've ever done," he laughed.

The laugh encouraged her. "Not to mention all *your* books, years ago. You see," she added, suddenly fearful lest she might have said something to offend him, "my mother never minded my reading your books. I mean, she really encouraged me, even when I was only seventeen or eighteen. My mother died last year," she explained. There was a silence. "I've lived with Aunt Edith ever since," she went on. "Aunt Edith's my father's sister. Older than he was. Father died in 1923."

"So you're all alone now?" he questioned. "Except, of course, for Aunt Edith."

"Whom I've now left." She was almost boasting again. "Because when I was twenty-one . . ."

"You stuck out your tongue at her and ran away. Poor Aunt Edith!"

"I won't have you being sorry for her," Pamela answered hotly. "She's really awful, you know. Like poor Joan's husband in *The Return of Eurydice*." How easy it was to talk to him!

"So you even know," said Fanning, laughing, "what it's like to be unhappily married. Already. Indissolubly wedded to a virtuous Aunt."

"No joke, I can tell you. *I'm* the one to be sorry for. Besides, she didn't mind my going away, whatever she might say."

"She did say something then?"

"Oh, yes. She always says things. More in sorrow than in anger, you know. Like head-mistresses. So gentle and good, I mean. When all the time she really thought me too awful. I used to call her Hippo, because she was such a hypocrite—*and* so fat. Enormous. Don't you *hate* enormous people? No, she's really delighted to get rid of me," Pamela concluded, "simply delighted." Her face was flushed and as though luminously alive; she spoke with a quick eagerness.

"What a tremendous hurry she's in," he was thinking, "to tell me all about herself. If she were older or uglier, what an intolerable egotism it would be! As intolerable as mine would be if I happened to be less intelligent. But as it is . . ." His face, as he listened to her, expressed a sympathetic attention.

"She always disliked me," Pamela had gone on. "Mother too. She couldn't abide my mother, though she was always sweetly hippo-ish with her."

"And your mother—how did she respond?"

"Well, not hippo-ishly, of course. She couldn't be that. She treated Aunt Edith—well, how *did* she treat Aunt Edith?" Pamela hesitated, frowning. "Well, I suppose you'd say she was just natural with the Hippo. I mean . . ." She bit her lip. "Well, if she ever *was* really natural. *I* don't know. Is anybody natural?" She looked up questioningly at Fanning. "Am I natural, for example?"

Smiling a little at her choice of an example, "I should think almost certainly not," Fanning answered, more or less at random.

"You're right, of course," she said despairingly, and her face was suddenly tragic, almost there were tears in her eyes. "But isn't it awful? I mean, isn't it simply hopeless?"

Pleased that his chance shot should have gone

home, "At your age," he said consolingly, "you can hardly expect to be natural. Naturalness is something you learn, painfully, by trial and error. Besides," he added, "there are some people who are unnatural by nature."

"Unnatural by nature." Pamela nodded, as she repeated the words, as though she were inwardly marshalling evidence to confirm their truth. "Yes, I believe that's us," she concluded. "Mother and me. Not hippos, I mean, not *poseuses*, but just unnatural by nature. You're quite right. As usual," she added, with something that was almost resentment in her voice.

"I'm sorry," he apologized.

"How is it you manage to know so much?" Pamela asked in the same resentful tone. By what right was he so easily omniscient, when she could only grope and guess in the dark?

Taking to himself a credit that belonged, in this case, to chance, "Child's play, my dear Watson," he answered banteringly. "But I suppose you're too young to have heard of Sherlock Holmes. And anyhow," he added, with an ironical seriousness, "don't let's waste any more time talking about me."

Pamela wasted no more time. "I get so depressed with myself," she said with a sigh. "And after what you've told me I shall get still more depressed. Unnatural by nature. And by upbringing too. Because I see now that my mother was like that. I mean, she was unnatural by nature too."

"Even with you?" he asked, thinking that this was becoming interesting. She nodded without speaking. He looked at her closely. "Were you very fond of her?" was the question that now suggested itself.

After a moment of silence, "I loved my father more," she answered slowly. "He was more . . . more reliable. I mean, you never quite knew where you were with my mother. Sometimes she almost forgot about me; or else she didn't forget me enough and spoiled me. And then sometimes she used to get into the most terrible rages with me. She really frightened me then. And said such terribly hurting things. But you mustn't think I didn't love her. I did." The words seemed to release a spring; she was suddenly moved. There was a little silence. Making an effort, "But that's what she was like," she concluded at last.

"But I don't see," said Fanning gently, "that there was anything speciàlly unnatural in spoiling you and then getting cross with you." They were crossing the Piazza del Popolo; the traffic of four thronged streets intricately merged and parted in the open space. "You must have been a charming child. And also . . . Look out!" He laid a hand on her arm. An electric bus passed noiselessly, a whispering monster. "Also maddeningly exasperating. So where the unnaturalness came in . . ."

"But if you'd known her," Pamela interrupted, "you'd have seen exactly where the unnaturalness . . ."

"Forward!" he called and, still holding her arm, he steered her on across the Piazza.

She suffered herself to be conducted blindly. "It came out in the way she spoiled me," she explained, raising her voice against the clatter of a passing lorry. "It's so difficult to explain, though; because it's something I felt. I mean, I've never really tried to put it into words till now. But it was as if . . . as if she weren't just herself spoiling me, but the picture of a young mother—do you see what I mean? —spoiling the picture of a little girl. Even as a child I kind of felt it wasn't quite as it should be. Later on I began to *know* it too, here." She tapped her forehead. "Particularly after father's death, when I was beginning to grow up. There were times when it was almost like listening to recitations—dreadful. One feels so blushy and prickly; you know the feeling."

He nodded. "Yes, I know. Awful!"

"Awful," she repeated. "So you can understand what a beast I felt, when it took me that way. So disloyal, I mean. So ungrateful. Because she was being so wonderfully sweet to me. You've no idea. But it was just when she was being her sweetest that I got the feeling worst. I shall never forget when she made me call her Clare—that was her christian name. 'Because we're going to be companions,' she said and all that sort of thing. Which was simply too sweet and too nice of her. But if you'd heard the way she said it! So dreadfully unnatural. I mean, it was almost as bad as Aunt Edith reading *Prospice*. And yet I know she meant it, I know she wanted me to be her companion. But somehow something kind of went wrong on the way between the wanting and the saying. And then the doing seemed to go just as wrong as the saying. She always wanted to do things excitingly, romantically, like in a play. But you can't *make* things be exciting and romantic, can you?" Fanning shook his head. "She wanted to kind of force things to be thrilling by thinking and wishing, like Christian Science. But it doesn't work. We had wonderful times together; but she always tried to make out that they were more wonderful than they really were. Which only made them less wonderful. Going to the Paris Opera on a gala night is wonderful; but it's never as wonderful as when Rastignac goes, is it?"

"I should think it wasn't!" he agreed. "What an insult to Balzac to imagine that it could be!"

"And the real thing's less wonderful," she went on, "when you're being asked all the time to see it as Balzac, and to *be* Balzac yourself. When you aren't anything of the kind. Because, after all, what am I? Just good, ordinary, middle-class English."

She pronounced the words with a kind of defiance. Fanning imagined that the defiance was for him and, laughing, prepared to pick up the ridiculous little glove. But the glove was not for him; Pamela had thrown it down to a memory, to a ghost, to one of her own sceptical and mocking selves. It had been on

the last day of their last stay together in Paris—
that exciting, exotic Paris of poor Clare's imagination, to which their tickets from London never seemed
quite to take them. They had gone to lunch at La
Pérouse. "Such a marvellous, *fantastic* restaurant!
It makes you feel as though you were back in the
Second Empire." (Or was it the First Empire?
Pamela could not exactly remember.) The rooms
were so crowded with Americans, that it was with
some difficulty that they secured a table. "We'll have
a marvellous lunch," Clare had said, as she unfolded
her napkin. "And some day, when you're in Paris
with your lover, you'll come here and order just the
same things as we're having to-day. And perhaps
you'll think of me. Will you, darling?" And she had
smiled at her daughter with that intense, expectant
expression that was so often on her face, and the very
memory of which made Pamela feel subtly uncomfortable. "How should I ever forget?" she had answered, laying her hand on her mother's and smiling.
But after a second her eyes had wavered away from
that fixed look, in which the intensity had remained
as desperately on the stretch, the expectancy as
wholly unsatisfied, as hungrily insatiable as ever. The
waiter, thank goodness, had created a timely diver-
sion; smiling at him confidentially, almost amorously,
Clare had ordered like a princess in a novel of high
life. The bill, when it came, was enormous. Clare had
had to scratch the bottom of her purse for the last
stray piece of nickel. "It looks as though we should

have to carry our own bags at Calais and Dover. I
didn't realize I'd run things so fine." Pamela had
looked at the bill. "But, Clare," she had protested,
looking up again at her mother with an expression
of genuine horror, "it's wicked! Two hundred and
sixty francs for a lunch! It wasn't worth it." The
blood had risen darkly into Clare's face. "How can
you be so disgustingly *bourgeoisie*, Pamela? So crass,
so crawling?" Incensed by the heaping up of this
abuse, "I think it's stupid to do things one can't
afford," the girl had answered; "stupid and vulgar."
Trembling with rage, Clare had risen to her feet.
"I'll never take you out again. Never." (How often
since then Pamela had recalled that terribly pro-
phetic word!) "You'll never understand life, you'll
never be anything but a sordid little middle-class
Englishwoman. Never, never." And she had swept
out of the room, like an insulted queen. Overheard
by Pamela, as she undignifiedly followed, "Gee!" an
American voice had remarked, "it's a regular cat
fight."

The sound of another, real voice overlaid the remembered Middle Western accents.

"But after all," Fanning was saying, "it's better
to be a good ordinary bourgeois than a bad ordinary
bohemian, or a sham aristocrat, or a second-rate intellectual. . . ."

"I'm not even third-rate," said Pamela mournfully. There had been a time when, under the influence of the now abhorred Miss Huss, she had

thought she would like to go up to Oxford and read
Greats. But Greek grammar was so awful . . . "Not
even fourth-rate."

"Thank goodness," said Fanning. "Do you know
what third- and fourth-rate intellectuals are?
They're professors of philology and organic chemis-
try at the minor universities, they're founders and
honorary life presidents of the Nuneaton Poetry
Society and the Baron's Court Debating Society;
they're the people who organize and sedulously at-
tend all those Conferences for promoting interna-
tional goodwill and the spread of culture that are
perpetually being held at Buda-Pesth and Prague
and Stockholm. Admirable and indispensable creatures, of course! But impossibly dreary; one simply
cannot have any relations with them. And how virtuously they disapprove of those of us who have something better to do than disseminate culture or foster
goodwill—those of us who are concerned, for example, with creating beauty—like me; or, like you,
my child, in deliciously *being* beauty."

Pamela blushed with pleasure and for that reason
felt it necessary immediately to protest. "All the
same," she said, "it's rather humiliating not to be
able to do anything but be. I mean, even a cow can
be."

"Damned well, too," said Fanning. "If I *were* as
intensely as a cow *is*, I'd be uncommonly pleased with
myself. But this is getting almost too metaphysical.
And do you realize what the time is?" He held out

his watch; it was ten past one. "And where we are?
At the Tiber. We've walked miles." He waved his
hand; a passing taxi swerved in to the pavement beside them. "Let's go and eat some lunch. You're
free?"

"Well . . ." She hesitated. It was marvellous, of
course; so marvellous that she felt she ought to refuse. "If I'm not a bore. I mean, I don't want to im-
pose . . . I mean . . ."

"You mean you'll come and have lunch. Good. Do
you like marble halls and bands? Or local colour?"

Pamela hesitated. She remembered her mother once
saying that Valadier and the Ulpia were the *only*
two restaurants in Rome.

"Personally," Fanning went on, "I'm slightly
avaricious about marble halls. I rather resent spending four times as much and eating about two-thirds
as well. But I'll overcome my avarice if you prefer
them."

Pamela duly voted for local colour; he gave an
address to the driver and they climbed into the cab.

"It's a genuinely Roman place," Fanning explained. "I hope you'll like it."

"Oh, I'm sure I shall." All the same, she did rather
wish they were going to Valadier's.

III

Fanning's old friend, Dodo del Grillo, was in Rome
for that one night and had urgently summoned him
to dine. His arrival was loud and exclamatory.

"Best of all possible Dodos!" he cried, as he advanced with outstretched hands across the enormous baroque saloon. "What an age! But what a pleasure!"

"At last, Miles," she said reproachfully; he was twenty minutes late.

"But I know you'll forgive me." And laying his two hands on her shoulders he bent down and kissed her. He made a habit of kissing all his women friends.

"And even if I didn't forgive, you wouldn't care two pins."

"Not one." He smiled his most charming smile. "But if it gives you the smallest pleasure, I'm ready to say I'd be inconsolable." His hands still resting on her shoulders, he looked at her searchingly, at arm's length. "Younger than ever," he concluded.

"I couldn't look as young as you do," she answered. "You know, Miles, you're positively indecent. Like Dorian Gray. What's your horrible secret?"

"Simply Mr. Hornibrooke," he explained. "The culture of the abdomen. So much more important than the culture of the mind." Dodo only faintly smiled; she had heard the joke before. Fanning was sensitive to smiles; he changed the subject. "And where's the marquis?" he asked.

The marchesa shrugged her shoulders. Her husband was one of those dear old friends whom somehow one doesn't manage to see anything of nowadays.

"Filippo's in Tanganyika," she explained. "Hunting lions."

"While you hunt them at home. And with what success! You've bagged what's probably the finest specimen in Europe this evening. Congratulations!"

"*Merci, cher maître!*" she laughed. "Shall we go in to dinner?"

The words invited, irresistibly. "If only I had the right to answer: *Oui, chère maîtresse!*" Though as a matter of fact, he reflected, he had never really found her at all interesting in that way. A woman without temperament. But very pretty once—that time (how many years ago?) when there had been that picnic on the river at Bray, and he had drunk a little too much champagne. "If only!" he repeated; and then was suddenly struck by a grotesque thought. Suppose she were to say yes, now—now! "If only I had the right!"

"But luckily," said Dodo, turning back towards him, as she passed through the monumental door into the dining-room, "luckily you haven't the right. You ought to congratulate me on my immense good sense. Will you sit there?"

"Oh, I'll congratulate. I'm always ready to congratulate people who have sense." He unfolded his napkin. "And to condole." Now that he knew himself safe, he could condole as much as he liked. "What you must have suffered, my poor sensible Dodo, what you must have missed!"

"Suffered less," she answered, "and missed **more**

unpleasantnesses than the women who didn't have the sense to say no."

"What a mouthful of negatives! But that's how sensible people always talk about love—in terms of negatives. Never of positives; they ignore those and go about sensibly avoiding the discomforts. Avoiding the pleasures and exultations too, poor sensible idiots! Avoiding all that's valuable and significant. But it's always like that. The human soul is a fried whiting. (What excellent red mullet this is, by the way! Really excellent.) Its tail is in its mouth. All progress finally leads back to the beginning again. The most sensible people—dearest Dodo, believe me—are the most foolish. The most intellectual are the stupidest. I've never met a really good metaphysician, for example, who wasn't in one way or another bottomlessly stupid. And as for the really spiritual people, look what they revert to. Not merely to silliness and stupidity, but finally to crass non-existence. The highest spiritual state is ecstasy, which is just not being there at all. No, no; we're all fried whitings. Heads are invariably tails."

"In which case," said Dodo, "tails must also be heads. So that if you want to make intellectual or spiritual progress, you must behave like a beast—is that it?"

Fanning held up his hand. "Not at all. If you rush too violently towards the tail, you run the risk of shooting down the whiting's open mouth into its stomach, and even further. The wise man . . ."

"So the whitings are fried without being cleaned?"

"In parables," Fanning answered reprovingly, "whitings are always fried that way. The wise man, as I was saying, oscillates lightly from head to tail and back again. His whole existence—or shall we be more frank and say 'my' whole existence?—is one continual oscillation. I am never too consistently sensible, like you; or too consistently feather-headed like some of my other friends. In a word," he wagged a finger, "I oscillate."

Tired of generalizations, "And where exactly," Dodo enquired, "have you oscillated to at the moment? You've left me without your news so long. . . ."

"Well, at the moment," he reflected aloud, "I suppose you might say I was at a dead point between desire and renunciation, between sense and sensuality."

"Again?" She shook her head. "And who is she this time?"

Fanning helped himself to asparagus before replying. "Who is she?" he echoed. "Well, to begin with, she's the writer of admiring letters."

Dodo made a grimace of disgust. "What a horror!" For some reason she felt it necessary to be rather venomous about this new usurper of Fanning's heart. "Vamping by correspondence—it's really the lowest. . . ."

"Oh, I agree," he said. "On principle and in theory I entirely agree."

"Then why," she began, annoyed by his agreement; but he interrupted her.

"Spiritual adventuresses," he said. "That's what they generally are, the women who write you letters. Spiritual adventuresses. I've suffered a lot from them in my time."

"I'm sure you have."

"They're a curious type," he went on, ignoring her sarcasms. "Curious and rather horrible. I prefer the good old-fashioned vampire. At least one knew where one stood with her. There she was—out for money, for power, for a good time, occasionally, perhaps, for sensual satisfactions. It was all entirely above-board and obvious. But with the spiritual adventuress, on the contrary, everything's most horribly turbid and obscure and slimy. You see, she doesn't want money or the commonplace good time. She wants Higher Things—damn her neck! Not large pearls and a large motor-car, but a large soul —that's what she pines for: a large soul and a large intellect, and a huge philosophy, and enormous culture, and out sizes in great thoughts."

Dodo laughed. "You're fiendishly cruel, Miles."

"Cruelty can be a sacred duty," he answered. "Besides, I'm getting a little of my own back. If you knew what these spiritual vamps had done to me! I've been one of their appointed victims. Yes, appointed; for, you see, they can't have their Higher Things without attaching themselves to a Higher Person."

"And are you one of the Higher People, Miles?"

"Should I be dining here with you, my dear, if I weren't?" And without waiting for Dodo's answer, "They attach themselves like lice," he went on. "The contact with the Higher Person makes them feel high themselves; it magnifies them, it gives them significance, it satisfies their parasitic will to power. In the past they could have gone to religion—fastened themselves on the nearest priest (that's what the priest was there for), or sucked the spiritual blood of some saint. Nowadays they've got no professional victims; only a few charlatans and swamis and higher-thought-mongers. Or alternatively the artists. Yes, the artists. They find our souls particularly juicy. What I've suffered! Shall I ever forget that American woman who got so excited by my book on Blake that she came specially to Tunis to see me? She had an awful way of opening her mouth very wide when she talked, like a fish. You were perpetually seeing her tongue; and, what made it worse, her tongue was generally white. Most distressing. And how the tongue wagged! In spite of its whiteness. Wagged like mad, and mostly about the Divine Mind."

"The Divine Mind?"

He nodded. "It was her specialty. In Rochester, N. Y., where she lived, she was never out of touch with it. You've no idea what a lot of Divine Mind there is floating about in Rochester, particularly in the neighbourhood of women with busy husbands and incomes of over fifteen thousand dollars. If only she could have stuck to the Divine Mind! But the Divine Mind has one grave defect: it won't make love to you. That was why she'd come all the way to Tunis in search of a merely human specimen."

"And what did you do about it?"

"Stood it nine days and then took the boat to Sicily. Like a thief in the night. The wicked flee, you know. God, how they can flee!"

"And she?"

"Went back to Rochester, I suppose. But I never opened any more of her letters. Just dropped them into the fire whenever I saw the writing. Ostrichism— it's the only rational philosophy of conduct. According to the Freudians we're all unconsciously trying to get back to . . ."

"But poor woman!" Dodo burst out. "She must have suffered."

"Nothing like what I suffered. Besides she had the Divine Mind to go back to; which was her version of the Freudians' pre-natal . . ."

"But I suppose you'd encouraged her to come to Tunis?"

Reluctantly, Fanning gave up his Freudians. "She could write good letters," he admitted. "Inexplicably good, considering what she was at close range."

"But then you treated her abominably."

"But if you'd seen her, you'd realize how abominably she'd treated me."

"You?"

"Yes, abominably—by merely existing. She taught me to be very shy of letters. That was why I was so pleasantly surprised this morning when my latest correspondent suddenly materialized at Cook's. Really ravishing. One could forgive her everything for the sake of her face and that charming body. Everything, even the vamping. For a vamp I suppose she is, even this one. That is, if a woman *can* be a spiritual adventuress when she's so young and pretty and well-made. Absolutely and *sub specie æternitatis,* I suppose she can. But from the very sublunary point of view of the male victim, I doubt whether, at twenty-one . . ."

"Only twenty-one?" Dodo was disapproving. "But Miles!"

Fanning ignored her interruption. "And another thing you must remember," he went on, "is that the spiritual vamp who's come of age this year is not at all the same as the spiritual vamp who came of age fifteen, twenty, twenty-five years ago. She doesn't bother much about Mysticism, or the Lower Classes, or the Divine Mind, or any nonsense of that sort. No, she goes straight to the real point—the point which the older vamps approached in such a tiresomely circuitous fashion—she goes straight to herself. But straight!" He stabbed the air with his fruit-knife. "A bee-line. Oh, it has a certain charm that directness. But whether it won't be rather frightful when they're older is another question. But then almost everything is rather frightful when people are older."

"Thank you," said Dodo. "And what about you?"

"Oh, an old satyr," he answered with that quick, brilliantly mysterious smile of his. "A superannuated faun. I know it; only too well. But at the same time, most intolerably, a Higher Person. Which is what draws the spiritual vamps. Even the youngest ones. Not to talk to me about the Divine Mind, of course, or their views about Social Reform. But about themselves. Their Individualities, their Souls, their Inhibitions, their Unconsciouses, their Pasts, their Futures. For them, the Higher Things are all frankly and nakedly personal. And the function of the Higher Person is to act as a sort of psycho-analytical father confessor. He exists to tell them all about their strange and wonderful psyches. And meanwhile, of course, his friendship inflates their egotism. And if there should be any question of love, what a personal triumph!"

"Which is all very well," objected Dodo. "But what about the old satyr? Wouldn't it also be a bit of a triumph for him? You know, Miles," she added gravely, "it would really be scandalous if you were to take advantage. . . ."

"But I haven't the slightest intention of taking any advantages. If only for my own sake. Besides, the child is too ingenuously absurd. The most hair-raising theoretical knowledge of life, out of books. You should hear her prattling away about inverts

and perverts and birth control—but prattling from
unplumbed depths of innocence and practical ignorance. Very queer. And touching too. Much more
touching than the old-fashioned innocences of the
young creatures who thought babies were brought
by storks. Knowing all about love and lust, but in
the same way as one knows all about quadratic equa-
tions. And her knowledge of the other aspects of life
is really of the same kind. What she's seen of the
world she's seen in her mother's company. The worst
guide imaginable, to judge from the child's account.
(Dead now, incidentally.) The sort of woman who
could never live on top gear, so to speak—only at
one or two imaginative removes from the facts. So
that, in her company, what was nominally real life
became actually just literature—yet more literature.
Bad, inadequate Balzac in flesh and blood instead of
genuine, good Balzac out of a set of nice green volumes. The child realizes it herself. Obscurely, of
course; but distressfully. It's one of the reasons why
she's applied to me: she hopes I can explain what's
wrong. And correct it in practice. Which I won't do
in any drastic manner, I promise you. Only mildly,
by precept—that is, if I'm not too bored to do it at
all."

"What's the child's name?" Dodo asked.

"Pamela Tarn."

"Tarn? But was her mother by any chance Clare
Tarn?"

He nodded. "That was it. She even made her

daughter call her by her christian name. The companion stunt."

"But I used to know Clare Tarn quite well," said Dodo in an astonished, feeling voice. "These last years I'd hardly seen her. But when I was more in London just after the War . . ."

"But this begins to be interesting," said Fanning. "New light on my little friend. . . ."

"Whom I absolutely forbid you," said Dodo emphatically, "to . . ."

"Tamper with the honour of," he suggested. "Let's phrase it as nobly as possible."

"No, seriously, Miles. I really won't have it. Poor Clare Tarn's daughter. If I didn't have to rush off to-morrow I'd ask her to come and see me, so as to warn her."

Fanning laughed. "She wouldn't thank you. And besides if any one is to be warned, I'm the one who's in danger. But I shall be firm, Dodo—a rock. I won't allow her to seduce me."

"You're incorrigible, Miles. But mind, if you dare. . . ."

"But I won't. Definitely." His tone was reassuring. "Meanwhile I must hear something about the mother."

The marchesa shrugged her shoulders. "A woman who couldn't live on top gear. You've really said the last word."

"But I want first words," he answered. "It's not the verdict that's interesting. It's the whole case, it's all the evidence. You're *sub-poenaed*, my dear. Speak up."

"Poor Clare!"

"Oh, *nil nisi bonum*, of course, if that's what disturbs you."

"She'd have so loved it to be not *bonum*, poor dear!" said the marchesa, tempering her look of vague condolence with a little smile. "That was her great ambition—to be thought rather wicked. She'd have liked to have the reputation of a vampire. Not a spiritual one, mind you. The other sort. Lola Montes —that was her ideal."

"It's an ideal," said Fanning, "that takes some realizing, I can tell you."

Dodo nodded. "And that's what she must have found out, pretty soon. She wasn't born to be a fatal woman; she lacked the gifts. No staggering beauty, no mysterious fascination or intoxicating vitality. She was just very charming, that was all; and at the same time rather impossible and absurd. So that there weren't any aspiring victims to be fatal to. And a vampire without victims is—well, *what?*"

"Certainly not a vampire," he concluded.

"Except, of course, in her own imagination, if she chooses to think so. In her own imagination Clare certainly was a vampire."

"Reduced, in fact, to being her own favourite character in fiction."

"Precisely. You always find the phrase."

"Only too fatally!" He made a little grimace. "I

often wish I didn't. The luxury of being inarticulate!
To be able to wallow indefinitely long in every feeling
and sensation, instead of having to clamber out at
once on to a hard, dry, definite phrase. But what
about your Clare?"

"Well, she started, of course, by being a riddle to
me. Unanswerable, or rather answerable, answered,
but so very strangely that I was still left wondering.
I shall never forget the first time Filippo and I went
to dine there. Poor Roger Tarn was still alive then.
While the men were drinking their port, Clare and
I were alone in the drawing-room. There was a little
chit-chat, I remember, and then, with a kind of determined desperation, as though she'd that second
screwed herself up to jumping off the Eiffel Tower,
suddenly, out of the blue, she asked me if I'd ever
had one of those *wonderful* Sicilian peasants—I can't
possibly reproduce the tone, the expression—as a
lover. I was a bit taken aback, I must confess. 'But we
don't live in Sicily,' was the only thing I could think
of answering—too idiotically! 'Our estates are all in
Umbria and Tuscany.' 'But the Tuscans are *superb*
creatures too,' she insisted. Superb, I agreed. But, as
it happens, I don't have affairs with even the superbest
peasants. Nor with anybody else, for that matter.
Clare was dreadfully disappointed. I think she'd expected the most romantic confidences—moonlight
and mandolins and *stretti, stretti, nell' estasì d'amor*.
She was really very ingenuous. 'Do you mean to say
you've really never . . . ?' she insisted. I ought to

have got angry, I suppose; but it was all so ridiculous, that I never thought of it. I just said, 'Never,' and felt as though I were refusing her a favour. But she made up for my churlishness by being lavish to herself. But lavish! You can't imagine what a tirade she let fly at me. How *wonderful* it was to get away from self-conscious, complicated, sentimental love! How profoundly *satisfying* to feel oneself at the mercy of the dumb, dark forces of physical passion! How *intoxicating* to humiliate one's culture and one's class feeling before some *magnificent* primitive, some *earthly* beautiful satyr, some *divine* animal! And so on, *crescendo*. And it ended with her telling me the story of her *extraordinary* affair with—was it a gamekeeper? or a young farmer? I forget. But there was something about rabbit-shooting in it, I know."

"It sounds like a chapter out of George Sand."

"It was."

"Or still more, I'm afraid," he said, making a wry face, "like a most deplorable parody of my *Endymion and the Moon*."

"Which I've never read, I'm ashamed to say."

"You should, if only to understand this Clare of yours."

"I will. Perhaps I'd have solved her more quickly, if I'd read it at the time. As it was I could only be amazed—and a little horrified. That rabbit-shooter!" She shook her head. "He ought to have been so romantic. But I could only think of that awful yellow kitchen soap he'd be sure to wash himself with, or

perhaps carbolic, so that he'd smell like washed dogs
—dreadful! And the flannel shirts, not changed quite
often enough. And the hands, so horny, with very
short nails, perhaps broken. No, I simply couldn't
understand her."

"Which is to your discredit, Dodo, if I may say
so."

"Perhaps. But you must admit, I never pretended
to be anything but what I am—a perfectly frivolous
and respectable member of the upper classes. With a
taste, I must confess, for the scandalous. Which was
one of the reasons, I suppose, why I became so intimate with poor Clare. I was really fascinated by
her confidences."

"Going on the tiles vicariously, eh?"

"Well, if you choose to put it grossly and vulgarly. . . ."

"Which I *do* choose," he interposed. "To be tactfully gross and appositely vulgar—that, my dear, is
one of the ultimate artistic refinements. One day I
shall write a monograph on the aesthetics of vulgarity. But meanwhile shall we say that you were
inspired by an intense scientific curiosity to . . ."

Dodo laughed. "One of the tiresome things about
you, Miles, is that one can never go on being angry
with you."

"Yet another subject for a monograph!" he answered, and his smile was at once confidential and
ironical, affectionate and full of mockery. "But let's
hear what the scientific curiosity elicited?"

"Well, to begin with, a lot of really rather embarrassingly intimate confidences and questions, which I needn't repeat."

"No, don't. I know what those feminine conversations are. I have a native modesty. . . ."

"Oh, so have I. And, strangely enough, so had Clare. But somehow she wanted to outrage herself. You felt it all the time. She always had that desperate jumping-off-the-Eiffel-Tower manner, when she began to talk like that. It was a kind of martyrdom. But enjoyable. Perversely." Dodo shook her head. "Very puzzling. I used to have to make quite an effort to change the conversation from gynaecology to romance. Oh, those lovers of hers! Such stories! The most fantastic adventures in East End opium dens, in aeroplanes, and even, I remember (it was that very hot summer of 'twenty-two), even in a refrigerator!"

"My dear!" protested Fanning.

"Honestly! I'm only repeating what she told me."

"But do you mean to say you believed her?"

"Well, by that time, I must admit, I was beginning to be rather sceptical. You see, I could never elicit the names of these creatures. Nor any detail. It was as though they didn't exist outside the refrigerator and the aeroplane."

"How many of them were there?"

"Only two at that particular moment. One was a Grand Passion, and the other a Caprice. A Caprice," she repeated, rolling the r. "It was one of poor

Clare's favourite words. I used to try and pump
her. But she was mum. 'I want them to be *mysterious*,' she told me the last time I pressed her for
details. 'Anonymous, without an *état civil*. Why
should I show you their passports and identity
cards?' 'Perhaps they haven't got any,' I suggested.
Which was malicious. I could see she was annoyed.
But a week later she showed me their photographs.
There they were; the camera cannot lie; I had to be
convinced. The Grand Passion, I must say, was a
very striking-looking creature. Thin-faced, worn, a
bit Roman and sinister. The Caprice was more ordinarily the nice young Englishman. Rather childish and simple, Clare explained; and she gave me to
understand that she was initiating him. It was the
other, the Grand P., who thought of such refinements
as the refrigerator. Also, she now confided to me for
the first time, he was mildly a sadist. Having seen
his face, I could believe it. 'Am I ever likely to meet
him?' I asked. She shook her head. He moved in a
very different world from mine."

"A rabbit-shooter?" Fanning asked.

"No: an intellectual. That's what I gathered."

"Golly!"

"So there was not the slightest probability, as you
can see, that *I* should ever meet him." Dodo laughed.
"And yet almost the first face I saw on leaving Clare
that afternoon was the Grand P.'s."

"Coming to pay his sadistic respects?"

"Alas for poor Clare, no. He was behind glass in

the show-case of a photographer in the Brompton
Road, not a hundred yards from the Tarns' house
in Ovington Square. The identical portrait. I
marched straight in. 'Can you tell me who that is?'
But it appears that photography is done under the
seal of confession. They wouldn't say. Could I order
a copy? Well, yes, as a favour, they'd let me have
one. Curiously enough, they told me, as they were
taking down my name and address, another lady had
come in only two or three days before and also ordered a copy. 'Not by any chance a rather tall lady
with light auburn hair and a rather amusing mole
on the left cheek?' That did sound rather like the
lady. 'And with a very confidential manner,' I suggested, 'as though you were her oldest friends?' Exactly, exactly; they were unanimous. That clinched
it. Poor Clare, I thought, as I walked on towards the
Park, poor, poor Clare!"

There was a silence.

"Which only shows," said Fanning at last, "how
right the Church has always been to persecute literature. The harm we imaginative writers do! Enormous! We ought all to be on the Index, every one.
Consider your Clare, for example. If it hadn't been
for books, she'd never have known that such things
as passion and sensuality and perversity even existed.
Never."

"Come, come," she protested.

But, "Never," Fanning repeated. "She was congenitally as cold as a fish; it's obvious. Never had a

spontaneous, untutored desire in her life. But she'd read a lot of books. Out of which she'd fabricated a theory of passion and perversity. Which she then consciously put into practice."

"Or rather didn't put into practice. Only day-dreamed that she did."

He nodded. "For the most part. But sometimes, I don't mind betting, she realized the day-dreams in actual life. Desperately, as you so well described it, with her teeth clenched and her eyes shut, as though she were jumping off the Eiffel Tower. That rabbit-shooter, for instance. . . ."

"But do you think the rabbit-shooter really existed?"

"Perhaps not that particular one. But *a* rabbit-shooter, perhaps several rabbit-shooters—at one time or another, I'm sure, they genuinely existed. Though never *genuinely*, of course, for her. For her, it's obvious, they were just phantoms, like the other inhabitants of her dreamery. Phantoms of flesh and blood, but still phantoms. I see her as a kind of Midas, turning everything she touched into imagination. Even in the embraces of a genuine, solid rabbit-shooter, she was still only indulging in her solitary sultry dream—a dream inspired by Shakespeare, or Mrs. Barclay, or the Chevalier de Nerciat, or D'Annunzio, or whoever her favourite author may have been."

"Miles Fanning, perhaps," Dodo mockingly suggested.

"Yes, I feared as much."

"What a responsibility!"

"Which I absolutely refuse to accept. What have I ever written but solemn warnings against the vice of imagination? Sermons against mental licentiousness of every kind—intellectual licentiousness, mystical licentiousness, fantastic-amorous licentiousness. No, no. I'll accept no responsibility. Or at least no special responsibility—only the generic responsibility of being an imaginative author, the original sin of writing in such a way as to influence people. And when I say 'influence,' of course I don't really mean *influence*. Because a writer can't influence people, in the sense of making them think and feel and act as he does. He can only influence them to be more, or less, like one of their own selves. In other words, he's never understood. (Thank goodness! because it would be very humiliating to be really understood by one's readers.) What readers get out of him is never, finally, *his* ideas, but theirs. And when they try to imitate him or his creations, all that they can ever do is to act one of their own potential rôles. Take this particular case. Clare read and, I take it, was impressed. She took my warnings against mental licentiousness to heart and proceeded to do—what? Not to become a creature of spontaneous, unvitiated impulses—for the good reason that that wasn't in her power—but only to imagine that she was such a creature. She imagined herself a woman like the one I put into *Endymion and the Moon* and acted accordingly—or else didn't act, only dreamed; it makes very little difference. In a word, she did exactly what all my books told her not to do. Inevitably; it was her nature. I'd influenced her, yes. But she didn't become more like one of my heroines. She only became more intensely like herself. And then, you must remember, mine weren't the only books on her shelves. I think we can take it that she'd read *Les Liaisons Dangereuses* and Casanova and some biography, shall we say, of the Maréchal de Richelieu. So that those spontaneous unvitiated impulses—how ludicrous they are, anyhow, when you *talk* about them!—became identified in her mind with the most elegant forms of 'caprice'—wasn't that the word? She was a child of nature—but with qualifications. The kind of child of nature that lived at Versailles or on the Grand Canal about 1760. Hence those rabbit-shooters and hence also those sadistic intellectuals, whether real or imaginary—and imaginary even when real. I may have been a favourite author. But I'm not responsible for the rabbit-shooters or the Grand P.'s. Not more responsible than any one else. She'd heard of the existence of love before she'd read me. We're all equally to blame, from Homer downwards. Plato wouldn't have any of us in his Republic. He was quite right, I believe. Quite right."

"And what about the daughter?" Dodo asked, after a silence.

He shrugged his shoulders. "In reaction against the mother, so far as I could judge. In reaction, but also influenced by her, unconsciously. And the influence is effective because, after all, she's her mother's daughter and probably resembles her mother, congenitally. But consciously, on the surface, she knows she doesn't want to live as though she were in a novel. And yet can't help it, because that's her nature, that's how she was brought up. But she's miserable, because she realizes that fiction-life *is* fiction. Miserable and very anxious to get out—out through the covers of the novel into the real world."

"And are you her idea of the real world?" Dodo enquired.

He laughed, "Yes, I'm the real world. Strange as it may seem. And also, of course, pure fiction. The Writer, the Great Man—the Official Biographer's fiction, in a word. Or, better still, the autobiographer's fiction. Chateaubriand, shall we say. And her breaking out—that's fiction too. A pure Miles Fanningism, if ever there was one. And, poor child, she knows it. Which makes her so cross with herself. Cross with me too, in a curious obscure way. But at the same time she's thrilled. What a thrilling situation! And herself walking about in the middle of it. She looks on and wonders and wonders what the next instalment of the feuilleton's going to contain."

"Well, there's one thing we're quite certain it's not going to contain, aren't we? Remember your promise, Miles."

"I think of nothing else," he bantered.

"Seriously, Miles, seriously."

"I think of nothing else," he repeated in a voice that was the parody of a Shakespearean actor's.

Dodo shook her finger at him. "Mind," she said, "mind!" Then, pushing back her chair, "Let's move into the drawing-room," she went on. "We shall be more comfortable there."

IV

"And to think," Pamela was writing in her diary, "how nervous I'd been beforehand, and the trouble I'd taken to work out the whole of our first meeting, question and answer, like the Shorter Catechism, instead of which I was like a fish in water, really at home, for the first time in my life, I believe. No, perhaps not more at home than with Ruth and Phyllis, but then they're girls, so they hardly count. Besides, when you've once been at home in the sea, it doesn't seem much fun being at home in a little glass bowl, which is rather unfair to Ruth and Phyllis, but after all it's not their fault and they can't help being little bowls, just as M. F. can't help being a sea, and when you've swum about a bit in all that intelligence and knowledge and really *devilish* understanding, well, you find the bowls rather narrow, though of course they're sweet little bowls and I shall always be very fond of them, especially Ruth. Which makes me wonder if what he said about Clare and me—unnatural by nature—is always true, because hasn't every unnatural person got somebody she can be natural with, or even that she can't help being natural with, like

213

oxygen and that other stuff making water? Of course it's not guaranteed that you find the other person who makes you natural, and I think perhaps Clare never did find her person, because I don't believe it was Daddy. But in my case there's Ruth and Phyllis and now to-day M. F.; and he really proves it, because I *was* natural with him more than with any one, even though he did say I was unnatural by nature. No, I feel that if I were with him always, I should always be my *real* self, just kind of easily spouting, like those lovely fountains we went to look at this afternoon, not all tied up in knots and squirting about vaguely in every kind of direction, and muddy at that, but beautifully clear in a big gushing spout, like what Joan in *The Return of Eurydice* finally became when she'd escaped from that awful, awful man and found Walter. But does that mean I'm in love with him?"

Pamela bit the end of her pen and stared, frowning, at the page before her. Scrawled large in orange ink, the question stared back. Disquietingly and insistently stared. She remembered a phrase of her mother's. "But if you knew," Clare had cried (Pamela could *see* her, wearing the black afternoon dress from Patou, and there were yellow roses in the bowl on the table under the window), "if you knew what certain writers were to me! *Shrines*—there's no other word. I could worship the Tolstoy of Anna Karenina." But Harry Braddon, to whom the words were addressed, had laughed at her. And, though she hated

Harry Braddon, so had Pamela, mockingly. For it
was absurd; nobody was a shrine, nobody. And anyhow, what *was* a shrine? Nothing. Not nowadays, not
when one had stopped being a child. She told herself
these things with a rather unnecessary emphasis, almost truculently, in the style of the professional
atheists in Hyde Park. One didn't worship—for the
good reason that she herself once had worshipped.
Miss Figgis, the classical mistress, had been her pash
for more than a year. Which was why she had gone
to Early Service so frequently in those days and been
so keen to go up to Oxford and take Greats. (Besides,
she had even, at that time, rather liked and admired
Miss Huss. Ghastly old Hussy! It seemed incredible
now.) But oh, that grammar! And Caesar was such a
bore, and Livy still worse, and as for Greek . . . She
had tried very hard for a time. But when Miss Figgis
so obviously preferred that priggish little beast
Kathleen, Pamela had just let things slide. The bad
marks had come in torrents and old Hussy had begun
being more sorrowful than angry, and finally more
angry than sorrowful. But she hadn't cared. What
made not caring easier was that she had her mother
behind her. "I'm so delighted," was what Clare had
said when she heard that Pamela had given up wanting to go to Oxford. "I'd have felt so terribly inferior if you'd turned out a blue-stocking. Having
my frivolity rebuked by my own daughter!" Clare
had always boasted of her frivolity. Once, under the
influence of old Hussy and for the love of Miss Fig-

gis, an earnest disapprover, Pamela had become an apostle of her mother's gospel. "After all," she had pointed out to Miss Figgis, "Cleopatra didn't learn Greek." And though Miss Figgis was able to point out, snubbingly, that the last of the Ptolemies had probably spoken nothing but Greek, Pamela could still insist that in principle she was quite right: Cleopatra hadn't learnt Greek, or what, if you were a Greek, corresponded to Greek. So why should she? She began to parade a violent and childish cynicism, a cynicism which was still (though she had learnt, since leaving school, to temper the ridiculous expression of it) her official creed. There were no shrines—though she sometimes, wistfully and rather shamefacedly, wished there were. One didn't, determinedly didn't worship. She herself might admire Fanning's books, *did* admire them, enormously. But as for worshipping—no, she absolutely declined. Clare had overdone it all somehow—as usual. Pamela was resolved that there should be no nonsense about *her* feelings.

"But does that mean I'm in love with him?" insisted the orange scrawl.

As though in search of an answer, Pamela turned back the pages of her diary (she had already covered nearly eight of them with her account of this memorable twelfth of June). "His face," she read, "is very brown, almost like an Arab's, except that he has blue eyes, as he lives mostly in the South, because he says that if you don't live in the sun, you go slightly mad,

which is why people in the North, like us and the
Germans and the Americans are so tiresome, though
of course you go still madder where there's too much
sun, like in India, where they're even more hopeless.
He's very good looking and you don't think of him
as being either old or young, but as just being there,
like that, and the way he smiles is really very extraordinary, and so are his eyes, and I simply *adored* his
white silk suit." But the question was not yet answered. His silk suit wasn't him, nor was his voice,
even though he had "an awfully nice one, rather like
that man who talks about books on the wireless, only
nicer." She turned over a page. "But M. F. is different from most clever people," the orange scrawl
proclaimed, "because he doesn't make you feel a fool,
even when he does laugh at you, and never, which is
so *ghastly* with men like Professor Cobley, talks down
to you in that awful patient, gentle way, which makes
you feel a million times more of a worm than being
snubbed or ignored, because, if you have any pride,
that sort of intelligence without tears is just loath-
some, as though you were being given milk pudding
out of charity. No, M. F. talks to you on the level
and the extraordinary thing is that, while he's talking to you and you're talking to him, you *are* on a
level with him, or at any rate you feel as though you
were, which comes to the same thing. He's like influenza, you catch his intelligence." Pamela let the
leaves of the notebook flick past, one by one, under
her thumb. The final words on the half-blank page

once more stared at her, questioningly. "But does that mean I'm in love with him?" Taking her pen from between her teeth, "Certainly," she wrote, "I do find him terribly attractive physically." She paused for a moment to reflect, then added, frowning as though with the effort of raising an elusive fact from the depths of memory, of solving a difficult problem in algebra: "Because really, when he put his hand on my shoulder, which would have been simply intolerable if any one else had done it, but somehow with him I didn't mind, I felt all thrilled with an absolute frisson." She ran her pen through the last word and substituted "thrill," which she underlined to make it seem less lamely a repetition. "Frisson" had been one of Clare's favourite words; hearing it pronounced in her mother's remembered voice, Pamela had felt a sudden mistrust of it; it seemed to cast a kind of doubt on the feelings it stood for, a doubt of which she was ashamed—it seemed so disloyal and the voice had sounded so startlingly, so heart-rendingly clear and near—but which she still couldn't help experiencing. She defended herself; "frisson" had simply had to go, because the thrill was genuine, absolutely genuine, she insisted. "For a moment," she went on, writing very fast, as though she were trying to run away from the sad, disagreeable thoughts that had intruded upon her, "I thought I was going to faint when he touched me, like when one's coming to after chloroform, which I've certainly never felt like with any one else." As a protest against the doubts inspired by that unfortunate frisson she underlined "never," heavily. Never; it was quite true. When Harry Braddon had tried to kiss her, she had been furious and disgusted —disgusting beast! Saddening and reproachful, Clare's presence hovered round her once more; Clare had liked Harry Braddon. Still, he was a beast. Pamela had never told her mother about that kiss. She shut her eyes excludingly and thought instead of Cecil Rudge, poor, timid, unhappy little Cecil, whom she liked so much, was so genuinely sorry for. But when, that afternoon at Aunt Edith's, when at last, after an hour's visibly laborious screwing to the sticking point, he had had the courage to take her hand and say "Pamela" and kiss it, she had just laughed, oh! unforgivably, but she simply couldn't help it; he was so ridiculous. Poor lamb, he had been terribly upset. "But I'm so sorry," she had gasped between the bursts of her laughter, "so dreadfully sorry. Please don't be hurt." But his face, she could see, was agonized. "Please! Oh, I feel so miserable." And she had gone off into another explosion of laughter which almost choked her. But when she could breathe again, she had run to him where he stood, averted and utterly unhappy, by the window, she had taken his hand and, when he still refused to look at her, had put her arm round his neck and kissed him. But the emotion that had filled her eyes with tears was nothing like passion. As for Hugh Davies—why, it certainly had been rather thrilling when Hugh kissed her. It had been thrilling, but certainly not to a fainting point. But then had she *really* felt like fainting to-day, a small voice questioned. She drowned the small voice with the scratching of her pen. "Consult the oracles of passion," she wrote and, laying down her pen, got up and crossed the room. A copy of *The Return of Eurydice* was lying on the bed; she picked it up and turned over the pages. Here it was! "Consult the oracles of passion," she read aloud and her own voice sounded, she thought, strangely oracular in the solitude. "A god speaks in them, or else a devil, one can never tell which beforehand, nor even, in most cases, afterwards. And, when all is said, does it very much matter? God and devil are equally supernatural, that is the important thing; equally supernatural and therefore, in this all too flatly natural world of sense and science and society, equally desirable, equally significant." She shut the book and walked back to the table. "Which is what he said this afternoon," she went on writing, "but in that laughing way, when I said I could never see why one shouldn't do what one liked, instead of all this Hussy and Hippo rigmarole about service and duty, and he said yes, that was what Rabelais had said" (there seemed to be an awful lot of "saids" in this sentence, but it couldn't be helped; she scrawled on;) "which I pretended I'd read—why can't one tell the truth? particularly as I'd just been saying at the same time that one ought to say what one thinks as well as do what one likes;

but it seems to be hopeless—and he said he entirely agreed, it was perfect, so long as you had the luck to like the sort of things that kept you on the right side of the prison bars and think the sort of things that don't get you murdered when you say them. And I said I'd rather say what I thought and do what I liked and be murdered and put in gaol than be a Hippo, and he said I was an idealist, which annoyed me and I said I certainly wasn't, all I was was some one who didn't want to go mad with inhibitions. And he laughed, and I wanted to quote him his own words about the oracles, but somehow it was so shy-making that I didn't. All the same, it's what I intensely feel, that one *ought* to consult the oracles of passion. And I shall consult them." She leaned back in her chair and shut her eyes. The orange question floated across the darkness: "But does that mean I'm in love with him?" The oracle seemed to be saying yes. But oracles, she resolutely refused to remember, can be rigged to suit the interests of the questioner. Didn't the admirer of *The Return of Eurydice* secretly *want* the oracle to say yes? Didn't she think she'd almost fainted, because she'd wished she'd almost fainted, because she'd come desiring to faint? Pamela sighed; then, with a gesture of decision, she slapped her notebook to and put away her pen. It was time to get ready for dinner; she bustled about efficiently and distractingly among her trunks. But the question returned to her as she lay soaking in the warm other-world of her bath. By the time she got out she had boiled herself to such a pitch of giddiness that she could hardly stand.

For Pamela, dinner in solitude, especially the public solitude of hotels, was a punishment. Companionlessness and compulsory silence depressed her. Besides, she never felt quite eye-proof; she could never escape from the obsession that every one was looking at her, judging, criticizing. Under a carapace of rather impertinent uncaringness she writhed distressfully. At Florence her loneliness had driven her to make friends with two not very young American women who were staying in her hotel. They were a bit earnest and good and dreary. But Pamela preferred even dreariness to solitude. She attached herself to them inseparably. They were touched. When she left for Rome, they promised to write to her, they made her promise to write to them. She was so young; they felt responsible; a steadying hand, the counsel of older friends. . . . Pamela had already received two steadying letters. But she hadn't answered them, never would answer them. The horrors of lonely dining cannot be alleviated by correspondence.

Walking down to her ordeal in the restaurant, she positively yearned for her dreary friends. But the hall was a desert of alien eyes and faces; and the waiter who led her through the hostile dining-room, had bowed, it seemed to her, with an ironical politeness, had mockingly smiled. She sat down haughtily at her table and almost wished she were under it. When the *sommelier* appeared with his list, she ordered half a bottle of something absurdly expensive, for fear he might think she didn't know anything about wine.

She had got as far as the fruit, when a presence loomed over her; she looked up. "You?" Her delight was an illumination; the young man was dazzled. "What marvellous luck!" Yet it was only Guy Browne, Guy whom she had met a few times at dances and found quite pleasant—that was all. "Think of your being in Rome!" She made him sit down at her table. When she had finished her coffee, Guy suggested that they should go out and dance somewhere. They went. It was nearly three when Pamela got to bed. She had had a most enjoyable evening.

V

But how ungratefully she treated poor Guy when, next day at lunch, Fanning asked her how she had spent the evening! True, there were extenuating circumstances, chief among which was the fact that Fanning had kissed her when they met. By force of habit, he himself would have explained, if any one had asked him why, because he kissed every presentable face. Kissing was in the great English tradition. "It's the only way I can be like Chaucer," he liked to affirm. "Just as knowing a little Latin and less Greek is my only claim to resembling Shakespeare and as lying in bed till ten's the nearest I get to Descartes." In this particular case, as perhaps in every other particular case, the force of habit had been seconded by a deliberate intention; he was accustomed to women being rather in love with him, he liked the amorous atmosphere and could use the simplest as well as the most complicated methods to create it. Moreover he was an experimentalist, he genuinely wanted to see what would happen. What happened was that Pamela was astonished, embarrassed, thrilled, delighted, bewildered. And what with her confused excitement and the enormous effort she had made to take it all as naturally and easily as he had done, she was betrayed into what, in other circumstances, would have been a scandalous ingratitude. But when one has just been kissed, for the first time and at one's second meeting with him, kissed offhandedly and yet (she felt it) significantly, by Miles Fanning—actually Miles Fanning!—little men like Guy Browne do seem rather negligible, even though one did have a very good time with them the evening before.

"I'm afraid you must have been rather lonely last night," said Fanning, as they sat down to lunch. His sympathy hypocritically covered a certain satisfaction that it should be his absence that had condemned her to dreariness.

"No, I met a friend," Pamela answered with a smile which the inward comparison of Guy with the author of *The Return of Eurydice* had tinged with a certain amused condescendingness.

"A friend?" He raised his eyebrows. "*Amico* or *amica?* Our English is so discreetly equivocal. With this key Bowdler locked up his heart. But I apologize. *Co* or *ca?*"

"*Co*. He's called Guy Browne and he's here learning Italian to get into the Foreign Office. He's a nice boy." Pamela might have been talking about a favourite, or even not quite favourite, retriever. "Nice; but nothing very special. I mean, not in the way of intelligence." She shook her head patronizingly over Guy's very creditable First in History as a guttersnipe capriciously favoured by an archduke might learn in his protector's company to shake his head and patronizingly smile at the name of a marquis of only four or five centuries' standing. "He can dance, though," she admitted.

"So I suppose you danced with him?" said Fanning in a tone which, in spite of his amusement at the child's assumption of an aged superiority, he couldn't help making rather disobligingly sarcastic. It annoyed him to think that Pamela should have spent an evening, which he had pictured as dismally lonely, dancing with a young man.

"Yes, we danced," said Pamela, nodding.

"Where?"

"Don't ask me. We went to about six different places in the course of the evening."

"Of course you did," said Fanning almost bitterly. "Moving rapidly from one place to another and doing exactly the same thing in each—that seems to be the young's ideal of bliss."

Speaking as a young who had risen above such

things, but who still had to suffer from the folly of her unregenerate contemporaries, "It's quite true," Pamela gravely confirmed.

"They go to Pekin to listen to the wireless and to Benares to dance the frox-trot. I've seen them at it. It's incomprehensible. And then the tooting up and down in automobiles, and the roaring up and down in aeroplanes and the stinking up and down in motor-boats. Up and down, up and down, just for the sake of not sitting still, of never having time to think or feel. No, I give them up, these young of yours." He shook his head. "But I'm becoming a minor prophet," he added; his good humour was beginning to return.

"But after all," said Pamela, "we're not *all* like that."

Her gravity made him laugh. "There's at least one who's ready to let herself be bored by a tiresome survivor from another civilization. Thank you, Pamela." Leaning across the table, he took her hand and kissed it. "I've been horribly ungrateful," he went on, and his face, as he looked at her was suddenly transfigured by the bright enigmatic beauty of his smile. "If you knew how charming you looked!" he said; and it was true. That ingenuous face, those impertinent little breasts—charming. "And how charming you *were!* But of course you *do* know," a little demon prompted him to add: "no doubt Mr. Browne told you last night."

Pamela had blushed—a blush of pleasure, and embarrassed shyness, and excitement. What he had just said and done was more significant, she felt, even than the kiss he had given her when they met. Her cheeks burned; but she managed, with an effort, to keep her eyes unwaveringly on his. His last words made her frown. "He certainly didn't," she answered. "He'd have got his face smacked."

"Is that a delicate hint?" he asked. "If so," and he leaned forward, "here's the other cheek."

Her face went redder than ever. She felt suddenly miserable; he was only laughing at her. "Why do you laugh at me?" she said aloud, unhappily.

"But I wasn't," he protested. "I really did think you were annoyed."

"But why should I have been?"

"I can't imagine." He smiled. "But if you would have smacked Mr. Browne's face. . . ."

"But Guy's quite different."

It was Fanning's turn to wince. "You mean he's young, while I'm only a poor old imbecile who needn't be taken seriously?"

"Why are you so stupid?" Pamela asked almost fiercely. "No, but I mean," she added in quick apology, "I mean . . . well, I don't care two pins about Guy. So you see, it would annoy me if he tried to push in, like that. Whereas with somebody who does mean something to me . . ." Pamela hesitated. "With *you*," she specified in a rather harsh, strained voice and with just that look of despairing determination. Fanning imagined, just that jumping-off-the-Eiffel-Tower expression, which her mother's face must have assumed in moments such as this, "it's quite different. I mean, with you of course I'm not annoyed. I'm pleased. Or at least I *was* pleased, till I saw you were just making a fool of me."

Touched and flattered, "But my dear child," Fanning protested, "I wasn't doing anything of the kind. I meant what I said. And much more than I said," he added, in the teeth of the warning and reproachful outcry raised by his common sense. It was amusing to experiment, it was pleasant to be adored, exciting to be tempted (and how young she was, how perversely fresh!). There was even something quite agreeable in resisting temptation; it had the charms of a strenuous and difficult sport. Like mountain climbing. He smiled once more, consciously brilliant.

This time Pamela dropped her eyes. There was a silence which might have protracted itself uncomfortably, if the waiter had not broken it by bringing the *tagliatelle*. They began to eat. Pamela was all at once exuberantly gay.

After coffee they took a taxi and drove to the Villa Giulia. "For we mustn't," Fanning explained, "neglect your education."

"Mustn't we?" she asked. "I often wonder why we mustn't. Truthfully now, I mean without any hipping and all that—why shouldn't I neglect it? Why should I go to this beastly museum?" She was preparing to play the cynical, boastfully unintellectual part which she had made her own. "Why?" she re-

peated truculently. Behind the rather vulgar low-
brow mask she cultivated wistful yearnings and concealed the uneasy consciousness of inferiority. "A lot
of beastly old Roman odds and ends!" she grumbled;
that was one for Miss Figgis.

"Roman?" said Fanning. "God forbid! Etruscan."

"Well, Etruscan then; it's all the same anyhow.
Why shouldn't I neglect the Etruscans? I mean,
what have they got to do with me—*me?*" And she
gave her chest two or three little taps with the tip of
a crooked forefinger.

"Nothing, my child," he answered. "Thank goodness, they've got absolutely nothing to do with you,
or me, or anybody else."

"Then why . . ."

"Precisely for that reason. That's the definition
of culture—knowing and thinking about things that
have absolutely nothing to do with us. About Etruscans, for example; or the mountains on the moon; or
cat's cradle among the Chinese; or the Universe at
large."

"All the same," she insisted, "I still don't see."

"Because you've never known people who weren't
cultured. But make the acquaintance of a few practical business-men—the kind who have no time to be
anything but alternately efficient and tired. Or of a
few workmen from the big towns. (Country people
are different; they still have the remains of the old
substitutes for culture—religion, folk-lore, tradition.

The town fellows have lost the substitutes without acquiring the genuine article.) Get to know those people; *they'll* make you see the point of culture. Just as the Sahara'll make you see the point of water. And for the same reason: they're arid."

"That's all very well; but what about people like Professor Cobley?"

"Whom I've happily never met," he said, "but can reconstruct from the expression on your face. Well, all that can be said about those people is: just try to imagine them if they'd never been irrigated. Gobi or Shamo."

"Well, perhaps." She was dubious.

"And anyhow the biggest testimony to culture isn't the soulless philistines—it's the soulful ones. My sweet Pamela," he implored, laying a hand on her bare brown arm, "for heaven's sake don't run the risk of becoming a soulful philistine."

"But as I don't know what that is," she answered, trying to persuade herself, as she spoke, that the touch of his hand was giving her a tremendous *frisson*—but it really wasn't.

"It's what the name implies," he said. "A person without culture who goes in for having a soul. An illiterate idealist. A Higher Thinker with nothing to think about but his—or more often, I'm afraid, *her*—beastly little personal feelings and sensation. They spend their lives staring at their own navels and in the intervals trying to find other people who'll take an interest and come and stare too. Oh, figura-

tively," he added, noticing the expression of astonishment which had passed across her face. *"En tout
bien, tout honneur.* At least, sometimes and to begin
with. Though I've known cases . . ." But he decided it would be better not to speak about the lady
from Rochester, N. Y. Pamela might be made
to feel that the cap fitted. Which it did, except that
her little head was such a charming one. "In the
end," he said, "they go mad, these soulful philistines.
Mad with self-consciousness and vanity and egotism
and a kind of hopeless bewilderment; for when
you're utterly without culture, every fact's an isolated, unconnected fact, every experience is unique
and unprecedented. Your world's made up of a few
bright points floating about inexplicably in the
midst of an unfathomable darkness. Terrifying! It's
enough to drive any one mad. I've seen them, lots of
them, gone utterly crazy. In the past they had organized religion, which meant that somebody had
once been cultured for them, vicariously. But what
with protestantism and the modernists, their philis-
tinism's absolute now. They're alone with their own
souls. Which is the worst companionship a human
being can have. So bad, that it sends you dotty. So
beware, Pamela, beware! You'll go mad, if you think
only of what has something to do with you. The
Etruscans will keep you sane."

"Let's hope so." She laughed. "But aren't we
there?"

The cab drew up at the door of the villa; they got out.

"And remember that the things that start with having nothing to do with you," said Fanning, as he counted out the money for the entrance tickets, "turn out in the long run to have a great deal to do with you. Because they become a part of you and you of them. A soul can't know or fully become itself without knowing and therefore to some extent becoming what isn't itself. Which it does in various ways. By loving, for example."

"You mean . . . ?" The flame of interest brightened in her eyes.

But he went on remorselessly. "And by thinking of things that have nothing to do with you."

"Yes, I see." The flame had dimmed again.

"Hence my concern about your education." He beckoned her through the turnstile into the museum. "A purely selfish concern," he added, smiling down at her. "Because I don't want the most charming of my young friends to grow into a monster, whom I shall be compelled to flee from. So resign yourself to the Etruscans."

"I resign myself," said Pamela, laughing. His words had made her feel happy and excited. "You can begin." And in a theatrical voice, like that which used to make Ruth go off into such fits of laughter, "I am all ears," she added, "as they say in the Best Books." She pulled off her hat and shook out the imprisoned hair.

To Fanning, as he watched her, the gesture brought a sudden shock of pleasure. The impatient, exuberant youthfulness of it! And the little head, so beautifully shaped, so gracefully and proudly poised on its long neck! And her hair was drawn back smoothly from the face to explode in a thick tangle of curls on the nape of the neck. Ravishing!

"All ears," she repeated, delightedly conscious of the admiration she was receiving.

"All ears." And almost meditatively. "But do you know," he went on, "I've never even seen your ears. May I?" And without waiting for her permission, he lifted up the soft, goldy-brown hair that lay in a curve, drooping, along the side of her head.

Pamela's face violently reddened; but she managed none the less to laugh. "Are they as long and furry as you expected?" she asked.

He allowed the lifted hair to fall back into its place and, without answering her question, "I've always," he said, looking at her with a smile which she found disquietingly enigmatic and remote, "I've always had a certain fellow-feeling for those savages who collect ears and thread them on strings, as necklaces."

"But what a horror!" she cried out.

"You think so?" He raised his eyebrows.

But perhaps, Pamela was thinking, he was a sadist. In that book of Krafft-Ebbing's there had been a lot about sadists. It would be queer, if he were . . .

"But what's certain," Fanning went on in another, business-like voice, "what's only too certain is that ears aren't culture. They've got too much to do with us. With me, at any rate. Much too much." He smiled at her again. Pamela smiled back at him, fascinated and obscurely a little frightened; but the fright was an element in the fascination. She dropped her eyes. "So don't let's waste any more time," his voice went on. "Culture to right of us, culture to left of us. Let's begin with this culture on the left. With the vases. They really have absolutely nothing to do with us."

He began and Pamela listened. Not very attentively, however. She lifted her hand and, under the hair, touched her ear. "A fellow-feeling for those savages." She remembered his words with a little shudder. He'd almost meant them. And "ears aren't culture. Too much to do with us. With me. Much too much." He'd meant that too, genuinely and wholeheartedly. And his smile had been a confirmation of the words; yes, and a comment, full of mysterious significance. What *had* he meant? But surely it was obvious what he had meant. Or wasn't it obvious?

The face she turned towards him wore an expression of grave attention. And when he pointed to a vase and said, "Look," she looked, with what an air of concentrated intelligence! But as for knowing what he was talking about! She went on confusedly thinking that he had a fellow-feeling for those savages, and that her ears had too much to do with him, much too much, and that perhaps he was in love with her, perhaps also that he was like those people in Krafft-Ebbing, perhaps . . .; and it seemed to her that her blood must have turned into a kind of hot, red soda-water, all fizzy with little bubbles of fear and excitement.

She emerged, partially at least, out of this bubbly and agitated trance to hear him say, "Look at that, now." A tall statue towered over her. "The Apollo of Veii," he explained. "And really, you know, it *is* the most beautiful statue in the world. Each time I see it, I'm more firmly convinced of that."

Dutifully, Pamela stared. The God stood there on his pedestal, one foot advanced, erect in his draperies. He had lost his arms, but the head was intact and the strange Etruscan face was smiling, enigmatically smiling. Rather like *him,* it suddenly occurred to her.

"What's it made of?" she asked; for it was time to be intelligent.

"Terracotta. Originally coloured."

"And what date?"

"Late sixth century."

"B.C.?" she queried, a little dubiously, and was relieved when he nodded. It really would have been rather awful if it had been A.D. "Who by?"

"By Vulca, they say. But as that's the only Etruscan sculptor they know the name of . . ." He shrugged his shoulders, and the gesture expressed a double doubt—doubt whether the archæologists were right and doubt whether it was really much good talking about Etruscan art to some one who didn't feel quite certain whether the Apollo of Veii was made in the sixth century before or after Christ.

There was a long silence. Fanning looked at the statue. So did Pamela, who also, from time to time, looked at Fanning. She was on the point, more than once, of saying something; but his face was so meditatively glum that, on each occasion, she changed her mind. In the end, however, the silence became intolerable.

"I think it's extraordinarily fine," she announced in the rather religious voice that seemed appropriate. He only nodded. The silence prolonged itself, more oppressive and embarrassing than ever. She made another and despairing effort. "Do you know, I think he's really rather like you. I mean, the way he smiles. . . ."

Fanning's petrified immobility broke once more into life. He turned towards her, laughing. "You're irresistible, Pamela."

"Am I?" Her tone was cold; she was offended. To be told you were irresistible always meant that you'd behaved like an imbecile child. But her conscience was clear; it was a gratuitous insult—the more intolerable since it had been offered by the man who, a moment before, had been saying that he had a fellow-feeling for those savages and that her ears had altogether *too* much to do with him.

Fanning noticed her sudden change of humour and obscurely divined the cause. "You've paid me the

most irresistible compliment you could have invented," he said, doing his best to undo the effect of
his words. For after all what did it matter, with little
breasts like that and thin brown arms, if she did
mix up the millenniums a bit? "You could hardly
have pleased me more if you'd said I was another
Rudolph Valentino."

Pamela had to laugh.

"But seriously," he said, "if you knew what this
lovely God means to me, how much . . ."

Mollified by being once more spoken to seriously,
"I think I can understand," she said in her most
understanding voice.

"No, I doubt if you can." He shook his head. "It's
a question of age, of the experience of a particular
time that's not your time. I shall never forget when
I came back to Rome for the first time after the War
and found this marvellous creature standing here.
They only dug him up in 'sixteen, you see. So there
it was, a brand new experience, a new and apocalyptic voice out of the past. Some day I shall try to get
it on to paper, all that this God has taught me." He
gave a little sigh; she could see that he wasn't
thinking about her any more; he was talking for
himself. "Some day," he repeated. "But it's not ripe
yet. You can't write a thing before it's ripe, before
it wants to be written. But you can talk about it, you
can take your mind for walks all round it and
through it." He paused and, stretching out a hand,
touched a fold of the God's sculptured garment, as

though he were trying to establish a more intimate, more real connection with the beauty before him. "Not that what he taught me was fundamentally new," he went on slowly. "It's all in Homer, of course. It's even partially expressed in the archaic Greek sculpture. Partially. But Apollo here expresses it wholly. He's *all* Homer, *all* the ancient world, concentrated in a single lump of terracotta. That's his novelty. And then the circumstances gave him a special point. It was just after the War that I first saw him—just after the apotheosis and the logical conclusion of all the things Apollo *didn't* stand for. You can imagine how marvellously new he seemed by contrast. After that horrible enormity, he was a lovely symbol of the small, the local, the kindly. After all that extravagance of beastliness— yes, and all that extravagance of heroism and self-sacrifice—he seemed so beautifully sane. A God who doesn't admit the separate existence of either heroics or diabolics, but somehow includes them in his own nature and turns them into something else—like two gases combining to make a liquid. Look at him," Fanning insisted. "Look at his face, look at his body, see how he stands. It's obvious. He's neither the God of heroics, nor the God of diabolics. And yet it's equally obvious that he knows all about both, that he includes them, that he combines them into a third essence. It's the same with Homer. There's no tragedy in Homer. He's pessimistic, yes; but never tragic. His heroes aren't heroic in our sense of the

word; they're men." (Pamela took a very deep
breath; if she had opened her mouth, it would have
been a yawn.) "In fact, you can say there aren't
any heroes in Homer. Nor devils, nor sins. And none
of our aspiring spiritualities and, of course, none of
our horrible, nauseating disgusts—because they're
the complement of being spiritual, they're the tails
to its heads. You couldn't have had Homer writing
'the expensive spirit in a waste of shame.' Though,
of course, with Shakespeare it may have been physiological; the passion violent and brief, and then the
most terrible reaction. It's the sort of thing that
colours a whole life, a whole work. Only of course one's
never allowed to say so. All that one isn't allowed to
say!" He laughed. Pamela also laughed. "But physiology or no physiology," Fanning went on, "he
couldn't have written like that if he'd lived before
the great split—the great split that broke life into
spirit and matter, heroics and diabolics, virtue and
sin and all the other accursed antitheses. Homer
lived before the split; life hadn't been broken when
he wrote. They're complete, his men and women,
complete and real; for he leaves nothing out, he
shirks no issue, even though there is no tragedy. He
knows all about it—*all*." He laid his hand again
on the statue. "And this God's his portrait. He's
Homer, but with the Etruscan smile. Homer smiling
at the sad, mysterious, beautiful absurdity of the
world. The Greeks didn't see that divine absurdity
as clearly as the Etruscans. Not even in Homer's

day; and by the time you get to any sculptor who was anything like as accomplished as the man who made this, you'll find that they've lost it altogether. True, the earliest Greek Gods used to smile all right —or rather grin; for subtlety wasn't their strong point. But by the end of the sixth century they were already becoming a bit too heroic; they were developing those athlete's muscles and those tiresomely noble poses and damned superior faces. But our God here refused to be a prize-fighter or an actor-manager. There's no *terribiltà* about him, no priggishness, no sentimentality. And yet without being in the least pretentious, he's beautiful, he's grand, he's authentically divine. The Greeks took the road that led to Michelangelo and Bernini and Thorwaldsen and Rodin. A rake's progress. These Etruscans were on a better track. If only people had had the sense to follow it! Or at least get back to it. But nobody has, except perhaps old Maillol. They've all allowed themselves to be lured away. Plato was the arch-seducer. It was he who first sent us whoring after spirituality and heroics, whoring after the complementary demons of disgust and sin. We needs must love—well, not the highest, except sometimes by accident—but always the most extravagant and exciting. Tragedy was much more exciting than Homer's luminous pessimism, than this God's smiling awareness of the divine absurdity. Being alternately a hero and a sinner is much more sensational than being an integrated man. So as men seem to have the Yellow Press in the blood, like syphilis, they went back on Homer and Apollo; they followed Plato and Euripides. And Plato and Euripides handed them over to the Stoics and the Neo-Platonists. And these in turn handed humanity over to the Christians. And the Christians have handed us over to Henry Ford and the machines. So here we are."

Pamela nodded intelligently. But what she was chiefly conscious of was the ache in her feet. If only she could sit down!

But, "How poetical and appropriate," Fanning began again, "that the God should have risen from the grave exactly when he did, in 1916! Rising up in the midst of the insanity, like a beautiful, smiling reproach from another world. It was dramatic. At least I felt it so, when I saw him for the first time just after the War. The resurrection of Apollo, the Etruscan Apollo. I've been his worshipper and self-appointed priest ever since. Or at any rate I've tried to be. But it's difficult." He shook his head. "Perhaps it's even impossible for us to recapture . . ." He left the sentence unfinished and, taking her arm, led her out into the great courtyard of the Villa. Under the arcades was a bench. Thank goodness, said Pamela inwardly. They sat down.

"You see," he went on, leaning forward, his elbows on his knees, his hands clasped, "you can't get away from the things that the God protests against. Because they've become a part of you. Tradition and education have driven them into your very bones. It's a case of what I was speaking about just now—of the things that have nothing to do with you coming by force of habit to have everything to do with you. Which is why I'd like you to get Apollo and his Etruscans into your system while you're still young. It may save you trouble. Or on the other hand," he added with a rueful little laugh, "it may not. Because I really don't know if he's everybody's God. He may do for me—and do, only because I've got Plato and Jesus in my bones. But does he do for you? *Chi lo sa?* The older one grows, the more often one asks that question. Until, of course, one's arteries begin to harden, and then one's opinions begin to harden too, harden till they fossilize into certainty. But meanwhile, *chi lo sa? chi lo sa?* And after all it's quite agreeable, not knowing. And knowing, and at the same time knowing that it's no practical use knowing—that's not disagreeable either. Knowing, for example, that it would be good to live according to this God's commandments, but knowing at the same time that one couldn't do it even if one tried, because one's very guts and skeleton are already pledged to other Gods."

"I should have thought that was awful," said Pamela.

"For you, perhaps. But I happen to have a certain natural affection for the accomplished fact. I like and respect it, even when it is a bit depressing. Thus, it's a fact that I'd like to think and live in the unsplit, Apollonian way. But it's also a fact—

and the fact as such is lovable—that I can't help indulging in aspirations and disgusts; I can't help
thinking in terms of heroics and diabolics. Because
the division, the splitness, has been worked right into
my bones. So has the microbe of sensationalism; I
can't help wallowing in the excitements of mysticism
and the tragic sense. Can't help it." He shook his
head. "Though perhaps I've wallowed in them rather
more than I was justified in wallowing—justified by
my upbringing, I mean. There was a time when I
was really quite perversely preoccupied with mystical experiences and ecstasies and private universes."

"Private universes?" she questioned.

"Yes, private, not shared. You create one, you
live in it, each time you're in love, for example."
(Brightly serious, Pamela nodded her understanding and agreement; yes, yes, she knew all about
that.) "Each time you're spiritually exalted," he
went on, "each time you're drunk, even. Everybody
has his own favourite short cuts to the other world.
Mine, in those days, was opium."

"Opium?" She opened her eyes very wide. "Do
you mean to say you smoked opium?" She was
thrilled. Opium was a vice of the first order.

"It's as good a way of becoming supernatural,"
he answered, "as looking at one's nose or one's
navel, or not eating, or repeating a word over and
over again, till it loses its sense and you forget how
to think. All roads lead to Rome. The only bother
about opium is that it's rather an unwholesome road.

I had to go to a nursing home in Cannes to get disintoxicated."

"All the same," said Pamela, doing her best to imitate the quiet casualness of his manner, "it must be rather delicious, isn't it? Awfully exciting, I mean," she added, forgetting not to be thrilled.

"*Too* exciting." He shook his head. "That's the trouble. We needs must love the excitingest when we see it. The supernatural *is* exciting. But I don't want to love the supernatural, I want to love the natural. Not that a little supernaturalness isn't, of course, perfectly natural and necessary. But you can overdo it. I overdid it then. I was all the time in 'tother world, never here. I stopped smoking because I was ill. But even if I hadn't been, I'd have stopped sooner or later for aesthetic reasons. The supernatural world is so terribly baroque—altogether too Counter-Reformation and Bernini. At its best it can be Greco. But you can have too much even of Greco. A big dose of him makes you begin to pine for Vulca and his Apollo."

"But doesn't it work the other way too?" she asked. "I mean, don't you sometimes *long* to start smoking again?" She was secretly hoping that he'd let her try a pipe or two.

Fanning shook his head. "One doesn't get tired of very good bread," he answered. "Apollo's like that. I don't pine for supernatural excitements. Which doesn't mean," he added, "that I don't in practice run after them. You can't disintoxicate yourself of

your culture. That sticks deeper than a mere taste
for opium. I'd like to be able to think and live in the
spirit of the God. But the fact remains that I can't."

"Can't you?" said Pamela with a polite sympathy.
She was more interested in the opium.

"No, no, you can't entirely disintoxicate yourself
of mysticism and the tragic sense. You can't take a
Turvey treatment for spirituality and disgust. You
can't. Not nowadays. Acceptance is impossible in a
split world like ours. You've got to recoil. In the circumstances it's right and proper. But absolutely it's
wrong. If only one could accept as this God accepts,
smiling like that . . ."

"But you *do* smile like that," she insisted.

He laughed and, unclasping his hands, straight-
ened himself up in his seat. "But unhappily," he
said, "a man can smile and smile and not be Apollo.
Meanwhile, what's becoming of your education?
Shouldn't we . . . ?"

"Well, if you like," she assented dubiously. "Only
my feet are rather tired. I mean, there's something
about sight-seeing. . . ."

"There is indeed," said Fanning. "But I was prepared to be a martyr to culture. Still, I'm thankful
you're not." He smiled at her, and Pamela was
pleased to find herself once more at the focus of his
attention. It had been very interesting to hear him
talk about his philosophy and all that. But all the
same . . .

"Twenty to four," said Fanning, looking at his

watch. "I've an idea; shouldn't we drive out to Monte Cavo and spend the evening up there in the cool? There's a view. And a really very eatable dinner."

"I'd love to. But . . ." Pamela hesitated. "Well, you see I did tell Guy I'd go out with him this evening."

He was annoyed. "Well, if you prefer . . ."

"But I don't prefer," she answered hastily. "I mean, I'd much rather go with you. Only I wondered how I'd let Guy know I wasn't. . . ."

"Don't let him know," Fanning answered, abusing his victory. "After all, what are young men there for, except to wait when young women don't keep their appointments? It's their function in life."

Pamela laughed. His words had given her a pleasing sense of importance and power. "Poor Guy!" she said through her laughter, and her eyes were insolently bright.

"You little hypocrite!"

"I'm not," she protested. "I really *am* sorry for him."

"A little hypocrite *and* a little devil," was his verdict. He rose to his feet. "If you could see your own eyes now! But *andiamo*." He held out his hand to help her up. "I'm beginning to be rather afraid of you."

"What nonsense!" She was delighted. They walked together towards the door.

Fanning made the driver go out by the Appian

Way. "For the sake of your education," he explained, pointing at the ruined tombs, "which we can continue, thank heaven, in comfort, and at twenty miles an hour."

Leaning back luxuriously in her corner, Pamela laughed. "But I must say," she had to admit, "it is really rather lovely."

From Albano the road mounted through the chestnut woods towards Rocca di Papa. A few miles brought them to a turning on the right; the car came to a halt.

"It's barred," said Pamela, looking out of the window. Fanning had taken out his pocket-book and was hunting among the bank-notes and the old letters. "The road's private," he explained. "They ask for your card—heaven knows why. The only trouble being, of course, that I've never possessed such a thing as a visiting-card in my life. Still, I generally have one or two belonging to other people. Ah, here we are! Good!" he produced two pieces of pasteboard. A gatekeeper had appeared and was waiting by the door of the car. "Shall we say we're Count Keyserling?" said Fanning, handing her the count's card. "Or alternatively," he read from the other, "that we're Herbert Watson, Funeral Furnisher, Funerals conducted with Efficiency and Reverence, Motor Hearses for use in every part of the Country." He shook his head. "The last relic of my poor old friend Tom Hatchard. Died last year. I had to bury him. Poor Tom! On the whole I think we'd better be Herbert Watson. *Ecco!*" He handed out the card; the man saluted and went to open the gate. "But give me back Count Keyserling." Fanning stretched out his hand. "He'll come in useful another time."

The car started and went roaring up the zig-zag ascent. Lying back in her corner, Pamela laughed and laughed, inextinguishably.

"But what *is* the joke?" he asked.

She didn't know herself. Mr. Watson and the Count had only been a pretext; this enormous laughter, which they had released, sprang from some other, deeper source. And perhaps it was a mere accident that it should be laughter at all. Another pretext, a different finger on the trigger, and it might have been tears, or anger, or singing "Constantinople" at the top of her voice—anything.

She was limp when they reached the top. Fanning made her sit down where she could see the view and himself went off to order cold drinks at the bar of the little inn that had once been the monastery of Monte Cavo.

Pamela sat where he had left her. The wooded slopes fell steeply away beneath her, down, down to the blue shining of the Alban Lake; and that toy palace perched on the hill beyond was the Pope's, that tiny city in a picture-book, Marino. Beyond a dark ridge on the left the round eye of Nemi looked up from its crater. Far off, behind Albano an expanse of blue steel, burnished beneath the sun, was the

Tyrrhenian, and flat like the sea, but golden with ripening corn and powdered goldenly with a haze of dust, the Campagna stretched away from the feet of the subsiding hills, away and up towards a fading horizon, on which the blue ghosts of mountains floated on a level with her eyes. In the midst of the expanse a half-seen golden chaos was Rome. Through the haze the dome of St. Peter's shone faintly in the sun with a glitter as of muted glass. There was an enormous silence, sad, sad but somehow consoling. A sacred silence. And yet when, coming up from behind her, Fanning broke it, his voice, for Pamela, committed no iconoclasms for it seemed, in the world of her feelings, to belong to the silence, it was made, as it were, of the same intimate and friendly substance. He squatted down on his heels beside her, laying a hand on her shoulder to steady himself.

"What a panorama of space and time!" he said. "So many miles, such an expanse of centuries! You can still walk on the paved road that led to the temple here. The generals used to march up sometimes in triumph. With elephants."

The silence enveloped them again, bringing them together; and they were alone and as though conspiratorially isolated in an atmosphere of solemn amorousness.

"*I signori son serviti,*" said a slightly ironic voice behind them.

"That's our drinks," said Fanning. "Perhaps

we'd better . . ." He got up and, as he unbent them, his knees cracked stiffly. He stooped to rub them, for they ached; his joints were old. "Fool!" he said to himself, and decided that to-morrow he'd go to Venice. She was too young, too dangerously and perversely fresh.

They drank their lemonade in silence. Pamela's face wore an expression of grave serenity which it touched and flattered and moved him to see. Still, he was a fool to be touched and flattered and moved.

"Let's go for a bit of a stroll," he said, when they had slaked their thirst. She got up without a word, obediently, as though she had become his slave.

It was breathless under the trees and there was a smell of damp, hot greenness, a hum and flicker of insects in the probing slants of sunlight. But in the open spaces the air of the heights was quick and nimble, in spite of the sun; the broom-flower blazed among the rocks; and round the bushes where the honeysuckle had clambered, there hung invisible islands of perfume, cool and fresh in the midst of the hot sea of bracken smell. Pamela moved here and there with little exclamations of delight, pulling at the tough sprays of honeysuckle. "Oh, look!" she called to him in her rapturous voice. "Come and look!"

"I'm looking," he shouted back across the intervening space. "With a telescope. With the eye of faith," he corrected; for she had moved out of sight. He sat down on a smooth rock and lighted a cigarette. Venice, he reflected, would be rather boring at this particular season. In a few minutes Pamela came back to him, flushed, with a great bunch of honeysuckle between her hands.

"You know, you ought to have come," she said reproachfully. "There were such *lovely* pieces I couldn't reach."

Fanning shook his head. "He also serves who only sits and smokes," he said and made room for her on the stone beside him. "And what's more," he went on, " 'let Austin have his swink to him reserved.' Yes, let him. How wholeheartedly I've always agreed with Chaucer's Monk! Besides, you seem to forget, my child, that I'm an old, old gentleman." He was playing the safe, the prudent part. Perhaps if he played it hard enough, it wouldn't be necessary to go to Venice.

Pamela paid no attention to what he was saying. "Would you like this one for your buttonhole, Miles?" she asked, holding up a many-trumpeted flower. It was the first time she had called him by his christian name and the accomplishment of this much-meditated act of daring made her blush. "I'll stick it in," she added, leaning forward, so that he shouldn't see her reddened cheeks, till her face was almost touching his coat.

Near and thus offered (for it was an offer, he had no doubt of that, a deliberate offer) why shouldn't he take this lovely, this terribly and desperately tempting freshness? It was a matter of stretching out one's hands. But no; it would be too insane. She was near, this warm young flesh, this scent of her hair, near and offered—with what an innocent perversity, what a touchingly ingenuous and uncomprehending shamelessness! But he sat woodenly still, feeling all of a sudden as he had felt when, a lanky boy, he had been too shy, too utterly terrified, in spite of his longings, to kiss that Jenny—what on earth was her name? —that Jenny Something-or-Other he had danced the polka with at Uncle Fred's one Christmas, how many centuries ago!—and yet only yesterday, only this instant.

"There!" said Pamela and drew back. Her cheeks had had time to cool a little.

"Thank you." There was a silence.

"Do you know," she said at last, efficiently, "you've got a button loose on your coat."

He fingered the hanging button. "What a damning proof of celibacy!"

"If only I had a needle and thread. . . ."

"Don't make your offer too lightly. If you knew what a quantity of unmended stuff I've got at home. . . ."

"I'll come and do it all to-morrow," she promised, feeling delightfully protective and important.

"Beware," he said. "I'll take you at your word. It's sweated labour."

"I don't mind. I'll come."

"Punctually at ten-thirty, then." He had forgotten about Venice. "I shall be a ruthless taskmaster."

Nemi was already in shadow when they walked

back; but the higher slopes were transfigured with
the setting sunlight. Pamela halted at a twist of the
path and turned back towards the Western sky.
Looking up, Fanning saw her standing there, goldenly flushed, the colours of her skin, her hair, her
dress, the flowers in her hands, supernaturally heightened and intensified in the almost level light.

"I think this is the most lovely place I've ever
seen." Her voice was solemn with a natural piety.
"But you're not looking," she added in a different
tone, reproachfully.

"I'm looking at you," he answered. After all, if he
stopped in time, it didn't matter his behaving like a
fool—it didn't finally matter and, meanwhile, was
very agreeable.

An expression of impertinent mischief chased away
the solemnity from her face. "Trying to see my ears
again?" she asked; and, breaking off a honeysuckle
blossom, she threw it down in his face, then turned
and ran up the steep path.

"Don't imagine I'm going to pursue," he called
after her. "The Pan and Syrinx business is a winter
pastime. Like football."

Her laughter came down to him from among the
trees; he followed the retreating sound. Pamela
waited for him at the top of the hill and they walked
back together towards the inn.

"Aren't there any ruins here?" she asked. "I mean,
for my education."

He shook his head. "The Young Pretender's

brother pulled them all down and built a monastery with them. For the Passionist Fathers," he added after a little pause. "I feel rather like a Passionist Father myself at the moment." They walked on without speaking, enveloped by the huge, the amorously significant silence.

But a few minutes later, at the dinner table, they were exuberantly gay. The food was well cooked, the wine, an admirable Falernian. Fanning began to talk about his early loves. Vaguely at first, but later, under Pamela's questioning, with an ever-increasing wealth of specific detail. They were indiscreet, impudent questions, which at ordinary times she couldn't have uttered, or at least have only despairingly forced out, with a suicide's determination. But she was a little tipsy now, tipsy with the wine and her own laughing exultation; she rapped them out easily, without a tremor. "As though you were the immortal Sigmund himself," he assured her, laughing. Her impudence and that knowledgeable, scientific ingenuousness amused him, rather perversely; he told her everything she asked.

When she had finished with his early loves, she questioned him about the opium. Fanning described his private universes and that charming nurse who had looked after him while he was being disintoxicated. He went on to talk about the black poverty he'd been reduced to by the drug. "Because you can't do journalism or write novels in the other world," he explained. "At least I never could." And he told her of the debts he still owed and of his present arrangements with his publishers.

Almost suddenly the night was cold and Fanning became aware that the bottle had been empty for a long time. He threw away the stump of his cigar. "Let's go." They took their seats and the car set off, carrying with it the narrow world of form and colour created by its head-lamps. They were alone in the darkness of their padded box. An hour before Fanning had decided that he would take this opportunity to kiss her. But he was haunted suddenly by the memory of an Australian who had once complained to him of the sufferings of a young colonial in England. "In Sydney," he had said, "when I get into a taxi with a nice girl, I know exactly what to do. And I know exactly what to do when I'm in an American taxi. But when I apply my knowledge in London— God, isn't there a row!" How vulgar and stupid it all was! Not merely a fool, but a vulgar, stupid fool. He sat unmoving in his corner. When the lights of Rome were round them, he took her hand and kissed it.

"Good-night."

She thanked him. "I've had the loveliest day." But her eyes were puzzled and unhappy. Meeting them, Fanning suddenly regretted his self-restraint, wished that he had been stupid and vulgar. And after all would it have been so stupid and vulgar? You could make any action seem anything you liked, from saintly to disgusting, by describing it in the appropriate words. But his regrets had come too late. Here was her hotel. He drove home to his solitude feeling exceedingly depressed.

VI

June 14th. Spent the morning with M., who lives in a house belonging to a friend of his who is a Catholic and lives in Rome, M. says, because he likes to get his popery straight from the horse's mouth. A nice house, old, standing just back from the Forum, which I said I thought was like a rubbish heap and he agreed with me, in spite of my education, and said he always preferred live dogs to dead lions and thinks it's awful the way the Fascists are pulling down nice ordinary houses and making holes to find more of these beastly pillars and things. I sewed on a lot of buttons, etc., as he's living in only two rooms on the ground floor and the servants are on their holiday, so he eats out and an old woman comes to clean up in the afternoons, but doesn't do any mending, which meant a lot for me, but I liked doing it, in spite of the darning, because he sat with me all the time, sometimes talking, sometimes just working. When he's writing or sitting with his pen in his hand thinking, his face is quite still and *terribly* serious and far, far away, as though he were a picture, or more like some sort of not human person, a sort of angel, if one can imagine them without nightdresses and long hair, really rather frightening, so that one longed to shout or throw a reel of cotton at him so as to change him back again into a man. He has very beautiful hands, rather long and bony, but strong. Sometimes, after he'd sat thinking for a long time, he'd get up and walk about the room, frowning and looking kind of angry, which was still more terrifying—sitting there while he walked up and down quite close to me, as though he were absolutely alone. But one time he suddenly stopped his walking up and down and said how profusely he apologized for his toes, because I was darning, and it was really very wonderful to see him suddenly changed back from that picture-angel sort of creature into a human being. Then he sat down by me and said he'd been spending the morning wrestling with the problem of speaking the truth in books; so I said, but haven't you always spoken it? because that always seemed to me the chief point of M.'s books. But he said, not much, because most of it was quite unspeakable in our world, as we found it too shocking and humiliating. So I said, all the same I didn't see why it shouldn't be spoken, and he said, nor did he in theory, but in practice he didn't want to be lynched. And he said, look for example at those advertisements in American magazines with the photos and life stories of people with unpleasant breath. So I said, yes, aren't they simply *too* awful. Because they really do make one shudder. And he said, precisely, there you are, and they're so successful because every one thinks them so perfectly awful. They're outraged by them, he said, just as you're outraged and they rush off and buy the stuff in sheer terror, because they're so terrified of being an outrage physically to other people. And he said, that's only one small sample of all the class of truths, pleasant and unpleasant, that you can't speak, except in scientific books, but that doesn't count, because you deliberately leave your feelings outside in the cloak-room when you're being scientific. And just because they're unspeakable, we pretend they're unimportant, but they aren't, on the contrary, they're terribly important and he said, you've only got to examine your memory quite sincerely for five minutes to realize it, and of course he's quite right. When I think of Miss Poole giving me piano lessons—but no, really, one *can't* write these things, and yet one obviously ought to, because they *are* so important, the humiliating physical facts, both pleasant and unpleasant (though I must say, most of the ones I can think of seem to be unpleasant), so important in all human relationships, he says, even in love, which is really rather awful, but of course one must admit it. And M. said it would take a whole generation of being shocked and humiliated and lynching the shockers and humiliaters before people could settle down to listening to that sort of truth calmly, which they did do, he says, at certain times in the past, at any rate much more so than now. And he says that when they can listen to it completely calmly, the world will be quite different from what it is now, so I asked, in what way? but he said he couldn't clearly imagine, only he knew it would be different. After that he went back to his table and wrote very quickly for about half an hour without stopping, and I longed to ask him if he'd been writing the truth and if so,

what about, but I didn't have the nerve, which was
stupid.

We lunched at our usual place, which I really don't
much like, as who wants to look at fat business-men
and farmers from the country simply *drinking* spaghetti? even if the spaghetti *is* good, but M. prefers
it to the big places, because he says that in Rome one
must do as the Romans do, not as the Americans.
Still, I must say I do like looking at people who dress
well and have good manners and nice jewels and
things, which I told him, so he said all right, we'd go
to Valadier to-morrow to see how the rich ate maca-
roni, which made me wretched, as it looked as though
I'd been cadging, and of course that's the last thing
in the world I meant to do, to make him waste a lot of
money on me, particularly after what he told me yesterday about his debts and what he made on the aver-
age, which still seems to me shockingly little, considering who he is, so I said no, wouldn't he lunch with
me at Valadier's and he laughed and said it was the
first time he'd heard of a gigolo of fifty being taken
out by a woman of twenty. That rather upset me—the
way it seemed to bring what we are to each other on
to the wrong level, making it all a sort of joke and
sniggery, like something in *Punch*. Which is hateful,
I can't bear it. And I have the feeling that he does it
on purpose, as a kind of protection, because he doesn't
want to care too much, and that's why he's always
saying he's so old, which is all nonsense, because
you're only as old as you feel, and sometimes I even

feel older than he does, like when he gets so amused and interested with little boys in the street playing that game of sticking out your fingers and calling a number, or when he talks about that awful old Dickens. Which I told him, but he only laughed and said age is a circle and you grow into a lot of the things you grew out of, because the whole world is a fried whiting with its tail in its mouth, which only confirms what I said about his saying he was old being all nonsense. Which I told him and he said, quite right, he only *said* he felt old when he *wished* that he felt old. Which made me see still more clearly that it was just a defence. A defence of *me*, I suppose, and all that sort of nonsense. What I'd have liked to say, only I didn't, was that I don't want to be defended, particularly if being defended means his defending himself against me and making stupid jokes about gigolos and old gentlemen. Because I think he really does rather care underneath—from the way he looks at me sometimes—and he'd like to say so and act so, but he won't on principle, which is really against all *his* principles and some time I *shall* tell him so. I insisted he should lunch with me and in the end he said he would, and then he was suddenly very silent and, I thought, glum and unhappy, and after coffee he said he'd have to go home and write all the rest of the day. So I came back to the hotel and had a rest and wrote this and now it's nearly seven and I feel terribly sad, almost like crying. *Next day.* Rang up Guy and had less difficulty than I expected getting him to forgive

me for yesterday, in fact he almost apologized himself. Danced till 2.15.

June 15th. M. still sad and didn't kiss me when we
met, *on purpose*, which made me angry, it's so humiliating to be defended. He was wearing an open shirt,
like Byron, which suited him; but I told him, you look
like the devil when you're sad (which is true, because
his face ought to move, not be still) and he said that
was what came of feeling and behaving like an angel;
so of course I asked why he didn't behave like a devil,
because in that case he'd look like an angel, and I
preferred his looks to his morals, and then I blushed,
like an idiot. But really it is too stupid that women
aren't supposed to say what they think. Why can't
we say, I like you, or whatever it is, without being
thought a kind of monster, if we say it first, and even
thinking ourselves monsters? Because one ought to
say what one thinks and do what one likes, or else one
becomes like Aunt Edith, hippo-ish and dead inside.
Which is after all what M.'s constantly saying in his
books, so he oughtn't to humiliate me with his beastly
defendings. Lunch at Valadier's was really rather a
bore. Afterwards we went and sat in a church, because
it was so hot, a huge affair full of pink marble and
frescoes and marble babies and gold. M. says that the
modern equivalent is Lyons' Corner House and that
the Jesuits were so successful because they gave the
poor a chance of feeling what it was like to live in a
palace, or something better than a palace, because he
says the chief difference between a Corner House and

the State rooms at Buckingham Palace is that the
Corner House is so much more sumptuous, almost as
sumptuous as these Jesuit churches. I asked him if he
believed in God and he said he believed in a great many
gods, it depended on what he was doing, or being, or
feeling at the moment. He said he believed in Apollo
when he was working and in Bacchus when he was drinking, and in Buddha when he felt depressed, and in
Venus when he was making love, and in the Devil when
he was afraid or angry, and in the Categorical Imperative, when he had to do his duty. I asked him which he
believed in now and he said he didn't quite know, but
he thought it was the Categorical Imperative, which
really made me furious, so I answered that I only believed in the Devil and Venus, which made him laugh
and he said I looked as though I were going to jump
off the Eiffel Tower, and I was just going to say what
I thought of his hippo-ishness. I mean I'd really made
up my mind, when a most horrible old verger rushed
up and said we must leave the church, because it seems
the Pope doesn't allow you to be in a church with
bare arms, which is really *too* indecent. But M. said
that after all it wasn't surprising, because every god
has to protect himself against hostile gods and the
gods of bare skin *are* hostile to the gods of souls and
clothes, and he made me stop in front of a shop window where there were some mirrors and said, you can
see for yourself, and I must say I really did look very
nice in that pale green linen which goes so awfully
well with the skin, when one's a bit sunburnt. But he

said, it's not merely a question of seeing, you must touch too, so I stroked my arms and said yes, they were nice and smooth, and he said, precisely, and then he stroked my arm very lightly, like a moth crawling, agonizingly creepy but delicious, once or twice, looking very serious and attentive, as though he were tuning a piano, which made me laugh, and I said I supposed he was experimenting to see if the Pope was in the right, and then he gave me the most horrible pinch and said, yes, the Pope was quite right and I ought to be muffled in Jaeger from top to toe. But I was so angry with the pain, because he pinched me really terribly, that I just rushed off without saying anything and jumped into a cab that was passing and drove straight to the hotel. But I was so wretched by the time I got there that I started crying in the lift and the lift man said he hoped I hadn't had any *dispiacere di famiglia*, which made me laugh and that made the crying much worse, and then I suddenly thought of Clare and felt such a horrible beast, so I lay on my bed and simply howled for about an hour, and then I got up and wrote a letter and sent one of the hotel boys with it to M.'s address, saying I was so sorry and would he come at once. But he didn't come, not for hours and hours, and it was simply too awful, because I thought he was offended, or despising, because I'd been such a fool, and I wondered whether he really did like me at all and whether this defending theory wasn't just my imagination. But at last, when I'd quite given him up and was so miserable I didn't know what I should do, he suddenly appeared—because he'd only that moment gone back to the house and found my note—and was too wonderfully sweet to me, and said he was so sorry, but he'd been on edge (though he didn't say why, but I know now that the defending theory wasn't just imagination) and I said I was so sorry and I cried, but I was happy, and then we laughed because it had all been so stupid and then M. quoted a bit of Homer which meant that after they'd eaten and drunk they wept for their friends and after they'd wept a little they went to sleep, so we went out and had dinner and after dinner we went and danced, and he dances really very well, but we stopped before midnight, because he said the noise of the jazz would drive him crazy. He was perfectly sweet, but though he didn't say anything sniggery, I could feel he was on the defensive all the time, sweetly and friendlily on the defensive, and when he said good-night he only kissed my hand.

June 18th. Stayed in bed till lunch re-reading *The Return of Eurydice*. I understand Joan so well now, better and better, she's *so* like me in all she feels and thinks. M. went to Tivoli for the day to see some Italian friends who have a house there. What is he like with other people, I wonder? Got two tickets for the fireworks to-morrow night, the hotel porter says they'll be good, because it's the first Girandola since the War. Went to the Villa Borghese in the afternoon for my education, to give M. a surprise when he comes back, and I must say some of the pictures and statues were very lovely, but the most awful looking fat man would follow me round all the time and finally the old beast even had the impertinence to speak to me, so I just said, *Lei è un porco*, which I must say was very effective. But it's extraordinary how things do just depend on looks and being sympathique, because if he hadn't looked such a pig, I shouldn't have thought him so piggish, which shows again what rot hippo-ism is. Went to bed early and finished *Eurydice*. This is the fifth time I've read it.

VII

"Oh, it was marvellous before the War, the Girandola. Really marvellous."

"But then what wasn't *marvellous* before the War?" said Pamela sarcastically. These references to a Golden Age in which she had had no part always annoyed her.

Fanning laughed. "Another one in the eye for the aged gentleman!"

There, he had slipped back again behind his defences! She did not answer for fear of giving him some excuse to dig himself in, impregnably. This hateful bantering with feelings! They walked on in silence. The night was breathlessly warm; the sounds of brassy music came to them faintly through the dim enormous noise of a crowd that thickened with every step they took towards the Piazza del Popolo. In the end they had to shove their way by main force.

Sunk head over ears in this vast sea of animal contacts, animal smells and noise, Pamela was afraid. "Isn't it awful?" she said, looking up at him over her shoulder; and she shuddered. But at the same time she rather liked her fear, because it seemed in some way to break down the barriers that separated them, to bring him closer to her—close with a physical closeness of protective contact that was also, increasingly, a closeness of thought and feeling.

"You're all right," he reassured her through the tumult. He was standing behind her, encircling her with his arms. "I won't let you be squashed"; and as he spoke he fended off the menacing lurch of a large back. "*Ignorante!*" he shouted at it.

A terrific explosion interrupted the distant selections from *Rigoletto* and the sky was suddenly full of coloured light; the Girandola had begun. A wave of impatience ran through the advancing crowd; they were violently pushed and jostled. But, "It's all right," Fanning kept repeating, "it's all right." They were squeezed together in a staggering embrace. Pamela was terrified, but it was with a kind of swooning pleasure that she shut her eyes and abandoned herself limply in his arms.

"*Ma piano!*" shouted Fanning at the nearest jostlers. "*Piano!*" and "'Sblood!" he said in English, for he had the affectation of using literary oaths. "Hell and Death!" But in the tumult his words were as though unspoken. He was silent; and suddenly, in the midst of that heaving chaos of noise and rough contacts, of movement and heat and smell, suddenly he became aware that his lips were almost touching her hair, and that under his right hand was the firm resilience of her breast. He hesitated for a moment on the threshold of his sensuality, then averted his face, shifted the position of his hand.

"At last!"

The haven to which their tickets admitted them was a little garden on the western side of the Piazza, opposite the Pincio and the source of the fireworks. The place was crowded, but not oppressively. Fanning was tall enough to overlook the interposed heads, and when Pamela had climbed on to a little parapet that separated one terrace of the garden from another, she too could see perfectly.

"But you'll let me lean on you," she said, laying a hand on his shoulder, "because there's a fat woman next to me who's steadily squeezing me off. I think she's expanding with the heat."

"And she almost certainly understands English. So for heaven's sake . . ."

A fresh volley of explosions from the other side of the great square interrupted him and drowned the answering mockery of her laughter. "Ooh! Ooh!" the crowd was moaning in a kind of amorous agony. Magical flowers in a delirium of growth, the rockets mounted on their slender stalks and, ah! high up above the Pincian Hill, dazzlingly, deafeningly, in a bunch of stars and a thunder-clap, they blossomed.

"Isn't it marvellous?" said Pamela looking down

at him with shining eyes. "Oh God!" she added, in another voice. "She's expanding again. Help!" And for a moment she was on the verge of falling. She leaned on him so heavily that he had to make an effort not to be pushed sideways. She managed to straighten herself up again into equilibrium.

"I've got you in case . . ." He put his arm round her knees to steady her.

"Shall I see if I can puncture the old beast with a pin?" And Fanning knew, by the tone of her voice, that she was genuinely prepared to make the experiment.

"If you do," he said, "I shall leave you to be lynched alone."

Pamela felt his arm tighten a little about her thighs. "Coward!" she mocked and pulled his hair.

"Martyrdom's not in my line," he laughed back. "Not even martyrdom for your sake." But her youth was a perversity, her freshness a kind of provocative vice. He had taken a step across that supernatural threshold. He had given—after all, why not?—a certain license to his desires. Amid their multitudinous uncoiling, his body seemed to be coming to a new and obscure life of its own. When the time came he would revoke the license, step back again into the daily world.

There was another bang, another, and the obelisk at the centre of the Piazza leapt out sharp and black against apocalypse after apocalypse of jewelled light. And through the now flushed, now pearly-brilliant, now emerald-shining smoke-clouds, a pine tree, a palm, a stretch of grass emerged, like strange unearthly visions of pine and palm and grass, from the darkness of the else invisible gardens.

There was an interval of mere lamplight—like sobriety, said Fanning, between two pipes of opium, like daily life after an ecstasy. And perhaps, he was thinking, the time to step back again had already come. "If only one could live without any lucid intervals," he concluded.

"I don't see why not." She spoke with a kind of provocative defiance, as though challenging him to contradict her. Her heart beat very fast, exultantly. "I mean, why shouldn't it be fireworks all the time?"

"Because it just isn't, that's all. Unhappily." It was time to step back again; but he didn't step back.

"Well, then it's a case of damn the intervals and enjoy . . . Oh!" She started. That prodigious bang had sent a large red moon sailing almost slowly into the sky. It burst into a shower of meteors that whistled as they fell, expiringly.

Fanning imitated their plaintive noise. "Sad, sad," he commented. "Even the fireworks can be sad."

She turned on him fiercely. "Only because you want them to be sad. Yes, you want them to be. Why do you want them to be sad?"

Yes, why? It was a pertinent question. She felt his arm tighten again round her knees and was triumphant. He was defending himself no more, he was listening to those oracles. But at the root of his deliberate recklessness, its contradiction and its cause, his sadness obscurely persisted. "But I *don't* want them to be sad," he protested.

Another garden of rockets began to blossom. Laughing, triumphant, Pamela laid her hand on his head.

"I feel so superior up here," she said.

"On a pedestal, what?" He laughed. " *'Guardami ben; ben son, ben son Beatrice!'* "

"Such a comfort you're not bald," she said, her fingers in his hair. "That must be a great disadvantage of pedestals—I mean, seeing the baldness of the men down below."

"But the great advantage of pedestals, as I now suddenly see for the first time . . ." Another explosion covered his voice. ". . . make it possible. . . ." Bang!

"Oh, look!" A blueish light was brightening, brightening.

". . . possible for even the baldest . . ." There was a continuous uninterrupted rattle of detonations. Fanning gave it up. What he had meant to say was that pedestals gave even the baldest men unrivalled opportunities for pinching the idol's legs.

"What were you saying?" she shouted through the battle.

"Nothing," he yelled back. He had meant, of course, to suit the action to the word, playfully. But the fates had decided otherwise and he wasn't really sorry. For he was tired; he had realized it almost suddenly. All this standing. He was no good at standing nowadays.

A cataract of silver fire was pouring down the slopes of the Pincian Hill, and the shining smoke-clouds rolled away from it like the spray from a tumbling river. And suddenly, above it, the eagle of Savoy emerged from the darkness, enormous, perched on the lictor's axe and rods. There was applause and patriotic music. Then, gradually, the brightness of the cataract grew dim; the sources of its silver streaming were one by one dried up. The eagle moulted its shining plumage, the axe and rods faded, faded and at last were gone. Lit faintly by only the common lamp-light, the smoke drifted slowly away towards the north. A spasm of motion ran through the huge crowd in the square below them. The show was over.

"But I feel," said Pamela, as they shoved their way back towards the open streets, "I feel as though the rockets were still popping off inside me." And she began to sing to herself as she walked.

Fanning made no comment. He was thinking of that Girandola he'd seen with Alice and Tony, and Laurina Frescobaldi—was it in 1907 or 1908? Tony was an ambassador now, and Alice was dead, and one of Laurina's sons (he recalled the expression of despair on that worn, but still handsome face, when she had told him yesterday, at Tivoli) was already old enough to be getting housemaids into trouble.

"Not only rockets," Pamela went on, interrupting her singing, "but even catherine wheels. I feel all catherine-wheely. You know, like when one's a little drunk." And she went on again with "Old Man River," tipsily happy and excited.

The crowd grew thinner around them and at last they were almost alone. Pamela's singing abruptly ceased. Here, in the open, in the cool of the dark night it had suddenly become inappropriate, a little shameful. She glanced anxiously at her companion; had he too remarked that inappropriateness, been shocked by it? But Fanning had noticed nothing; she wished he had. Head bent, his hands behind his back, he was walking at her side, but in another universe.—When had his spirit gone away from her, and why? She didn't know, hadn't noticed. Those inward fireworks, that private festival of exultation had occupied her whole attention. She had been too excitedly happy with being in love to be able to think of the object of that love. But now, abruptly sobered, she had become aware of him again, repentantly at first, and then, as she realized his new remoteness, with a sinking of the heart. What had happened in these few moments? She was on the point of addressing him, then checked herself. Her apprehension grew and grew till it became a kind of terrified certainty that he'd never loved her at all, that he'd suddenly begun to hate her. But why, but why? They walked on.

"How lovely it is here!" she said at last. Her voice was timid and unnatural. "And so deliciously cool."

They had emerged on to the embankment of the Tiber. Above the river, a second invisible river of air flowed softly through the hot night. "Shall we stop for a moment?" He nodded without speaking. "I mean, only if you want to," she added. He nodded again.

They stood, leaning on the parapet, looking down at the black water. There was a long, long silence. Pamela waited for him to say something, to make a gesture; but he did not stir, the word never came. It was as though he were at the other end of the world. She felt almost sick with unhappiness. Heart-beat after heart-beat, the silence prolonged itself.

Fanning was thinking of to-morrow's journey. How he hated the train! And in this heat. . . . But it was necessary. The wicked flee, and in this case the fleeing would be an act of virtue—painful. Was it love? Or just an itch of desire, of the rather crazy, dirty desire of an aging man? "*A cinquant' anni si diventa un po' pazzo.*" He heard his own voice speaking, laughingly, mournfully, to Laurina. "*Pazzo e porco. Si, anch' io divento un porco. Le minorenni —a cinquant' anni, sa sono un ossessione. Proprio un' ossessione.*" Was that all—just an obsession of crazy desire? Or was it love? Or wasn't there any difference, was it just a question of names and approving or disapproving tones of voice? What was certain was that you could be as desperately unhappy when you were robbed of your crazy desire as when you were robbed of your love. A *porco* suffers as much as Dante. And perhaps Beatrice too was lovely, in Dante's memory, with the perversity of youth, the shamelessness of innocence, the vice of freshness. Still, the wicked flee, the wicked flee. If only he'd had the strength of mind to flee before! A touch made him start. Pamela had taken his hand.

"Miles!" Her voice was strained and abnormal. Fanning turned towards her and was almost frightened by the look of determined despair he saw on her face. The Eiffel Tower . . . "Miles!"

"What is it?"

"Why don't you speak to me?"

He shrugged his shoulders. "I didn't happen to be feeling very loquacious. For a change," he added, self-mockingly, in the hope (he knew it for a vain one) of being able to turn away her desperate attack with a counter-attack of laughter.

She ignored his counter-attack. "Why do you shut yourself away from me like this?" she asked. "Why do you hate me."

"But, my sweet child . . ."

"Yes, you hate me. You shut me away. Why are you so cruel, Miles?" Her voice broke; she was crying. Lifting his hand, she kissed it, passionately, despairingly. "I love you so much, Miles. I love you." His hand was wet with her tears when, almost by force, he managed to draw it away from her.

He put his arm round her, comfortingly. But he was annoyed as well as touched, annoyed by her despairing determination, by the way she had made up her mind to jump off the Eiffel Tower, screwed up her courage turn by turn. And now she was jumping —but how gracelessly! The way he had positively had to struggle for his hand! There was something forced and unnatural about the whole scene. She was being a character in fiction. But characters in fiction suffer. He patted her shoulder, he made consolatory murmurs. Consoling her for being in love with him! But the idea of explaining and protesting and being lucidly reasonable was appalling to him at the moment, absolutely appalling. He hoped that she'd just permit herself to be consoled and ask no further questions, just leave the whole situation comfortably inarticulate. But his hope was again disappointed.

"Why do you hate me, Miles?" she insisted.

"But, Pamela . . ."

"Because you did care a little, you did. I mean, I could see you cared. And now, suddenly . . . What have I done, Miles?"

"But nothing, my child, nothing." He could not keep a note of exasperation out of his voice. If only she'd allow him to be silent!

"Nothing? But I can hear from the way you speak that there's something." She returned to her old refrain. "Because you did care, Miles; a little, you did." She looked up at him, but he had moved away from her, he had averted his eyes towards the street. "You did, Miles."

Oh, God! he was groaning to himself, God! And aloud (for she had made his silence untenable, she had driven him out into articulateness), "I cared too much," he said. "It would be so easy to do something stupid and irreparable, something mad, yes and bad, bad. I like you too much in other ways to want to run that risk. Perhaps, if I were twenty years younger. . . . But I'm too old. It wouldn't do. And you're too young, you can't really understand, you . . . Oh, thank God, there's a taxi." And he darted forward, waving and shouting. Saved! But when they had shut themselves into the cab, he found that the new situation was even more perilous than the old.

"Miles!" A flash of lamplight through the window of the cab revealed her face to him. His words had consoled her; she was smiling, was trying to look happy; but under the attempted happiness her expression was more desperately determined than ever. She was not yet at the bottom of her Tower. "Miles!" And sliding across the seat towards him, she threw her arms round his neck and kissed him. "Take me, Miles," she said, speaking in quick abrupt little spurts, as though she were forcing the words out with violence against a resistance. He recognized the suicide's voice, despairing, strained, and at the same time flat, lifeless. "Take me. If you want me. . . ."

Fanning tried to protest, to disengage himself, gently, from her embrace.

"But I want you to take me, Miles," she insisted. "I want you. . . ." She kissed him again, she pressed herself against his hard body. "I want you, Miles. Even if it is stupid and mad," she added in another little spurt of desperation, making answer to the expression on his face, to the words she wouldn't permit him to utter. "And it isn't. I mean, love isn't stupid or mad. And even if it were, I don't care. Yes, I want to be stupid and mad. Even if it were to kill me. So take me, Miles." She kissed him again. "Take me."

He turned away his mouth from those soft lips. She was forcing him back across the threshold. His body was uneasy with awakenings and supernatural dawn.

Held up by a tram at the corner of a narrow street, the cab was at a standstill. With quick strong gestures Fanning unclasped her arms from round his neck and, taking her two hands in his, he kissed first one and then the other. "Good-bye, Pamela," he whispered and, throwing open the door, he was half out of the cab before she realized what he was doing.

"But what are you doing, Miles? Where . . ." The door slammed. He thrust some money into the driver's hand and almost ran. Pamela rose to her feet to follow him, but the cab started with a sudden jerk that threw her off her balance, and she fell back on to the seat.

"Miles!" she called, and then, "Stop!"

But the driver either didn't hear, or else paid no attention. She did not call again, but sat, covering her face with her hands, crying and feeling so agonizingly unhappy that she thought she would die of it.

VIII

"By the time you receive this letter, I shall be—no, not dead, Pamela, though I know how thrilled and proud you'd be, through your temporary inconsolability, if I were to blow my brains out—not dead, but (what will be almost worse in these dog-days) in the train, bound for some anonymous refuge. Yes, a refuge, as though you were my worst enemy. Which in fact you almost are at the moment, for the good reason that you're acting as your own enemy. If I were less fond of you, I'd stay and join forces with you against yourself. And, frankly, I wish I were less fond of you. Do you know how desirable you are? Not yet, I suppose, not consciously, in spite of Prof. Krafft-Ebbing and the novels of Miles F. You can't yet know what a terrible army with banners you are, you and your eyes and your laughter and your impertinent breasts, like La Maja's, and those anti-educational ears in ambush under the hair. You can't know. But I know. Only too well. Just *how* well you'll realize, perhaps, fifteen or twenty years from now. For a time will come when the freshness of young bodies, the ingenuousness of young minds will begin to strike you as a scandal of shining beauty and attractiveness, and then finally as a kind of maddeningly alluring perversity, as the exhibition of a kind of irresistibly dangerous vice. The madness of the desirer—for middle-aged desires are mostly more or less mad desires—comes off on the desired object, staining it, degrading it. Which isn't agreeable if you happen to be fond of the object, as well as desiring. Dear object, let's be a little reasonable—oh, entirely against all my principles; I accept all the reproaches you made me the other day. But what are principles for but to be gone against in moments of crisis? And this *is* a moment of crisis. Consider: I'm thirty years older than you are; and even if one doesn't look one's age, one is one's age, somehow, somewhere; and even if one doesn't feel it, fifty's always fifty and twenty-one's twenty-one. And when you've considered that, let me put a few questions. First: are you prepared to be a disreputable woman? To which, of course, you answer yes, because you don't care two pins about what the old cats say. But I put another question: Do you know, by experience, what it's like to be a disreputable woman? And you must answer, no. Whereupon I retort: If you can't answer yes to the second, you've got no right to answer yes to the first. And I don't intend to give you the opportunity of answering yes to the second question. Which is all pure Podsnapism. But there are certain circumstances in which Podsnap is quite right.

"Sweet Pamela, believe me when I say it would be fatal. For when you say you love me, what do you mean? Who and what is it you love? I'll tell you. You love the author of *Eurydice* and of all those portraits of yourself he's filled his books with. You love the celebrated man, who was not only unsnubbing and attentive, but obviously admiring. Even before you saw him, you vaguely loved his reputation, and now you love his odd confidences. You love a kind of conversation you haven't heard before. You love a weakness in him which you think you can dominate and protect. You love—as I, of course, intended you to love—a certain fascinating manner. You even love a rather romantic and still youthful appearance. And when I say (which as yet, you know, I haven't said) that I love you, what do *I* mean? That I'm amused, and charmed, and flattered, and touched, and puzzled, and affectionate, in a word, a Passionist Father. But chiefly that I find you terribly desirable —an army with banners. Bring these two loves together and what's the result? A manifold disaster. To begin with, the nearer you come to me and the longer you remain with me, the more alien you'll find me, the more fundamentally remote. Inevitably. For you and I are foreigners to one another, foreigners in time. Which is a greater foreignness than the foreignness of space and language. You don't realize it now, because you don't know me—you're only in love, at first sight (like Joan in *Eurydice!*) and, what's more, not really with me, with your imagination of me. When you come to know me better—well, you'll find that you know me much worse. And then one day you'll be attracted by a temporal compatriot. Perhaps, indeed, you're attracted already, only your imagination won't allow you to admit it. What about that long-suffering Guy of yours? Of whom I was, and am, so horribly jealous—jealous with the malignity of a weaker for a stronger rival; for though I seem to hold all the cards at the moment, the ace of trumps is his: he's young. And one day, when you're tired of living at cross-purposes with me, you'll suddenly realize it; you'll perceive that he speaks your language, that he inhabits your world of thought and feeling, that he belongs, in a word, to your nation—that great and terrible nation, which I love and fear and hate, the nation of Youth. In the end, of course, you'll leave the foreigner for the compatriot. But not before you've inflicted a good deal of suffering on every one concerned, including yourself. And meanwhile, what about me? Shall I be still there for you to leave? Who knows? Not I, at any rate. I can no more answer for my future desires than for the Shah of Persia. For my future affection, yes. But it may last (how often, alas, affections do last that way!) only on condition of its object being absent. There are so many friends whom one's fond of when they're not there. Will you be one of them? It's the more possible since, after all, you're just as alien to me as I am to you. My country's called Middle-Ageia and every one who was out of the egg of childhood before 1914 is my compatriot. Through all my desires, shouldn't I also pine to hear my own language, to speak with those who share the national traditions? Of course. But the tragedy of middle-aged life is that its army with banners is hardly ever captained by a compatriot. Passion is divorced from understanding, and the aging man's desire attaches itself with an almost insane violence to precisely those outrageously fresh young bodies that house the most alien souls. Conversely, for the body of an understood and understanding soul, he seldom feels desire. And now, Pamela, suppose that my sentiment of your alienness should come to be stronger (as some time it must) than my desire for the lovely scandal of your young body. What then? This time I can answer; for I am answering for a self that changes very little through every change of circumstances—the self that doesn't intend to put up with more discomfort than it can possibly avoid; the self that, as the Freudians tell us, is homesick for that earthly paradise from which we've all been banished, our mother's womb, the only place on earth where man is genuinely omnipotent, where his every desire is satisfied, where he is perfectly at home and adapted to his surroundings, and therefore perfectly happy. Out of the womb, we're in an unfriendly world, in which our wishes aren't anticipated, where we're no longer magically omnipotent, where we don't fit, where we're not snugly at home. What's to be done in this world? Either face out the reality, fight with it, resignedly or heroically accept to suffer or struggle. Or else flee. In practice even the strongest heroes do a bit of fleeing—away from responsibility into deliberate ignorance, away from uncomfortable fact into imagination. Even the strongest. And conversely even the weakest fleers can make themselves strong. No, not the weakest; that's a mistake. The weakest become day-dreamers, masturbators, paranoiacs. The strong fleer is one who starts with considerable advantages. Take my case. I'm so endowed by nature that I can have a great many of the prizes of life for the asking—success, money in reasonable quantities, love. In other words I'm not entirely out of the womb; I can still, even in the extra-uterine world, have at least some of my desires magically satisfied. To have my wishes fulfilled I don't have to rush off every time to some imaginary womb-substitute. I have the power to construct a womb for myself out of the materials of the real world. But of course it's not a completely perfect and water-tight womb; no post-natal uterus can ever in the nature of things be that. It lets in a lot of unpleasantness and alienness and obstruction to wishes. Which I deal with by flight, systematic flight into unawareness, into deliberate ignorance, into irresponsibility. It's a weakness which is a source of strength. For when you can flee at will and with success (which is only possible if nature has granted you, as she has to me, the possibility of anarchic independence of society), what quantities of energy you save, what an enormous amount of emotional and mental wear and tear is spared you! I flee from business by leaving all my affairs in the hands of lawyers and agents, I flee from criticism (both from the humiliations of misplaced and wrongly motived praise and from the pain of even the most contemptible vermin's blame) by simply not reading what anybody writes of me. I flee from time by living as far as possible only in and for the present. I flee from cold weather by taking the train or ship to places where it's warm. And from women I don't love any more, I flee by just silently vanishing. For, like Palmerston, I never explain and never apologize. I just fade out. I decline to admit their existence. I consign their letters to the waste-paper basket, along with the press cuttings. Simple, crude even, but incredibly effective, if one's ready to be ruthless in one's weakness, as I am. Yes, quite ruthless, Pamela. If my desire grew weary or I felt homesick for the company of my compatriots, I'd just run away, determinedly, however painfully much you might still be in love with me, or your imagination, or your own hurt pride and humiliated self-love. And you, I fancy, would have as little mercy on my desires if they should happen to outlive what you imagine to be your passion for me. So that our love affair, if we were fools enough to embark on it, would be a race towards a series of successive goals—a race through boredom, misunderstanding, disillusion, towards the final winning-post of cruelty and betrayal. Which of us is likely to win the race? The betting, I should say, is about even, with a slight tendency in favour of myself. But there's not going to be a winner or a loser, for the good reason that there's not going to be any race. I'm too fond of you, Pamela, to . . ."

"Miles!"

Fanning started so violently that a drop of ink was jerked from his pen on to the paper. He felt as though his heart had fallen into an awful gulf of emptiness.

"Miles!"

He looked round. Two hands were clutching the bars of the unshuttered window and, as though desperately essaying to emerge from a subterranean captivity, the upper part of a face was peering in, over the high sill, with wide unhappy eyes.

"But Pamela!" There was reproach in his astonishment.

It was to the implied rebuke that she penitently answered. "I couldn't help it, Miles," she said; and, behind the bars, he saw her reddened eyes suddenly brighten and overflow with tears. "I simply had to come." Her voice trembled on the verge of breaking. "*Had* to."

The tears, her words and that unhappy voice were moving. But he didn't want to be moved, he was angry with himself for feeling the emotion, with her for inspiring it. "But, my dear child!" he began, and the reproach in his voice had shrilled to a kind of exasperation—the exasperation of one who feels himself hemmed in and helpless, increasingly helpless, against circumstances. "But I thought we'd settled," he began and broke off. He rose, and walked agitatedly towards the fireplace, agitatedly back again, like a beast in a cage; he was caught, hemmed in between those tearful eyes behind the bars and his own pity, with all those dangerous feelings that have their root in pity. "I thought," he began once more.

But, "Oh!" came her sharp cry, and looking again towards the window he saw that only the two small hands and a pair of straining wrists were visible. The tragical face had vanished.

"Pamela?"

"It's all right." Her voice came rather muffled and remote. "I slipped. I was standing on a little kind of ledge affair. The window's so high from the ground," she added plaintively.

"My poor child!" he said on a little laugh of amused commiseration. The reproach, the exasperation had gone out of his voice. He was conquered by the comic patheticness of her. Hanging on to the bars with those small, those rather red and childishly untended hands! And tumbling off the perch she had had to climb on, because the window was so high from the ground! A wave of sentimentality submerged him. "I'll come and open the door." He ran into the hall.

Waiting outside in the darkness, she heard the bolts being shot back, one by one . . . Clank, clank! and then "Damn!" came his voice from the other side of the door. "These things are so stiff. . . . I'm barricaded up as though I were in a safe." She stood there waiting. The door shook as he tugged at the recalcitrant bolt. The waiting seemed interminable. And all at once a huge, black weariness settled on her. The energy of wrought-up despair deserted her and she was left empty of everything but a tired misery. What was the good, what was the good of coming like this to be turned away again? For he *would* turn her away; he didn't want her. What was the good of renewing suffering, of once more dying?

"Hell and Death!" On the other side of the door, Fanning was cursing like an Elizabethan.

Hell and Death. The words reverberated in Pamela's mind. The pains of Hell—the darkness and dissolution of Death. What was the good.

Clank! Another bolt had gone back. "Thank goodness. We're almost . . ." A chain rattled. At the sound, Pamela turned and ran in a blind terror down the dimly-lighted street.

"At last!" The door swung back and Fanning stepped out. But the sentimental tenderness of his outstretched hands wasted itself on empty night. Twenty yards away a pair of pale legs twinkled in the darkness. "Pamela!" he called in astonishment. "What the devil . . . ?" The wasting on emptiness of his feelings had startled him into annoyance. He felt like one who has put forth all his strength to strike something and, missing his aim, swipes the unresisting air, grotesquely. "Pamela!" he called again, yet louder.

She did not turn at the sound of his voice, but ran on. These wretched high-heeled shoes! "Pamela!" And then came the sound of his pursuing footsteps. She tried to run faster. But the pursuing footsteps came nearer and nearer. It was no good. Nothing was any good. She slackened her speed to a walk.

"But what on earth?" he asked from just behind her, almost angrily. Pursuing, he called up within him the soul of a pursuer, angry and desirous. "What on earth?" And suddenly his hand was on her shoulder. She trembled a little at the touch. "But why?" he insisted. "Why do you suddenly run away?"

But Pamela only shook her averted head. She wouldn't speak, wouldn't meet his eyes. Fanning looked down at her intently, questioningly. Why? And as he looked at that weary hopeless face, he began to divine the reason. The anger of the pursuit subsided in him. Respecting her dumb, averted misery, he too was silent. He drew her comfortingly towards him. His arm round her shoulders, Pamela suffered herself to be led back towards the house.

Which would be best, he was wondering with the surface of his mind: to telephone for a taxi to take her back to the hotel, or to see if he could make up a bed for her in one of the upstairs rooms? But in the depths of his being he knew quite well that he would do neither of these things. He knew that he would be her lover. And yet, in spite of this deep knowledge, the surface mind still continued to discuss its little problem of cabs and bed-linen. Discussed it sensibly, discussed it dutifully. Because it would be a madness, he told himself, a criminal madness if he didn't send for the taxi or prepare that upstairs room. But the dark certainty of the depths rose suddenly and exploded at the surface in a bubble of ironic laughter, in a brutal and cynical word. "Comedian!" he said to himself, to the self that agitatedly thought of telephones and taxis and pillow-slips. "Seeing that it's obvious I'm going to have her." And, rising from the depths, her nakedness presented itself to him palpably in an integral and immediate contact with his whole being. But this was shameful, shameful. He pushed the naked Anadyomene back into the depths. Very well, then (his surface mind resumed its busy efficient rattle), seeing that it was perhaps rather late to start telephoning for taxis, he'd rig up one of the rooms on the first floor. But if he couldn't find any sheets . . . ? But here was the house, the open door.

Pamela stepped across the threshold. The hall was almost dark. Through a curtained doorway on the left issued a thin blade of yellow light. Passive in her tired misery, she waited. Behind her the chain rattled, as it had rattled only a few moments before, when she had fled from the ominous sound, and clank, clank! the bolts were thrust back into place.

"There," said Fanning's voice. "And now . . ." With a click, the darkness yielded suddenly to brilliant light.

Pamela uttered a little cry and covered her face with her hands. "Oh, please," she begged, "please." The light hurt her, was a sort of outrage. She didn't want to see, couldn't bear to be seen.

"I'm sorry," he said, and the comforting darkness returned. "This way." Taking her arm he led her towards the lighted doorway on the left. "Shut your eyes," he commanded, as they approached the curtain. "We've got to go into the light again; but I'll turn it out the moment I can get to the switch. Now!"

She shut her eyes and suddenly, as the curtain rings rattled she saw, through her closed eyelids, the red shining of transparent blood. Still holding her arm, he led her forward into the room.

Pamela lifted her free hand to her face. "Please don't look at me," she whispered. "I don't want you to see me like this. I mean, I couldn't bear . . ." Her voice faded to silence.

"I won't look," he assured her. "And anyhow," he added, when they had taken two or three more steps across the room, "now I can't." And he turned the switch.

The pale translucent red went black again before her eyes. Pamela sighed. "I'm so tired," she whispered. Her eyes were still shut; she was too tired to open them.

"Take off your coat." A hand pulled at her sleeve. First one bare arm, then the other slipped out into the coolness.

Fanning threw the coat over a chair. Turning back, he could see her, by the tempered darkness that entered through the window, standing motionless before him, passive, wearily waiting, her face, her limp arms pale against the shadowy blackness.

"Poor Pamela," she heard him say, and then suddenly light finger-tips were sliding in a moth-winged caress along her arm. "You'd better lie down and rest." The hand closed round her arm, she was pushed gently forward. That taxi, he was still thinking, the upstairs room. . . . But his fingers preserved the silky memory of her skin, the flesh of her arm was warm and firm against his palm. In the darkness, the supernatural world was coming mysteriously, thrillingly into existence; he was once more standing upon its threshold.

"There, sit down," came his voice. She obeyed; a low divan received her. "Lean back." She let herself fall on to pillows. Her feet were lifted on to the couch. She lay quite still. "As though I were dead," she thought, "as though I were dead." She was aware, through the darkness of her closed eyes, of his warm breathing presence, impending and very near. "As though I were dead," she inwardly repeated with a kind of pleasure. For the pain of her misery had ebbed away into the warm darkness and to be tired, she found, to be utterly tired and to lie there utterly still were pleasures. "As though I were dead." And the light reiterated touch of his finger-tips along her arm—what were those caresses but another mode, a soothing and delicious mode, of gently dying?

In the morning, on his way to the kitchen to prepare their coffee, Fanning caught sight of his littered writing-table. He halted to collect the scattered sheets. Waiting for the water to boil, he read, "By the time you receive this letter, I shall be, no, not dead, Pamela . . ." He crumpled up each page as he had finished reading it and threw it into the dust-bin.

IX

The architectural background was like something out of Alma Tadema. But the figures that moved

across the sunlit atrium, that lingered beneath the
colonnades and in the coloured shadow of the awnings,
the figures were Hogarthian and Rowlandsonian,
were the ferocious satires of Daumier and Rouveyre.
Huge jellied females overflowed the chairs on which
they sat. Sagging and with the gait of gorged bears,
old men went slowly shambling down the porticoes.
Like princes preceded by their outriders, the rich
fat burgesses strutted with dignity behind their bel-
lies. There was a hungry prowling of gaunt emaci-
ated men and women, yellow-skinned and with tragical, blue-injected eyes. And, conspicuous by their
trailing blackness, these bloated or cadaverous pen-
cillings from an anti-clerical notebook were priests.

In the midst of so many monsters Pamela was a
lovely miracle of health and beauty. These three
months had subtly transformed her. The rather
wavering and intermittent *savoir-vivre*, the child's
forced easiness of manner, had given place to a
woman's certainty, to that repose even in action, that
decision even in repose, which are the ordinary fruits
of the intimate knowledge, the physical understanding of love.

"For it isn't only murder that will out," as Fanning had remarked some few days after the evening
of the fireworks. "It isn't only murder. If you could
see yourself, my child! It's almost indecent. Any one
could tell that you'd been in bed with your lover.
Could tell in the dark even; you're luminous, positively luminous. All shining and smooth and pearly

with love-making. It's really an embarrassment to walk about with you. I've a good mind to make you wear a veil."

She had laughed, delightedly. "But I don't mind them seeing. I *want* them to see. I mean, why should one be ashamed of being happy?"

That had been three months since. At present she had no happiness to be ashamed of. It was by no shining of eyes, no luminous soft pearliness of smoothed and rounded contour that she now betrayed herself. All that her manner, her pose, her gestures proclaimed was the fact that there *had* been such shinings and pearly smoothings, once. As for the present, her shut and sullen face announced only that she was discontented with it and with the man who, sitting beside her, was the symbol and the embodiment of that unsatisfactory present. A rather sickly embodiment at the moment, a thin and jaundiced symbol. For Fanning was hollow-cheeked, his eyes darkly ringed, his skin pale and sallow under the yellow tan. He was on his way to becoming one of those pump-room monsters at whom they were now looking, almost incredulously. For, "Incredible!" was Fanning's comment. "Didn't I tell you that they simply weren't to be believed?"

Pamela shrugged her shoulders, almost imperceptibly, and did not answer. She did not feel like answering, she wanted to be uninterested, sullen, bored.

"How right old Butler was!" he went on, rousing himself by the stimulus of his own talk from the depression into which his liver and Pamela had plunged him. "Making the Erewhonians punish illness as a crime—how right! Because they *are* criminals, all these people. Criminally ugly and deformed, criminally incapable of enjoyment. Look at them. It's a caution. And when I think that I'm one of them . . ." He shook his head. "But let's hope this will make me a reformed character." And he emptied, with a grimace of disgust, his glass of tepid salt water. "Revolting! But I suppose it's right that Montecatini should be a place of punishment as well as cure. One can't be allowed to commit jaundice with impunity. I must go and get another glass of my punishment— my purgatory, in every sense of the word," he added, smiling at his own joke. He rose to his feet painfully (every movement was now a painful effort for him) and left her, threading his way through the crowd to where, behind their marble counters, the pump-room barmaids dispensed warm laxatives from rows of polished brass taps.

The animation had died out of Fanning's face, as he turned away. No longer distracted and self-stimulated by talk, he relapsed at once into melancholy. Waiting his turn behind two bulging monsignori at the pump, he looked so gloomily wretched, that a passing connoisseur of the waters pointed him out to his companion as a typical example of the hepatic pessimist. But bile, as a matter of fact, was not the only cause of Fanning's depression. There was also Pamela. And Pamela—he admitted it, though the fact belonged to that great class of humiliating phenomena, whose existence we are always trying to ignore—Pamela, after all, was the cause of the bile. For if he had not been so extenuated by that crazy love-making in the narrow cells of the Passionist Fathers at Monte Cavo, he would never have taken chill and the chill would never have settled on his liver and turned to jaundice. As it was, however, that night of the full moon had finished him. They had gone out, groping their way through the terrors of the nocturnal woods, to a little grassy terrace among the bushes, from which there was a view of Nemi. Deep sunk in its socket of impenetrable darkness and more than half eclipsed by shadow, the eye of water gleamed up at them secretly, as though through eye-lids almost closed. Under the brightness of the moon the hills, the woods seemed to be struggling out of ghostly greyness towards colour, towards the warmth of life. They had sat there for a while, in silence, look-ing. Then, taking her in his arms, " *'Ceda al tatto la vista, al labro il lume,'* " he had quoted with a kind of mockery—mocking her for the surrender to which he knew he could bring her, even against her will, even though, as he could see, she had made up her mind to sulk at him, mocking himself at the same time for the folly which drove him, weary and undesiring, to make the gesture. " *'Al labro il lume,'* " he repeated with that undercurrent of derision in his voice, and leaned towards her. Desire returned to him as he touched her and with it a kind of exultation, a re-

newal (temporary, he knew, and illusory) of all his
energies.

"No, Miles. Don't. I don't want . . ." And she had
averted her face, for she was angry, resentful, she
wanted to sulk. Fanning knew it, mockingly, and
mockingly he had turned back her face towards him
—"'*al labro il lume*'"—and had found her lips. She
struggled a little in his arms, protested and then
was silent, lay still. His kisses had had the power to
transform her. She was another person, different
from the one who had sulked and been resentful. Or
rather she was two people—the sulky and resentful
one, with another person superimposed, a person who
quiveringly sank and melted under his kisses, melted
and sank down, down towards that mystical death,
that apocalypse, that almost terrible transfigura-
But beneath, to one side, stood always the an
sulker, unappeased, unreconciled, ready to em
again (full of a new resentment for the way she h
been undignifiedly hustled off the stage), the mome
the other should have retired. His realization of th
made Fanning all the more perversely ardent, quicl
ened the folly of his passion with a kind of derisi
hostility. He drew his lips across her cheek and sud
denly their soft electrical touch on her ear made her
shudder. "Don't!" she implored, dreading and yet
desiring what was to come. Gently, inexorably his
teeth closed and the petal of cartilage was a firm
elastic resistance between them. She shuddered yet
more violently. Fanning relaxed the muscles of his

jaws, then tightened them once more, gently, against
that exquisite resistance. The felt beauty of rounded
warmth and resilience was under his hand. In the
darkness they were inhabitants of the supernatural
world.

But at midnight they had found themselves, almost suddenly, on earth again, shiveringly cold under
the moon. Cold, cold to the quick, Fanning had picked
himself up. They stumbled homewards through the
woods, in silence. It was in a kind of trance of chilled
and sick exhaustion that he had at last dropped
down on his bed in the convent cell. Next morning he
was ill. The liver was always his weak point. That
had been nearly three weeks ago.

The second of the two monsignori moved away;
Fanning stepped into his place. The barmaid handed
him his hot dilute sulphate of soda. He deposited fifty
centesimi as a largesse and walked off, meditatively
sipping. But returning to the place from which he
had come, he found their chairs occupied by a pair
of obese Milanese business-men. Pamela had gone. He
explored the Alma Tadema background; but there
was no sign of her. She had evidently gone back to
the hotel. Fanning, who still had five more glasses of
water to get through, took his place among the
monsters around the band-stand.

In her room at the hotel Pamela was writing up her
diary. "September 20th. Montecatini seems a beastly
sort of hole, particularly if you come to a wretched

little hotel like this, which M. insisted on doing, because he knows the proprietor, who is an old drunkard and also cooks the meals, and M. has long talks with him and says he's like a character in Shakespeare, which is all very well, but I'd prefer better food and a room with a bath, not to mention the awfulness of the other people in the hotel, one of whom is the chief undertaker in Florence, who's always boasting to the other people at meal times about his business and what a fine motor hearse with gilded angels he's got and the number of counts and dukes he's buried. M. had a long conversation with him and the old drunkard after dinner yesterday evening about how you preserve corpses on ice and the way to make money by buying up the best sites at the cemetery and holding them till you could ask five times as much as you paid, and it was the first time I'd seen him looking cheerful and amused since his illness and even for some time before, but I was so horrified that I went off to bed. This morning at eight to the pump-room, where M. has to drink eight glasses of different kinds of water before breakfast and there are hundreds of hideous people all carrying mugs, and huge fountains of purgatives, and a band playing the "Geisha," so I came away after half an hour, leaving M. to his waters, because I really can't be expected to watch him drinking, and it appears there are six hundred W.C.'s."

She laid down her pen and, turning round in her chair, sat for some time pensively staring at her own reflection in the wardrobe mirror. "If you look long enough," (she heard Clare's voice, she saw Clare, inwardly, sitting at her dressing-table), "you begin to wonder if it isn't somebody else. And perhaps, after all, one *is* somebody else, all the time." Somebody else, Pamela repeated to herself, somebody else. But was that a spot on her cheek, or a mosquito bite? A mosquito, thank goodness. "Oh God," she said aloud, and in the looking-glass somebody else moved her lips, "if only I knew what to do! If only I were dead!" She touched wood hastily. Stupid to say such things. But if only one knew, one were certain! All at once she gave a little stiff sharp shudder of disgust, she grimaced as though she had bitten on something sour. Oh, oh! she groaned; for she had suddenly seen herself in the act of dressing, there, in that moon-flecked darkness, among the bushes, that hateful night just before Miles fell ill. Furious because he'd humiliated her, hating him; she hadn't wanted to and he'd made her. Somebody else had enjoyed beyond the limits of enjoyment, had suffered a pleasure transmuted into its opposite. Or rather *she* had done the suffering. And then that further humiliation of having to ask him to help her look for her suspender belt! And there were leaves in her hair. And when she got back to the hotel, she found a spider squashed against her skin under the chemise. Yes, *she* had found the spider, not somebody else.

· · · · ·

Between the brackish sips Fanning was reading

in his pocket edition of the Paradiso. "*L'acqua che prendo giammai non si corse,*" he murmured;

> *Minerva spira e conducemi Apollo,*
> *e nove Muse mi dimostran l'Orse.*

He closed his eyes. "*E nove Muse mi dimostran l'Orse.*" What a marvel! "And the nine Muses point me to the Bears." Even translated the spell did not entirely lose its potency. "How glad I shall be," he thought, "to be able to do a little work again."

"*Il caffè?*" said a voice at his elbow. "*Non lo bevo mai, mai. Per il fegato, sa, è pessimo. Si dice anche che per gl'intestini. . . .*" The voice receded out of hearing.

Fanning took another gulp of salt water and resumed his reading.

> *Voi altri pochi che drizzante il collo*
> *per tempo al pan degli angeli, del quale*
> *vivesi qui ma non sen vien satollo . . .*

The voice had returned. "*Pesce bollito, carne ai ferri o arrostita, patate lesse. . . .*"

He shut his ears and continued. But when he came to:—

> *la concreata e perpetua sete*
> *del deiforme regno,*

he had to stop again. This craning for angels' bread, this thirsting for the god-like kingdom . . . The words reverberated questioningly in his mind. After all, why not? Particularly when man's bread made you sick (he thought with horror of that dreadful vomiting of bile), when it was a case of *pesce bollito* and you weren't allowed to thirst for anything more palatable than this stuff. (He swigged again.) These were the circumstances when Christianity became appropriate. Christians, according to Pascal, ought to live like sick men; conversely, sick men can hardly escape being Christians. How pleased Colin Judd would be! But the thought of Colin was depressing, if only all Christians were like Dante! But in that case, what a frightful world it would be! Frightful.

> *La concreata e perpetua sete*
> *del deiforme regno cen portava*
> *Veloci, quasi come il ciel vedete.*
> *Beatrice in suso ed io in lei guardava. . . .*

He thought of Pamela at the fireworks. On that pedestal. *Ben son, ben son Beatrice* on that pedestal. He remembered what he had said beneath the blossoming of the rockets; and also what he had meant to say about those legs which the pedestal made it so easy for the worshipper to pinch. Those legs how remote now, how utterly irrelevant! He finished off his third glass of Torretta and, rising, made his way to the bar for his first of Regina. Yes, how utterly irrelevant! he thought. A complete solution of continuity. You were on the leg level, then you vomited bile and as soon as you were able to think of anything but vomiting, you found yourself on the Dante level. He handed his mug to the barmaid. She rolled black eyes at him as she filled it. Some liverish gentlemen, it seemed, could still feel amorous. Or perhaps it was only the

obese ones. Fanning deposited his offering and retired. Irrelevant, irrelevant. It seemed, now, the unlikeliest story. And yet there it was, a fact. And
Pamela was solid, too solid.

Phrases floated up, neat and ready-made, to the
surface of his mind.

"What does he see in her? What on earth can she
see in him?"

"But it's not a question of sight, it's a question of
touch."

And he remembered—*sentiments-centimètres*—
that French pun about love, so appallingly cynical,
so humiliatingly true. "But only humiliating," he assured himself, "because we choose to think it so, arbi-
trarily, only cynical because *Beatrice in suso ed io in
lei guardava;* only appalling because we're creatures
who sometimes vomit bile and because, even without
vomiting, we sometimes feel ourselves naturally Christians." But in any case, *nove Muse mi dimostran
l'Orse.* Meanwhile, however. . . . He tilted another
gill of water down his throat. And when he was well
enough to work, wouldn't he also be well enough to
thirst again for that other god-like kingdom, with its
different ecstasies, its other peace beyond all understanding? But *tant mieux, tant mieux,* so long as the
Bears remained unmoved and the Muses went on
pointing.

.   .   .   .   .

Pamela was looking through her diary. "June
24th," she read. "Spent the evening with M. and

afterwards he said how lucky it was for me that I'd been seduced by him, which hurt my feelings (that word, I mean) and also rather annoyed me, so I said he certainly hadn't seduced me, and he said, all right, if I liked to say that I'd seduced him, he didn't mind, but anyhow it was lucky because almost anybody else wouldn't have been such a good psychologist as he, not to mention physiologist, and I should have hated it. But I said, how could he say such things? because it wasn't that at all and I was happy because I loved him, but M. laughed and said, you don't, and I said, I do, and he said, you don't, but if it gives you any pleasure to imagine you do, imagine, which upset me still more, his not believing, which is due to his not wanting to love himself, because I *do* love . . ."

Pamela quickly turned the page. She couldn't read that sort of thing now.

"June 25th. Went to the Vatican where M. . . ." She skipped nearly a page of Miles's remarks on classical art and the significance of orgies in the ancient religions; on the duty of being happy and having the sun inside you, like a bunch of ripe grapes; on making the world appear infinite and holy by an improvement of sensual enjoyment; on taking things untragically, unponderously.

"M. dined out and I spent the evening with Guy, the first time since the night of the fireworks, and he asked me what I'd been doing all this time, so I said, nothing in particular, but I felt myself blushing, and he said, anyhow you look extraordinarily well and happy and pretty, which also made me rather uncomfortable, because of what M. said the other day about murder will out, but then I laughed, because it was the only thing to do, and Guy asked what I was laughing about, so I said, nothing, but I could see by the way he looked at me that he was rather thrilled, which pleased me, and we had a very nice dinner and he told me about a girl he'd been in love with in Ireland and it seems they went camping together for a week, but he was never her lover because she had a kind of terror of being touched, but afterwards she went to America and got married. Later on, in the taxi, he took my hand and even tried to kiss me, but I laughed, because it was somehow very funny, I don't know why, but afterwards, when he persisted, I got angry with him.

"June 27th. Went to look at mosaics to-day, rather fine, but what a pity they're all in churches and always pictures of Jesus and sheep and apostles and so forth. On the way home we passed a wine shop and M. went in and ordered a dozen bottles of champagne, because he said that love can exist without passion, or understanding, or respect, but not without champagne. So I asked him if he really loved me, and he said, *Je t'adore*, in French, but I said, no, do you really *love* me? But he said, silence is golden and it's better to use one's mouth for kissing and drinking champagne and eating caviar, because he'd also bought some caviar; and if you start talking about love and thinking about love, you get everything wrong, because

it's not *meant* to be talked about, but acted, and if
people want to talk and think, they'd better talk
about mosaics and that sort of thing. But I still went
on asking him if he loved me. . . ."

"Fool, fool!" said Pamela aloud. She was ashamed
of herself. Dithering on like that! At any rate Miles
had been honest; she had to admit that. He'd taken
care to keep the thing on the champagne level. And
he'd always told her that she was imagining it all.
Which had been intolerable, of course; he'd been
wrong to be so right. She remembered how she had
cried when he refused to answer her insistent question; had cried and afterwards allowed herself to be
consoled. They went back to his house for supper;
he opened a bottle of champagne, they ate the caviar.
Next day he sent her that poem. It had arrived at the
same time as some flowers from Guy. She reopened
her notebook. Here it was.

At the red fountain's core the thud of drums
Quickens; for hairy-footed moths explore
This aviary of nerves; the woken birds
Flutter and cry in the branched blood; a bee
Hums with his million-times-repeated stroke
On lips your breast promotes geometers
To measure curves, to take the height of mountains,
The depth and silken slant of dells unseen.
I read your youth, as the blind student spells
With finger-tips the song from *Cymbeline*.
Caressing and caressed, my hands perceive
(In lieu of eyes) old Titian's paradise
With Eve unaproned; and the Maja dressed

Whisks off her muslins, that my skin may know
The blind night's beauty of brooding heat and cool,
Of silk and fibre, of molten-moist and dry,
Resistance and resilience.
                    But the drum
Throbs with yet faster beat, the wild birds go
Through their red liquid sky with wings yet more
Frantic and yet more desperate crying. Come!
The magical door its soft and breathing valves
Has set ajar. Beyond the threshold lie
Worlds after worlds receding into light,
As rare old wines on the ravished tongue renew
A miracle that deepens, that expands,
Blossoms, and changes hue, and chimes, and shines.
Birds in the blood and doubled drums incite
Us to the conquest of these new, strange lands
Beyond the threshold, where all common times,
Things, places, thoughts, events expire, and life
Enters eternity.

The darkness stirs, the trees are wet with rain;
Knock and it shall be opened, oh, again,
Again! The child is eager for its dam
And I the mother am of thirsty lips,
Oh, knock again!
Wild darkness wets this sound of strings.
How smooth it slides among the clarinets,
How easily slips through the trumpetings!
Sound glides through sound and lo! the apocalypse,
The burst of wings above a sunlit sea.
Must this eternal music make an end?
Prolong, prolong these all but final chords!
Oh, wounded sevenths, breathlessly suspend

Our fear of dying, our desire to know
The song's last words!
Almost Bethesda sleeps, uneasily.
A bubble domes the flatness; gyre on gyre,
The waves expand, expire, as in the deeps
The woken spring subsides
                              Play, music, play!
Reckless of death, a singing giant rides
His storm of music, rides; and suddenly
The tremulous mirror of the moon is broken;
On the farthest beaches of our soul, our flesh,
The tides of pleasure foaming into pain
Mount, hugely mount; break; and retire again.
The final word is sung, the last word spoken.

"Do I like it, or do I rather hate it? I don't know."

"June 28th. When I saw M. at lunch to-day, I told
him I didn't really know if I liked his poem, I mean
apart from literature, and he said, yes, perhaps the
young *are* more romantic than they think, which
rather annoyed me, because I believe he imagined I
was shocked, which is too ridiculous. All the same,
I *don't* like it."

Pamela sighed and shut her eyes, so as to be able
to think more privately, without distractions. From
this distance of time she could see all that had happened in perspective, as it were, and as a whole. It
was her pride, she could see, her fear of looking ridiculously romantic that had changed the quality of her
feelings towards Miles—a pride and a fear on which
he had played, deliberately. She had given herself

with passion and desperately, tragically, as she imagined that Joan would have desperately given herself, at first sight, to a reluctant Walter. But the love he had offered her in return was a thing of laughter and frank, admitted sensuality, was a gay and easy companionship enriched, but uncomplicated, by pleasure. From the first, he had refused to come up to her emotional level. From the first, he had taken it for granted—and his taking it for granted was in itself an act of moral compulsion—that she should descend to his. And she had descended—reluctantly at first, but afterwards without a struggle. For she came to realize, almost suddenly, that after all she didn't really love him in the tragically passionate way she had supposed she loved him. In a propitious emotional climate her belief that she was a despairing Joan might perhaps have survived, at any rate for a time. But it was a hot-house growth of the imagination; in the cool dry air of his laughter and cheerfully cynical frankness it had withered. And all at once she had found herself, not satisfied, indeed, with what he offered, but superficially content. She returned him what he gave. Less even than he gave. For soon it became apparent to her that their rôles were being reversed, that the desperate one was no longer herself, but Miles. For "desperate"—that was the only word to describe the quality of his desires. From light and gay—and perhaps, she thought, the lightness had been forced, the gaiety fabricated for the occasion as a defence against the tragical vehemence of her attack and of his own desires—his sensuality had become heavy, serious, intense. She had found herself the object of a kind of focussed rage. It had been frightening sometimes, frightening and rather humiliating; for she had often felt that, so far as he was concerned, she wasn't there at all; that the body between those strong, those ruthless and yet delicate, erudite, subtly intelligent hands of his, that were like a surgeon's or a sculptor's hands, was not her body, was no one's body, indeed, but a kind of abstraction, tangible, yes, desperately tangible, but still an abstraction. She would have liked to rebel; but the surgeon was a master of his craft, the sculptor's fingers were delicately learned and intelligent. He had the art to overcome her reluctances, to infect her with some of his strange, concentrated seriousness. Against her will. In the intervals he resumed his old manner; but the laughter was apt to be bitter and spiteful, there was a mocking brutality in the frankness.

Pamela squeezed her eyes more tightly shut and shook her head, frowning at her memories. For distraction she turned back to her diary.

"June 30th. Lunched with Guy, who was really rather tiresome, because what is more boring than somebody being in love with you, when you're not in love with them? Which I told him quite frankly, and I could see he was dreadfully upset, but what was I to do?"

Poor Guy! she thought, and she was indignant, not

with herself, but with Fanning. She turned over several pages. It was July now and they were at Ostia for the bathing. It was at Ostia that that desperate seriousness had come into his desire. The long hot hours of the siesta were propitious to his earnest madness. Propitious also to his talents, for he worked well in the heat. Behind her lowered eyelids Pamela had a vision of him sitting at his table, stripped to a pair of shorts, sitting there, pen in hand, in the next room and with an open door between them, but somehow at an infinite distance. Terrifyingly remote, a stranger more foreign for being known so well, the inhabitant of other worlds to which she had no access. They were worlds which she was already beginning to hate. His books were splendid of course; still, it wasn't much fun being with a man who, for half the time, wasn't there at all. She saw him sitting there, a beautiful naked stranger, brown and wiry, with a face like brown marble, stonily focussed on his paper. And then suddenly this stranger rose and came towards her through the door, across the room. "Well?" she heard herself saying. But the stranger did not answer. Sitting down on the edge of her bed, he took the sewing out of her hands and threw it aside on to the dressing-table. She tried to protest, but he laid a hand on her mouth. Wordlessly he shook his head. Then, uncovering her mouth, he kissed her. Under his surgeon's, his sculptor's hands, her body was moulded to a symbol of pleasure. His face was focussed and intent, but not on her, on something else, and serious, serious, like a martyr's, like a mathematician's, like a criminal's. An hour later, he was back at his table in the next room, in the next world, remote, a stranger once again—but he had never ceased to be a stranger.

Pamela turned over two or three more pages. On July 12th they went sailing and she had felt sick; Miles had been provokingly well all the time. The whole of the sixteenth had been spent in Rome. On the nineteenth they drove to Cerveteri to see the Etruscan tombs. She had been furious with him, because he had put out the lamp and made horrible noises in the cold sepulchral darkness, underground —furious with terror, for she hated the dark.

Impatiently, Pamela went on turning the pages. There was no point in reading; none of the really important things were recorded. Of the earnest madness of his love-making, of those hands, that reluctantly suffered pleasure she hadn't been able to bring herself to write. And yet those were the things that mattered. She remembered how she had tried to imagine that she was like her namesake of *Pastures New* —the fatal woman whose cool detachment gives her such power over her lovers. But the facts had proved too stubborn; it was simply impossible for her to pretend that this handsome fancy-picture was her portrait. The days flicked past under her thumb.

"July 30th. On the beach this morning we met some friends of M.'s, a journalist called Pedder, who has just come to Rome as correspondent for some paper or other, and his wife, rather awful, I thought, both of them, but M. seemed to be extraordinarily pleased to see them, and they bathed with us and afterwards came and had lunch at our hotel, which was rather boring so far as I was concerned, because they talked a lot about people I didn't know and then there was a long discussion about politics and history, and so forth, *too* highbrow, but what was intolerable was that the woman thought she ought to be kind and talk to me meanwhile about something I could understand, so she talked about shops in Rome and the best places for getting clothes, which was rather ridiculous, as she's obviously one of those absurd arty women, who appeared in M.'s novels as young girls just before and during the War, so advanced in those days, with extraordinary coloured stockings and frocks like pictures by Augustus John. Anyhow, what she was wearing at lunch was really too fancy-dress, and really at her age one ought to have a little more sense of the decencies, because she must have been quite thirty-five. So that the idea of talking about smart shops in Rome was quite ludicrous to start with, and anyhow it was so insulting to me, because it implied that I was too young and half-witted to be able to take an interest in their beastly conversation. But afterwards, apropos of some philosophical theory or other, M. began talking about his opium smoking, and he told them all the things he'd told me and a lot more besides, and it made me feel very uncomfortable and then miserable and rather angry, because I thought it was only me he talked to like that, so confidentially, but now I see he makes confidences to everybody and it's not a sign of his being particularly fond of a person, or in love with them, or anything like that. Which made me realize that I'm even less important to him than I thought and I found I minded much more than I expected I should mind, because I thought I'd got past minding. But I *do* mind."

Pamela shut her eyes again. "I ought to have gone away then," she said to herself. "Gone straight away." But instead of retiring, she had tried to come closer. Her resentment—for oh, how bitterly she resented those Pedders and his confidential manner towards them!—had quickened her love. She wanted to insist on being more specially favoured than a mere Pedder; and, loving him, she had the right to insist. By a process of imaginative incubation, she managed to revive some of the emotions she had felt before the night of the fireworks. Tragically, with a suicide's determination, she tried to force herself upon him. Fanning fought a retreating battle, ruthlessly. Oh, how cruel he could be, Pamela was thinking, how pitilessly cruel! The way he could shut himself up as though in an iron box of indifference! The way he could just fade out into absent silence, into another world! The way he could flutter out of an embarrassing emotional situation on the wings of some brilliant irrelevance! And the way he could flutter back again, the way he could compel you, with his charm, with the touch of his hands, to reopen the gates of your

life to him, when you'd made up your mind to shut
them against him for ever! And not content with
forcing you to yield, he would mock you for your
surrender, mock himself too for having attacked—
jeering, but without seeming to jeer, indirectly, in
some terrible little generalization about the weakness
of the human soul, the follies and insanities of the
body. Yes, how cruel he could be! She reopened her
eyes.

"August 10th. M. still very glum and depressed
and silent, like a wall when I come near. I think he
sometimes hates me for loving him. At lunch he said
he'd got to go into Rome this afternoon and he went
and didn't come back till late, almost midnight. Waiting for him, I couldn't help crying.

"August 11th. Those Pedders came to lunch again
to-day and all M.'s glumness vanished the moment he
saw them and he was charming all through lunch
and so amusing, that I couldn't help laughing,
though I felt more like crying, because why should
he be so much nicer and more *friendly* with them than
with me? After lunch, when we went to rest, he came
into my room and wanted to kiss me, but I wouldn't
let him, because I said, I don't want to owe your fits
of niceness to somebody else, and I asked him, why?
why was he so much nicer to them than to me? And he
said they were his people, they belonged to the same
time as he did and meeting them was like meeting
another Englishman in the middle of a crowd of Kaf-

firs in Africa. So I said, I suppose I'm the Kaffirs, and he laughed and said, no, not quite Kaffirs, not more than a Rotary Club dinner in Kansas City, with the Pedders playing the part of a man one had known at Balliol in 'ninety-nine. Which made me cry, and he sat on the edge of the bed and took my hand and said he was very sorry, but that's what life was like, and it couldn't be helped, because time was always time, but people weren't always the same people, but sometimes one person and sometimes another, sometimes Pedder-fanciers and sometimes Pamela-fanciers, and it wasn't my fault that I hadn't heard the first performance of *Pelléas* in 1902 and it wasn't Pedder's fault that he had, and therefore Pedder was his compatriot and I wasn't. But I said, after all, Miles, you're my lover, doesn't that make any difference? But he said, it's a question of speech, and bodies don't speak, only minds, and when two minds are of different ages it's hard for them to understand each other when they speak, but bodies can understand each other, because they don't talk, thank God, he said, because it's such a comfort to stop talking sometimes, to stop thinking and just *be*, for a change. But I said that might be all right for him, but just *being* was my ordinary life and the change for me was talking, was being friends with somebody who knew how to talk and do all the other things talking implies, and I'd imagined I was that, besides just being somebody he went to bed with, and that was why I was so miserable, because I found I wasn't, and those beastly Pedders were. But he said, damn the Pedders, damn the Pedders for making you cry! and he was so *divinely* sweet and gentle that it was like gradually sinking, sinking and being drowned. But afterwards he began laughing again in that rather hurting way, and he said, your body's so much more beautiful than their minds—that is, so long as one's a Pamela-fancier; which I am he said, or rather was and shall be, but now I must go and work, and he got up and went to his room, and I was wretched again."

The entries of a few days later were dated from Monte Cavo. A superstitious belief in the genius of place had made Pamela insist on the change of quarters. They had been happy on Monte Cavo; perhaps they would be happy there again. And so, suddenly, the sea didn't suit her, she needed mountain air. But the genius of place is an unreliable deity. She had been as unhappy on the hill-top as by the sea. No, not quite so unhappy, perhaps. In the absence of the Pedders, the passion which their coming had renewed declined again. Perhaps it would have declined even if they had still been there. For the tissue of her imagination was, at the best of times, but a ragged curtain. Every now and then she came to a hole and through the hole she could see a fragment of reality, such as the bald and obvious fact that she didn't love Miles Fanning. True, after a peep through one of these indiscreet holes she felt it necessary to repent for having seen the facts, she would work herself up again into believing her fancies. But her faith was

never entirely whole-hearted. Under the superficial
layer of imaginative suffering lay a fundamental and
real indifference. Looking back now, from the further shore of his illness, Pamela felt astonished that
she could have gone on obstinately imagining, in spite
of those loop-holes on reality, that she loved him.
"Because I didn't," she said to herself, clear-sighted,
weeks too late. "I didn't." But the belief that she did
had continued, even on Monte Cavo, to envenom those
genuinely painful wounds inflicted by him on her
pride, her self-respect, inflicted with a strange malice
that seemed to grow on him with the passage of the
days.

"August 23d." She had turned again to the notebook. "M. gave me this at lunch to-day.

> Sensual heat and sorrow cold
>   Are undivided twins;
> For there where sorrow ends, consoled,
>   Lubricity begins.

I told him I didn't exactly see what the point of it
was, but I supposed it was meant to be hurting, because he's always trying to be hurting now, but he
said, no, it was just a Great Thought for putting
into Christmas crackers. But he did mean to hurt,
and yet in one way he's crazy about me, he's . . ."

Yes, crazy was the right word. The more and the
more crazily he had desired her, the more he had
seemed to want to hurt her, to hurt himself too—for
every wound he inflicted on her was inflicted at the

same time on himself. "Why on earth didn't I leave him?" she wondered as she allowed a few more days to flick past.

"August 29th. A letter this morning from Guy in Scotland, so no wonder he took such an endless time to answer mine, which is a relief in one way, because I was beginning to wonder if he wasn't answering on purpose, but also rather depressing, as he says he isn't coming back to Rome till after the middle of September and goodness knows what will have happened by that time. So I felt very melancholy all the morning, sitting under the big tree in front of the monastery, such a marvellous huge old tree with very bright bits of sky between the leaves and bits of sun on the ground and moving across my frock, so that the sadness somehow got mixed up with the loveliness, which it often does do in a queer way, I find. M. came out unexpectedly and suggested going for a little walk before lunch, and he was very sweet for a change, but I dare say it was because he'd worked well. And I said, do you remember the first time we came up to Monte Cavo? and we talked about that afternoon and what fun it had been, even the museum, I said, even my education, because the Apollo was lovely. But he shook his head and said, *Apollo, Apollo, lama sabach-thani,* and when I asked why he thought his Apollo had abandoned him he said it was because of Jesus and the Devil, and you're the Devil, I'm afraid, and he laughed and kissed my hand, but I ought to wring your neck, he said. For something that's *your* fault,

I said, because it's you who make me a Devil for yourself. But he said it was me who made him make me into a Devil. So I asked how? And he said just by existing, just by having my particular shape, size, colour, and consistency, because if I'd looked like a beetle and felt like wood, I'd have never made him make me into a Devil. So I asked him why he didn't just go away seeing that what was wrong with me was that I was there at all. But that's easier said than done, he said, because a Devil's one of the very few things you can't run away from. And I asked why not? And he said because you can't run away from yourself and a Devil is at least half you. Besides, he said, the essence of a vice is that it *is* a vice—it holds you. Unless it unscrews itself, I said, because I'd made up my mind that minute that I'd go away, and it was such a relief having made up my mind, that I wasn't furious or miserable any more, and when M. smiled and said, if it *can* unscrew itself, I just laughed."

A little too early, she reflected, as she read the words; she had laughed too early. That night had been the night of the full moon (oh, the humiliation of that lost suspender belt, the horror of that spider squashed against her skin!) and the next day he had begun to be ill. It had been impossible, morally impossible to leave him while he was ill. But how ghastly illness was! She shuddered with horror. Ghastly! "I'm sorry to be so repulsive," he had said to her one day, and from her place at his bedside she had protested, but hypocritically, hypocritically. As Aunt Edith might have protested. Still, one's *got* to be hippo-ish, she excused herself, simply *got* to be sometimes. "But, thank goodness," she thought, "he's better now." In a day or two he'd be quite fit to look after himself. These waters were supposed to be miraculous.

She took a sheet of writing-paper from the box on the table and uncorked the bottle of ink.

"Dear Guy," she began, "I wonder if you're back in Rome yet?"